The Hemingway Thief

The Hemingway Thief

SHAUN HARRIS

SEVENTH STREET BOOKS®

AN IMPRINT OF PROMETHEUS BOOKS

59 JOHN GLENN DRIVE • AMHERST, NY 14228
www.seventhstreetbooks.com

Published 2016 by Seventh Street Books®, an imprint of Prometheus Books

Cover photo © rackishnewzealand/Dreamstime
Cover design by Jacqueline Nasso Cooke
Cover design © Prometheus Books

Inquiries should be addressed to
Seventh Street Books
59 John Glenn Drive
Amherst, New York 14228
VOICE: 716–691–0133 • FAX: 716–691–0137
WWW.SEVENTHSTREETBOOKS.COM

20 19 18 17 16 • 5 4 3 2 1

Library of Congress Cataloging-in-Publication Data

Names: Harris, Shaun, 1980-
Title: The Hemingway thief / by Shaun Harris.
Description: Amherst, NY : Seventh Street Books, 2016.
Identifiers: LCCN 2016007219 (print) | LCCN 2016018414 (ebook) |
    ISBN 9781633881754 (pbk.) | ISBN 9781633881761 (ebook)
Subjects: LCSH: Hemingway, Ernest, 1899-1961—Manuscripts—Fiction. |
    Lost articles—Fiction. | GSAFD: Mystery fiction | Suspense fiction
Classification: LCC PS3608.A783283 H46 2016 (print) |
    LCC PS3608.A783283 (ebook) | DDC 813/.6—dc23
LC record available at https://lccn.loc.gov/2016007219

Printed in the United States of America

For Anne

PART 1

In Another Country

Chapter One

I sat in the cantina at the Hotel Baja, putting away rum with lime and scratching out the crossword in a three-week-old Tijuana newspaper. The crossword was pure hubris. I barely spoke enough Spanish to order coffee. I was just about to pack it in when Grady Doyle arrived for his evening tequila.

"Been looking all over for you," he said, hanging like an ape from the doorframe with the setting sun surrounding him in a bloody corona. "You still thinking about offing yourself?"

"Authors sell better after they're dead," I replied without looking up.

"You're not really gonna do it though, right?" he said.

"Depends on how this crossword goes."

Grady sauntered behind the bar and leaned over to look at the paper spread out on the bar top's chipped lacquer.

"I got bad news for you," Grady said feigning commiseration. "None of your answers are written in what I would strictly call the Spanish language."

"Then what the hell is it?" I said.

"Looks like Esperanto. Maybe Apache Indian? Definitely not Spanish."

"Suicide it is," I said, and threw my pen across the room.

"You Catholic? Cause Catholics don't let suicides into heaven you know," Grady said with a frown.

"Technically it's murder. When you ice your nom de plume, it's murder. The Pope got a problem with murder?"

"Not if you're sorry you did it."

"Ah, there's the rub," I said. "I'll never be sorry." I've written thirty-two romance novels starring Alasdair MacMerkin, the Scottish vampire detective. All of them were under the pseudonym Toulouse Velour, and I was hoping to publish my thirty-third novel—one bereft of Scots, vampires, and genital euphemisms—under my own name, Henry Cooper. The second part of my plan was to issue a press release detailing poor Toulouse's gruesome death. My agent was not a great supporter of either part.

I snapped my fingers and pointed at the cooler next to Grady's feet. He kicked off the cheap lid and sent it careening into the corner, where it scared a gecko that had been offering silent support for my cruciverbal efforts. The gecko flicked its tongue at him and scurried away to the safety of a crack in the wall.

"See what you did," I said. "That gecko was my only friend."

Grady fished out my personal bottle of Sailor Jerry and kicked the cooler over, dumping the slushy contents out to mingle with the dust. He scratched his nose and considered the mess he'd made.

"Don't it bother you the booze here sucks so bad you have to bring your own?" Grady asked.

It did bother me, but it wasn't something I felt compelled to change. I was only down here on advice from my agent. I was supposed to clear my head and make a decision on my literary future, maybe even find some inspiration for a new book. It was only supposed to have been for a few days, maybe a week. That was a month ago.

"Yeah, but what are you gonna do?" I said.

"Buy the place," Grady said. He slapped the bar and hopped on the balls of his feet. "Which I did this morning. The hotel too." He was proud of this, though I couldn't fathom why. I thought the joint was a shit hole. I turned around on my stool to reexamine the place. Maybe I had missed something.

The cantina hung off the Hotel Baja like a broken ornament on a burnt-out Christmas tree. About the size of a barn and furnished in the same fashion, it was empty save for a young American trying not to pass out in the corner. The hotel was located in the center of Pendira,

Mexico, a town with a population of sixty people and ninety-two stray dogs. The closest city was Ensenada, and that was two hours of mountain-hugging, crumbling road away. Low patronage was common.

The decor consisted of a poster-sized Tecate ad tacked to the wooden paneling behind the bar. A half dozen splintered wood tables and a set of plastic lawn chairs scrounged from someone's porch filled out the floor space. There wasn't a roof, but Butch Wilson, the hotel's erstwhile proprietor, had hung a corrugated-metal billboard precariously above the bar as a jerry-rigged awning. There was a fair amount of garbage on the floor, carried in by the wind or left behind by the intermittent patrons.

I hadn't missed anything. The place was a shit hole.

"You bought the hotel?" I said. "You got that kind of money?" I hadn't pegged Grady for a guy with cash to spare. I hadn't pegged him as anything, really. All I knew about him was he was an ex-pat American, had been some sort of cop in his former life, and liked tequila at sunset. This had been enough to sustain a solid friendship over the past four weeks.

"Oh, I got it for a song," Grady said. "Butch's been trying to get out of here since the cartel wars started heating up in Tijuana. I lowballed him and he took it."

"You're not concerned about what's going on up north?" I asked. Though I couldn't read the article, the front page of the paper had a grisly photo of the latest carnage between the rival cartels near the border.

"That shit'll blow over. And when it does I'm gonna fix this place up nice. Get some of those pothead surfers down here from San Diego. You want some limes?" He bounded out from behind the bar and to the door, where a lime tree stood just outside. It was a homely, gnarled-looking beast, and it pushed against the edge of the doorframe like a medieval siege tower threatening to breach the entire west wall. Still, it had good limes and Grady studied it closely to find a few of the riper ones.

He moved with a lazy athleticism, dulled by years of disuse. He was of the age that I would describe as older, but not old, which put him somewhere between forty and whatever. His white T-shirt was soiled to a nice dirt color, its V-neck stretched to the breaking point. His skin was tanned into Naugahyde from days spent lying in the sun. His pants had once been chinos but were now simply vestiges of material ending just below his knees. He wore a pair of leather sandals so old and filthy they seemed to sprout from his hirsute, hobbit-like feet. Dark explosions of hair fell out from under his Miller Lite baseball cap and mixed into his unkempt beard. Back home, this man would have gotten thrown out of a McDonald's. Here, he just bought a hotel.

A man with a deep-orange spray-on tan and an absurdly tight sleeveless T-shirt brushed past Grady as he picked the limes. A pasty counterpart in a tailored three-piece followed closely after the first man. They moved predatorily to the table where the drunk American had lost his battle with consciousness. I watched them over my shoulder between sips of rum. The tanned one reached into the impossible mess of the drunken man's hair and pulled his head up. The one in the suit leaned over to examine his face. After a moment of deep consideration, he nodded and the other one let the drunk's head fall back on the table with a hard thud, like a pumpkin falling off a porch. They pulled chairs from a nearby table. The suit brushed his chair with a handkerchief and inspected it thoroughly before sitting. The tanned one turned his around and straddled the back.

"You know them?" Grady asked. He had returned to his place behind the bar and was slicing limes with a hunting knife. Keeping all of his fingers attached to his hand didn't seem to be a concern, as all of his attention was directed at the three men in the corner.

"Butch checked the kid in this morning," I said. I had been using the hotel's only phone, located in a booth in the miniscule lobby, to call my agent for my daily bread of praise and abuse. The kid looked to be in his late teens, dressed in jeans and one of those Army-surplus jackets I'd heard were making a comeback, and moved with a fidgety wariness. He checked in as Richard Kimble, which made me laugh out loud. I never understood why someone would be so clever with a fake name. Just open a phonebook and pick one. Guy should've just called himself

Johnny McAlias for all the good a name like Richard Kimble would do him. It was pretty clear he was on the run, and Butch, smelling the pungent aroma of desperation mixed with fear on the poor bastard, had charged him an extra fifty bucks.

"Kimble?" Grady said. He finished cutting the limes and dropped a slice in my glass before refilling it. There was a swallow at the bottom of the bottle, and he took it for himself. "What the hell kind of name is that?"

"A fake one, I suppose," I said, taking a smaller sip than usual. I wanted to prolong the hundred-foot Bataan Death March back to my room for another bottle. "He told Butch he's a writer, but something about him makes me think he's on the run from somebody."

"A writer, huh?" Grady said. "He gonna kill himself, too?"

"I hope not. I don't want the market to get saturated," I said. Grady slid the hunting knife under the bar and grabbed the empty bottle of rum by the neck. He dropped it down by his thigh and held it there.

"Do me a favor and keep still," he said. Behind me, I heard a crash and the sound of chairs falling over. There was incoherent muttering followed by a hand slapping flesh and a thud like someone getting punched in the stomach. I kept my head still and shifted my eyes to my right. The tanned man had his arms hooked under Richard Kimble's armpits and was dragging him out the door into the failing light. I felt and then smelled the man in the suit standing just behind me. He smelled like Listerine and tobacco.

"You guys didn't see nothing, right?" the man said. His voice was smooth and jovial as if he were asking about the drink specials. Grady didn't respond. The man chuckled, a cold, mirthless sound, and reached inside his jacket. Grady's muscles tensed. A massive revolver hung from the man's shoulder holster like salami in a deli window. He reached past it into his pocket and pulled out a wad of bills as thick as my arm. He counted out a half dozen fifties and reached over the bar to stuff them into Grady's shirt pocket. That was his mistake.

Grady grabbed his wrist, pulled him across the bar, and swung the rum bottle at his head with a forehand shot that would've made Roger

Federer stand up and cheer. The bottle erupted in a fountain of broken glass that showered over me like jagged raindrops. Grady spun him around and pinned him against the bar. He grabbed the hunting knife and held the gleaming tip a hair away from the man's eye.

"Get his gun would you, Coop," Grady said. There was blood on the bar and in my rum. "Coop, you there, buddy?" Grady had a serene smile on his face that was somehow unsettling. I didn't look quite so peaceful, but I was able to reach gingerly across the man's chest, unclip the holster, and ease the gun out. It was heavier than I expected and I almost dropped it. I held it out for Grady, but he shook his head.

"Just hold onto it a minute. Keep an eye on the door in case his friend comes back." He grabbed a fistful of the man's hair and pulled his head up while moving the knife to his throat. "I don't like men who throw their money around," Grady growled. "And I don't like people coming into my place and roughing up my customers."

The man let out a groggy groan as blood leaked from his scalp onto the bar. Grady took hold of his oxford shirt, heaved him off the bar, and onto his feet. He held his prisoner in a half nelson, the knife close to his throat, as he walked him around the bar.

"I don't think this one's up to talking. If we want information, we'll have to ask the one outside."

"We need information?" I asked.

"Take the gun and try to look like you know how to use it," Grady said, then waited a moment and started for the door. I followed.

It could have been the four tumblers of rum. It could have been loyalty to Grady, who, even though I had only known him for a few weeks, I considered a friend. It could have been that I felt it was wrong for two armed men to pick on an unconscious drunk. It could have been those things, but it wasn't. It was the story.

I envisioned myself recounting the tale to some gorgeous young blond in a crowded bar. I imagined commanding a boothful of friends and colleagues on the third floor of Chicago's Chop House with a whiskey in one hand and pantomiming the gun with the other. I thought about the countless people who would ask me to regale them with my "Mexico" anecdote at innumerable cocktail parties for years to come. I followed Grady into the dark, dangerous abyss for nothing more than the story I could tell.

It was dusk when we stepped out of the cantina. "Magic hour," they call it. Everything took on a blurred, fuzzy quality, like an old photograph found in the bottom of a steamer trunk. The tanned man stood next to a new-looking Ford pickup. The burning red tip of his cigarette danced as he spoke.

"The fuck is this?" he said. It was a Texas accent and it sounded more angry than surprised.

"You've got my customer there," Grady said from over his prisoner's shoulder.

"Well, that's my partner there, *amigo*," the Texan said. "You okay, Dell?" Dell gave an indecipherable groan as he started to come around, and Grady adjusted his grip on him.

"Fucking guy hit me with something, Andy," Dell said with a horse croak.

"It was a bottle," Grady said. "Where's my guy?"

"Right here," Andy said, and he opened the Ford's door. Richard Kimble tumbled out and landed face-up and limp on the gravel. There wasn't a part of him showing that wasn't bloody or bruised. His breathing was shallow and raspy, like an old man climbing stairs. Andy must have been working him over while we were dealing with Dell inside. Andy flicked cigarette ash onto the poor bastard's face. Kimble didn't even flinch. He was done for the night. "You a friend of his?"

"Like I said, he's a customer," Grady said. "Fella paid for safe lodging. I'm just making sure he gets what he paid for."

"And who the hell is this?" Andy said, and pointed at me. "The bellboy?" Grady didn't answer. Unfortunately, I've never been able to stand a silence, especially if there was a question hanging in the air.

"Henry Cooper," I said. The words fell out of my mouth like Jenga blocks. "People call me Coop. I'm a writer, you know, books."

"A writer? You write anything I'd know?" Andy said. It may seem like a strange question for someone standing over a beaten and bloody stranger to ask another man holding a gun on him, but it wasn't really. It's the inevitable question every writer gets asked when he tells someone what he does for a living.

"Does it matter?" I said.

"Look, man," Andy said, and reached inside his jacket. I flinched and almost pulled the trigger. Grady tensed and tightened his grip on Dell. Andy grinned and slipped a second Pall Mall next to the one already in his mouth. He gripped the lit one between his thumb and forefinger and placed its dying ember against the end of the fresh one. He exhaled as he spoke. "I just want to know what I'm dealing with."

"Just tell him, Coop," Grady said, and I could have sworn I saw him smirk.

"I write the *Alasdair MacMerkin* series," I said.

"The what?"

"Romance novels about a Scottish vampire detective," Grady said, and snorted.

"No shit," Andy said, and then tilted his chin up in thought. "Yeah, my girlfriend reads that shit. There's like a thousand of them. You write those?" I nodded in the way a guilty child admits he wet his pants. "But the name on the book ain't Cooper. It's uh, shit, help me out."

"Toulouse Velour," I mumbled.

"Toulouse Velour," Andy repeated relishing each tacky syllable. "Ain't Toulouse a chick's name though?"

"I'm pretty sure it's a guy's name," I said.

"Pretty sure?'

"I never officially checked," I admitted with a shrug.

"Can we focus on the issue at hand, fellas?" Grady growled. Andy placed his boot on top of Richard Kimble's chest, claiming him like a conquistador planting a flag, and leaned down with his forearms crossed over his knee.

"I got paid good money to find this kid," Andy said, "and I'm not about to hand him over to some fag writes chick books."

"Don't let the books fool you, Andy," Grady said. "Coop's not above shooting an unarmed man." Andy laughed.

"I gotta say, I ain't too convinced," he said. "He can barely hold the thing straight, let alone shoot. Ain't man enough to shoot, I bet. Ain't even man enough to write a man's book. You know who's good, Toulouse? You know who writes some real good shit? That guy, aw fuck, who's that guy. Wrote the thing they made into the movie with the guy who did that other movie. Grisham! You should write something like John Grisham."

That's when I shot him.

I have nothing against John Fucking Grisham. I enjoy his books, even some of the movies, as much as anyone else. He's never done anything to me personally. I've never even met the man. The only thing John Fucking Grisham ever did was to catch the literary fancy of my father. Dad was a newspaperman, and when a newspaperman reads for leisure it's almost always nonfiction. John Fucking Grisham was Dad's one indulgence in the field of fiction and, according to him, John Fucking Grisham was the pinnacle of not only the legal thriller, but all fiction. When I showed him my first short story, the one that had won first prize in the high school literary contest, he looked it over with barely feigned interest, grunted, and gave a four-word review: "It's no John Grisham."

Dad left us that same year. I was fourteen. When I published my first book under my real name a decade later, he sent a Hallmark card—he always cared enough to send the very best—with Snoopy reading a book on the front. Inside, he had scrawled in his epileptic handwriting, "I read your book. It was no John Grisham." Since then, whenever I publish a book I get a card. Don't ask me how he knows my pen name. I suspect my mother told him, but I've never broached the subject with her. Sometimes Snoopy is on the cover. Sometimes it's Garfield. Once it was a busty woman in a bikini, reading on a beach. Regardless of the cover, the message is always the same.

Some people grow up in the shadow of a sibling. They have to listen to their parents lament, "Why can't you be more like your brother?" I didn't have a brother. I had John. Fucking. Grisham.

It takes exactly five pounds of pressure to pull the trigger of a

.40-calliber semiautomatic Glock 22, which, Grady later told me, was the gun I held in my hand. He also told me the gun had been involved in several lawsuits over its likelihood to go off by accident. I like to think it was an accident, shooting the Texan. I like to think I flinched or panicked, or whatever, but I know better. This wasn't the first time someone had called out my masculinity, or my writing chops, or both together. There had been dozens of cocktail parties where this exact exchange had taken place. The difference was that I had never been holding a gun at the cocktail parties.

I shot Andy in the foot, but not the foot sitting on top of Richard Kimble. This piece of luck had nothing do with my aim—my eyes had been closed when I squeezed the trigger. Andy jumped in the air and fell on his ass, howling in pain and holding his Wolverine boot as blood poured through his fingers. Grady moved fast. He shoved Dell to the ground next to Andy and told me to grab our new unconscious friend. I stood over the poor schlub as I tried to decide where to put the gun. I started to shove it down the front of my pants but thought better of it. I didn't want my crotch to look like Andy's foot. Grady grabbed the gun away.

"Just get this asshole inside and call Digby. Wake him up if you have to," he said. I grabbed Kimble's shirt with both hands and dragged him into the relative safety of the cantina. Ten minutes later Grady entered, wiping the knife on his pants.

"They're gone," he said.

"Where did they go?" I asked. I had pulled the guy onto a chair and was trying to wake him up to take a drink of water. He was moaning steadily, which I took as a good sign.

"I'm guessing Ensenada. There's a hospital there. Dell, the one in the suit, seemed okay to drive. They should make it there before Andy loses his foot."

"You let them go?" I asked.

"They're not in any shape to try anything else tonight."

"But they'll be back, won't they? Shouldn't we have called the cops?"

"Shooting a man is an expensive problem in Mexico. I'm a little short on cash after the hotel and all." He walked over to the bar sink and turned on the water. There was a plaintive groan from the pipes, but only a trickle of water dribbled out. Grady cursed and used what he could to wash his face and the back of his neck. He dried them both with the hem of his shirt. Our poor friend groaned again and leaned forward in his chair. I caught him just before he fell, and eased him back upright.

"You call Digby?" Grady asked.

"Got his voice mail. I'm not going down to his place in the dark. You don't know for sure those guys left town."

"They're gone," Grady said, and waved his hand at me to dismiss my fears. "If you can't get Digby, will you at least help me take him up to Doc's room?"

"Those assholes are gonna come back for this asshole, Grady," I said.

"Probably," Grady said, lifting the man's feet. I grabbed his arms. "After we drop him at Doc's, I'm going to bed. I want to get out to the race route early tomorrow."

"Are you listening?" I said. "Those guys are gonna come back here, and a rum bottle won't be enough to stop them."

"What should I have done?" Grady said, walking backward, avoiding the bar and kicking open the rear door with his foot. "Should I have slit their throats and dumped them in a couple of shallow graves out in the desert?"

"No, I guess not," I said, struggling to lift my half of our comatose charge. Less than a day later, I would be wishing he had done that very thing.

Chapter Two

I awoke to the sound of someone cutting toenails. It was Digby, the concierge, although the title was applied loosely. He was sitting on a stool in the corner of my room, with his shoes and socks off. He wore his usual plaid trousers with suspenders over a sleeveless Flying Burrito Brothers T-shirt. According to Butch, Digby had literally come down out of the mountains a few years ago. He'd been covered with dirt, carrying a frayed canvas backpack containing a hunting knife, the same one Grady used to cut limes, and a half-finished book of crossword puzzles. He had asked for a job, and Butch hired him on as a sort of Man Friday. This meant climbing into Butch's wheezing pickup truck twice a month to get supplies in Ensenada. Other than that, Digby spent his time smoking weed and giving the occasional surfing lesson to the infrequent guests.

Digby's story changed with the tide. No one could pin down where he was from, what he had been doing in the Sierra Madres, or anything else about his past. He had once referenced a rich ex-wife in California who actually paid *him* alimony, but who knows if any of the women he spoke of existed outside of his own fevered imagination. He may have spent time in the military, but which branch, and for that matter which country, remained a mystery. His accent changed not only from day to day, but from sentence to sentence. He told stories about chaos and beauty from all seven continents, but it was always unclear whether he had experienced these vignettes himself, or was simply repeating things he'd heard. He never spoke of any occupation before coming to the Hotel Baja, and it seemed wrong to ask him flat out. I engaged him in conversation whenever possible to suss out his origins, but even after a month I hadn't found any answers. Grady thought it was becoming an unhealthy obsession.

"Is there a reason you're doing that right here?" I asked wiping the crusts of sleep from my eyes. Digby plucked an emery board from behind his ear and gently swiped it across his big toe.

"I can't find my clippers. I knew you had one," Digby said, as if we had been clothes-swapping roommates for years. "Boss says you gotta get up. You're gonna miss the race."

"Why would Butch give a shit about the race?" I said, and remembered Grady had bought the hotel yesterday, which made him Digby's new boss. Digby was a man who adapted quickly. He tossed the clippers aside and ran his hand through his mop of tangled dirty-blond hair.

"Had some excitement last night, didn't you, Mr. Cooper?"

"I've told you, Digby. Call me Coop," I said. I stretched out until I nearly fell off the bed and reached for the remains of last night's rum. It wasn't nearly enough, but Grady would have a cooler of beer up at the race so it was no tragedy.

"You had some excitement last night, *Coop*," Digby said. He stood up, leaned against the wall, and shoved his hands in his trouser pockets, looking like a surfer's version of Dillinger.

"There was some commotion," I said. "What do you know of it?"

"I know there's a guy nearly in a coma over in Doc's room," Digby said. He reached in his pocket and pulled out a small pistol with a pearl handle. He tossed it on the bed between my bare feet. "And I know the guys who put him there will be back."

"I was kind of thinking the same thing," I said. "And I was kind of hoping I was wrong."

"No, they'll be back. You shot the guy's toe off. A man doesn't let something like that stand," Digby said. "Take the gun, Coop. That's my favorite derringer. It only gets two shots, but I figure if you haven't hit anything by then it ain't gonna make a difference."

"That's what you figure, huh? What if there're more than two of them?"

"You ever a fire a gun before? I mean before last night."

"Nope."

"Then if there were more than two, you'd be fucked if I gave you a Uzi," Digby said, and strolled to the door. As he passed the threshold he turned on his heel, his hands stuck in his gabardine pockets. "Boss is waiting for you up on the bluff. Oh, and the water truck didn't come today. So no showers."

He left whistling an old tune I couldn't quite place. It didn't surprise me Digby carried around a two-shot pistol in his pocket. It wouldn't have surprised me if he carried a flame-thrower in his sock. What surprised me was how my world suddenly had an abundance of guns in it. Twenty-four hours earlier I had never even held a firearm. Now I was living like somebody found in the pages of Mickey Spillane's wastebasket.

I got up and kicked open the door to my bathroom. Pendira was so far off the map that it didn't have regular running water. Every two weeks a tanker came through and filled up the tower. This meant the people of Pendira practiced a forced form of water conservation made worse whenever the truck was delayed.

My agent, Peter Oxblood, had warned me to pick up a few gallons of bottled water on the way down. I was glad I had taken his advice. I plugged the sink and dumped a bottle in the basin so I could wash my face and brush my teeth. The Hotel Baja had been Ox's suggestion. He had been dragged there once by one of his clients for a bachelor party. He insisted its brand of low-tide charm would help me get my head out of my ass. His words.

After four years of perfecting the art of pretension in a place called college, I was lucky enough to publish my first novel. It was a long literary affair about a bovine veterinarian's encounter with a PETA-like vegan cult. I called it *Madge*, and I have no idea how many copies it sold because Ox never had the heart to tell me.

He couldn't, however, hide the reviews from me. The book critic for the *Washington Post* suggested my novel made a solid case to reconsider book burning. The *Chicago Reader* merely printed the first page with the suggestion it be used to line birdcages throughout the greater

Chicagoland area. My favorite of all was the little New England paper, one that did not have a book reviewer nor had it ever in its history printed a book review prior to this one, which described my book as the combined failure of delusional ego and lack of talent. The review ended with the terse yet grammatically suspect sentence: It's no John Grisham.

I fled to the one place that had always been a sanctuary for me: the bookstore. I huddled in the corner of the Romance section, where I wouldn't be confronted by anyone I knew, either in person or on book covers. I sipped on black coffee and wondered if high school kids might respect me enough to let me teach them English. I was about to take a stroll down the Career Help aisle when I heard a scuffle behind me. A seventy-year-old woman was leaning against her walker and slapping a teenaged bookseller twice her size with a trade paperback.

"I already read this one, idiot," she wailed. "I want the new one!"

"That is the new one," the poor clerk replied with surprising calm. He had turned to take the brunt of her tirade with his back. Another clerk, a mousy-looking girl with a ponytail, peeked around the bookshelf. The clerk under fire looked at her pleadingly, but she tilted her head up as if she heard someone call her name and quickly disappeared.

"How could it be new?" the incensed old woman said. "I already read it."

"It came out last month, ma'am. They can't write them as fast as you read them."

"I've had it with this nonsense," the woman said, and threw the book at him. He dodged and the paperback landed next to me. "I want to see your manager." She didn't wait for a reply and stalked off, walker clanging like a battle staff, presumably to harass the manager. I picked up the book, curious to see what could inspire such an insatiable need in an otherwise-frail old woman.

The cover showed a bare-chested man with abs that could cut glass. He was bending over a woman in a flowing gown as she reached for a wooden stake at the side of her bed. I found that the author had well over twenty books on the shelf above me, all in the same series. I remembered hearing a story about a *Newsday* columnist who'd written a romance novel as a joke and it became a bestseller. At the time I took it as a bitter grad-student yarn designed to deride the low-born genre novel, but looking down the aisle filled with bustiers and cod pieces I was struck with inspiration. I left the store with the complete series, along with the beginnings of several others.

Henry Cooper, for all intents and purposes, was dead to the publishing industry. What better place to reinvent myself than in the polar opposite of literary fiction? I locked myself in my garden apartment and read every romance novel available, of which there was legion. I ate up every convention and every trope. I read and I wrote. I absorbed and I disseminated. After four months locked up like Don Quixote in his attic, my only contact with the outside world being delivery guys and Ox's messages on my answering machine, I emerged just as addled as the man of La Mancha, but my quest was already finished. The first *MacMerkin* novel was complete. I had fallen as Henry Cooper and stood up again as Toulouse Velour. Ox sold the book within two weeks. It became a phenomenon within two months of hitting the shelves. As the ink flowed, so did the money, and things went pretty well for a few years.

About a year ago, I found a fruit basket on my doorstep. An assistant or intern at my publisher sent me a fruit basket, a congratulations on *MacMerkin's Regret* hitting the *New York Times* Best Seller List. It would have been a thoughtful gesture if the basket hadn't been filled with an assortment of fruit wrapped in pink tissue and surrounded by bath gels and scents not meant for anyone with a Y chromosome. The basket was also pink, and the graphic on the card was a silhouette of a woman taking a bubble bath. The caption read "For when you need a day just to be a girl." It was after the basket's arrival that I started to call my masculinity into question. The doubts continued to creep in until it culminated on the morning after a party at Ox's place. I woke up with a hangover and a brunette. Usually this was something to be happy about, but I made the mistake of taking her to breakfast. A friend of hers had brought her to the party because they were both enormous fans of Toulouse Velour, who was supposed to be there.

"I've read all her books," she had said between bites of Belgian waffle.

"Toulouse is a man," I said, realizing she had no idea who I was. Toulouse's identity was not exactly an open secret in the publishing industry. Only I, Ox, the publisher, and a handful of others knew. Knowing Toulouse's real name was like knowing that Carly Simon was really singing about Warren Beatty, or David Geffen, or whoever it was. "It's a man's name."

"Oh, that's just a pen name," she had laughed. "Like a joke, you know. A man doesn't write that way. A man can't write that way. At least not a straight man."

I had called Ox from the cab on the way home from breakfast and asked him if he thought our publisher might be interested in something new. Maybe something edgy or even gritty? A noir tour de force. Maybe I could even publish it under my real name? He informed me that my head was up my ass and suggested a long holiday in Baja.

In my suite at the Hotel Baja I dragged my toothbrush across my teeth and considered the small pistol sitting at the edge of my bed. I kept my eye on it as I slipped into my jeans and a fairly clean T-shirt. I told myself there was no need for a gun. I am not a gun person. I live a life devoid of guns. If you live by the gun, you die by the gun. You'll shoot someone's eye out. Just say no, and so forth. I was flat out not going to carry a gun.

I almost made it to the door before I turned back and stuffed the derringer in my pocket.

Chapter Three

The race was the Baja 500. Grady was nuts about it. It was his third favorite subject to talk about after women and college football. Few women ever came to the Hotel Baja, and in June with two months until kick-off the race shot up to number one with a bullet. The contingent of trucks, cars, and motorcycles took off from Ensenada to bust through five hundred kilometers of desert, scrub brush, broken roads, hills, valleys, and anything else that was never supposed to support a vehicle. It attracted thrill seekers and hangers-on from all over looking for glory in the small subculture that was into that sort of thing. According to Grady there was little, if any, money in it, but there were enough women in pleather pants and bikini tops to make it worthwhile.

A tiny sliver of the route ran by a spot up on a bluff about a mile away from the hotel. The actual race wasn't until next week, but Grady had been dragging me up there with a cooler of Tecate and sandwiches to watch the practice racers for the last couple of days. He had been trying to educate me on the different models of large bore motorcycles, stock VWs, and all the rest to no avail. I didn't give a shit about any of it. I went because the spot was up on a bluff that overlooked the Pacific. I liked having a brew in the sunshine and watching the surf crash into the cliff. The occasional blast of neon and motor oil that each vehicle brought was really more of an annoyance than anything else.

"Now what was that last one called, Coop?" Grady asked. He leaned back in his canvas folding chair and put his thumb and fore-finger under his beard.

"That would be a 1972 Ford Who-Gives-A-Fuck," I said, and

shoved my hand into the icy cooler water. I came up with a can of Tecate and popped the top.

"Wrong," Grady said. "It was a stock VW. Can you tell me what type of engine it might have had?"

"I can't. Can you tell me what happened to the drunk guy after I left last night?"

"You need to apply yourself, Coop, or else you'll never graduate from Grady's School of Off-Road Racing," he said, wagging his finger at me. He chuckled and locked his fingers behind his head. "Don't worry about that guy. Doc's got him on a cot in his room. He sedated him, but he should be up for talking by supper time."

"Digby agrees that the guys from last night will be back," I said.

"Probably," Grady said. "He say anything else?"

"No. If they're coming back, then why are we just sitting here?"

"You wanna go up to Ensenada and make a complaint?" Grady said, and tossed his beer can at the orange crate we used for empties. He missed and waved at it with his hand as if it would jump up into the crate on its own power if properly beckoned.

"Yes, goddamn it, something," I said, getting up and properly disposing of the empty for him.

"OK, fine, but be prepared to spend some time in jail for shooting the guy's toe off. Either that or bring enough cash to pay off every cop from here to there. That's if we even make it to Ensenada."

"Why wouldn't we make it to Ensenada?" I asked. Grady looked at me as if I were a child who just said something cute and incredibly naive.

"Dell and Andy were dumb, but they weren't stupid," Grady said, and grabbed another beer. "Ain't much traffic between here and the city. All they have to do is camp out on the mountain road and wait for us to come by. Wouldn't take much to stop a car up there. They take us out and they can take their time getting to the kid."

"Can't we call somebody?"

"Anyone we call is gonna want you to answer for the guy's toe. Had to shoot him, didn't you? Couldn't handle a little criticism?"

"I'm just a roiling ball of rage, Grady. I can't help it," I said. "So we're stuck here, is that it?"

"Were you planning on leaving anytime soon?"

"No."

"Then what do you care?" Grady said, rolling the cold can along his sweaty forehead. "Don't worry about it. I don't want to do shit until the guy wakes up and we can talk to him. We got plenty of supplies and they don't. Water truck'll be here tomorrow. We'll wait 'em out for a couple of days. Sound good?"

"I still think we should do something." I grumbled.

"I did do something," Grady said. "I did a little investigating. I found this." He leaned over the side of his chair and the aluminum legs squeaked a complaint about the weight shift. He grabbed a knapsack, placed it on his lap, and started going through it. He pulled out a bag of weed, a post-card, and a small leather portfolio. He handed me the portfolio.

"Where did these come from?" I asked. The portfolio was cracked soft brown leather and looked like something you'd find in your grand-father's desk. I untied the string, pulled open the flap, and reached inside, finding a wad of yellowed papers. It didn't have a title, it was handwritten, and at most there was enough for possibly one-third of a book, but I recognized it at once as a manuscript.

"Recognize it?" Grady asked. He had produced a pack of rolling papers and was getting to work on a fresh joint. I flipped through the stiff, crackling pages. Some of them were typewritten and some were in a rolling loopy handwriting. I found a heading about a quarter of the way through that read, *Chapter 17 (Forward to Scott)*. It sounded familiar, but I couldn't quite place it.

"What makes you think I should recognize it," I said.

"Because you're supposed to be a writer," he said with a smirk. "Here, I found this with it too." He handed me a copy of Ernest Hemingway's *A Moveable Feast*.

"They go together?" I said. I held the relic of a manuscript away from me as if a wider perspective were needed. At arm's length it still looked like an old bundle of paper.

"Doc thinks so. I showed it to him this morning 'cause you hadn't gotten up yet. Says chapter seventeen is about Scott Fitzgerald. It matches the copy of the book. You read it?"

"*A Moveable Feast*? Yeah, in college."

"I tried to read him once. The one about the fish and the old fart."

"What did you think?"

"I gave up halfway through. I don't like fishing, let alone reading about it. I found that in Richard Kimble's room. It was in his suitcase under the bed."

"I can't believe you tossed his room."

"Hey, I helped him out of a jam last night because he was a customer. I'm not going in whole hog unless I know what he's involved in."

"Why are we involved at all? It had nothing to do with us until you went all Billy Jack on the guy." Grady adjusted himself in his lawn chair so that he could look me in the eye.

"People need help, and if you can help them, then you do it," he said. "You don't, then you're not a man, are you?"

"I guess."

"No guessing. That's the fact of it. Are you a man, Coop?"

"The way I pee would seem to suggest so, yes."

"Then there you have it," he said, and slapped his bare thigh for emphasis.

"You didn't have to go through his things," I said. A truck that looked like Optimus Prime and a praying mantis had a love child roared by, drowning out Grady's answer, but I could tell from the look on his face he didn't care much for the man's privacy.

"Goddamn it," Grady said when the truck passed by. We had placed our chairs under the shade of a rock wall that nearly blocked out the sound of the racers until they were almost on top of us. "What was that? I missed it." I raised my hands to show I had no idea. Grady threw his empty can in the road, and I turned back to the manuscript.

Red pencil marks littered the pages along with extensive notations in the margins. At the top of each page, the initials *HB* were scrawled in quick and impatient handwriting. I looked back at the leather portfolio it came in. A brass plate with the same initials was stamped on the outside.

"This looks like it could have been one of the first drafts of the book," I said, thumbing through to the last page. A final note was written there in the same impatient bloody scrawl as the others. It read *"I won't let him ruin all that we have left."*

"Is it worth something?" Grady asked.

"I don't know," I said absently. The note was odd. I was pretty sure HB was the editor, probably a name I had once known and had forgotten. The question was: for whom was the note written? The date at the top of the page was January 1962. Hemingway shot himself in '61. I doubted the note was meant for a dead man. I slid the pages back in the portfolio and dropped it back into Grady's bag. I looked down to find a business card in my lap. It must have fallen out of the portfolio when I pulled out the manuscript. "It might be worth something if it's real."

"How much?" Grady asked. The card looked expensive, thick stock, embossed lettering. The information, however, was rather spartan. It consisted of a name, N. Thandy, not even a full name, a PO box in Atlanta, and an occupation: Collector—Rare Books and Antiquities.

"You mean, would it be worth enough to kill for?" I said, sliding the card into my pocket.

"We don't know they were gonna kill him," Grady said, reaching into the cooler for a new beer. I noted it was his fourth since I'd arrived. I had no idea how many he'd had while waiting for me. "They may've just wanted to rough him up until he spilled where he stashed the book."

"You don't know they were after the book," I said. "He could've knocked up some rich guy's daughter for all we know."

"You got a point there," Grady said with a chuckle. "You're a smart guy. Guess that's what makes your books so popular."

"The name on the cover is what makes my books so popular," I said, and took the remains of the joint Grady proffered. "I don't know much about rare books and what they go for, but my agent does. I'll give him a call. See what he has to say. If I can get him to stop . . ." I thought I saw the edge of the rock wall move, and for a moment I wondered how good Grady's weed was. Could it have hit me that quickly? Was I being paranoid? I decided to err on the side of caution and slid the derringer out of my pocket, holding it close to my thigh.

"Stop what?" Grady said.

"Anybody there?" I yelled to the shadows.

"You got me," a voice said from behind the wall. I saw the gun first. It made my tiny derringer look like an action-figure accessory. Its nickel plating gleamed in the sun, and a cruel grin followed it.

"Bet you motherfuckers didn't expect to see me again, huh," Dell said, and racked a round into the chamber.

Chapter Four

"We certainly didn't expect to see you this soon," Grady said casually. "Where's your buddy?"

Dell stood with his legs shoulder width apart, leaning back on his heels. A long, ugly gash was sutured up the left side of his face. It would leave a scar that no woman, despite the saying, would dig. He wore the same suit as last night, evidenced by the blood on it, some from his head and some from his partner's foot.

"Hospital up the road," Dell said. His non-gun hand was stuck in his pocket, and every part of him was relaxed save the eyes. They were alive with a hateful electric fervor. I had no doubt he'd pull the trigger. He'd do Grady first and then me; probably take his time with me. The derringer hidden against my thigh felt infinitesimally small. There was a layer of greasy sweat between my palm and the handle, and I suspected that if I were to draw the gun, it would fly out of my hand and land innocuously next to his Italian loafers. "But we still got a job to do, ya know?"

"I admire your work ethic," I said, which was the truth. I doubt I would have tried to write anything the day after a night like Dell had.

"I can't wait to hurt you dead," Dell growled. Perhaps he thought my admiration was insincere.

"Ok, Dell," Grady said, taking a sip from his beer. "What now?" Dell turned his attention and his gun on Grady.

"What happens now is you tell me which eye you want a bullet in," Dell said.

"That's a stupid fucking question, and I'm not going to answer it," Grady said.

"Look, man," I said raising my hand and leveling the little two-shot at Dell's chest. "I got a gun. You got a gun. Let's just talk this out. I mean Grady and I don't even really know what's going on here, you know? Maybe this doesn't have to get violent."

"Sure it does," Dell said. He took another step from the shadow of the rock wall and into the sunshine. He stood in the middle of the little dirt track. I heard a high, insect-like whine from somewhere in the distance. Dell was too focused on our standoff to hear it. "Andy wanted me to kill you slow, but I'll kill you quick and make something up to tell him."

"I appreciate that." Grady said. The whine was getting louder now, but it could have just been the sound of the surf as it traveled up the bluff. "It's mighty white of you."

"Honestly," Dell said. "I just don't have the time. I gotta kill you two, then kill the asshole with the book, then find the book. You're lucky you caught me with a full dance card, is all."

"Who you working for?" Grady said. Dell's head dropped back and he launched into a theatrical guffaw. When it waned down to a giggle he shook his head.

"Buddy, you don't wanna kn—" Dell started, but stopped when he heard the buzzing roar coming around the rocks. It was too late. He only had time to drop his jaw as a VW pickup slammed into him. His body spun over the hood like an epileptic ballerina, catapulted into the air, and came to rest at the edge of the cliff. The VW slid to a stop, kicking up a cloud of dust that drifted back up the road toward us. Grady burst out of his chair and sprinted to Dell with a speed I wouldn't have expected from him. In a moment he had Dell's gun in his hand. He slid it into his belt at the small of his back and dropped his T-shirt over it as the VW's driver approached.

"Oh fuck, man," the driver said, pulling his helmet off. He was dressed in white and neon-green leather and I wondered how he could stand the heat in an outfit like that. He held his helmet in one hand and in the other a small plastic box I assumed was a first aid kit. Grady held his empty hand up to the driver's chest.

"Just a second, friend," Grady said. The driver took a step back and ran his gloved hand through his sweat-tangled hair.

"You fucking kidding me?" he said with wild eyes. "That guy needs help."

"You can't help a dead man," Grady said, placing his hand on the driver's shoulder. I looked down at Dell. His shirt was torn across his chest and there was a deep gash running the length of his sternum. His face was an oleo of blood, grime, and dust. There was a sickening crater above his ear, but I could hear a blood-filled gurgle wheezing from his crushed larynx. He wasn't dead, but he was on his way.

"Oh, Jesus," the driver whimpered. "I killed him?"

"Not your fault, man," Grady said. "But you do know you're in Mexico, right?"

"Is he fucking dead?" the driver said.

"Yeah, which goes back to my point," Grady said. "You're in Mexico and you killed a man." The driver started to protest and Grady put up his hands. "Not your fault, I know. And it doesn't matter that we're witnesses. The authorities down here only see a gringo in trouble, get me?"

The driver tried to look over Grady's shoulder, and Grady shifted his body to keep Dell's broken body out of sight. I shuffled over to it, careful to keep my gun out of the driver's eye line. I knelt next to Dell's cracked skull, and breath escaped him like a draft through an old house. His one open eye looked back at me with a cow's dull focus. And then it was gone. He was gone. No more Dell.

"What do I do?" the driver asked. Grady patted him on the back with his big, reassuring paw. He hadn't given Dell a second glance after his first cursory check of the mangled body. Dell was dead, that was true, but there was no way Grady could have known that. I wondered if it even mattered to him.

"Lucky for you, we're here," Grady said. "Our hotel is just down the road. Can you help us move him, you know, out of the way? Just to the side of the road. There's gonna be other drivers coming and we don't want any more accidents, right? After that we'll take care of the rest."

"I'm sorry," the driver said, rubbing the back of his neck with a blue bandana. "Was he a friend of yours?"

"No, he was a piece of shit, buddy," Grady said with a smile. "Don't give him a second thought."

≋

When we arrived at the hotel, my body felt like I had just played four quarters in Soldier Field without pads. Apparently the VW only had room enough for two, while the truck bed could hold a romance novelist and a cooler full of beer quite nicely.

"Sorry, dude, you drew the short straw," the driver had said to me, nodding toward the truck bed while sliding his helmet over his head. His name was Glenn, and after his initial shock he seemed to be taking the situation in stride. It was the Grady effect. He seemed to have a way of getting you to accept the unacceptable and move on. He had done it with me last night. How else could I explain sleeping so soundly after putting a hole in a guy's foot?

Grady was out of the truck before it came to a stop, but I had to roll out of the bed with help from the driver. My legs felt atrophied, and I leaned against the tailgate to keep from falling. Grady sprinted across the parking lot and kicked open the front door with one leg.

"Is he some kind of cop or something?" the driver asked, looking after him. He had his helmet off and held it against his chest like a teddy bear.

"That's what he tells me," I said. I reached into my shirt pocket and pulled out a pulverized pack of cigarettes. I tossed the useless mess aside with an angry grunt. "You got any smokes?"

"Ain't you gonna go help him?" the driver asked, reaching into his jacket pocket and coming up with a pack of Marlboros.

"I'd just get in the way," I said. The driver shrugged, and we stared at the hotel's front door like two husbands waiting for their wives outside of Victoria's Secret. Time ran by and the only sound was the breeze stirring the parking-lot dust, the driver pulling in gulps of air, and my cigarette burning.

Grady reappeared with Digby in tow. They conversed in hushed

tones as they approached. Digby pointed to the ocean and then the
hills. Grady nodded and threw up his hands in an annoyed "whatever"
gesture. They parted, and Digby stalked up to Glenn the Driver and
put an arm around him. As I watched Digby steer poor Glenn back to
the truck, Grady sidled up next to me.

"Doc says Richard Kimble is up and wants to talk to us," he said.

"What for?" I asked. Digby climbed into the passenger seat of the
truck and it pulled out in a cloud of dust.

"To thank us, probably," Grady said, and headed back for the hotel.
I watched the truck pass over the rise and out of sight. Somehow I knew
Mr. Kimble's gratitude would not be the only thing discussed.

Chapter Five

The man we knew as Richard Kimble was sitting up against a white pillow on a steel-frame bed, trying to choke down a cup of coffee. His head was wrapped with an Ace bandage holding a cotton pad against his temple, and a patch covered one eye. He looked like the fife player from Willard's *Spirit of '76*. His naked torso was a relief map of misery. Yellow, blue, and purple bruises fit together like jigsaw pieces, and when he moved it was with a symphony of agonized grunts. His suitcase sat open on an orange crate in the corner, clothes tossed about as if someone had been hurrying through it. He looked up when we came in the room, and he set his mug down on the wicker nightstand.

A late-middle-aged man in a canvas work shirt and slacks sat at the desk in the corner, taking notes. There was no reason for the record keeping. Doc hadn't had a genuine practice in over two decades. He looked up at us, nodded to his patient, and went back to writing the notes no one would ever look at.

"Gentlemen," Kimble said as Grady walked across the room, leaving me by the door. He kicked the suitcase off the orange crate, grabbed the crate, threw it next to the bed, and sat down on it.

"My name's Grady Doyle. This is Coop. You met Doc and Digby," Grady said. His voice was even, but there was a flavor of animosity in each word. "Listen, pal, you know that feeling you get when you're walking in a big city and all off a sudden you're lost and in a bad neighborhood? You know that sucking feeling in your gut that says your ass is in some trouble?"

"Yeah," the bruised man said.

"You got that feeling now?"

"Not really."

"You should," Grady said.

"How about you start with your name and go from there," I said. Grady rolled his eyes at me. The injured man tugged at the bandage on his head, exposing more tufts of wavy black hair. His one good eye was a deep, shimmering blue, and it jumped around the room.

"Ebbie Milch," he said.

"Where you from, Ebbie?" I asked. Grady gave a low grunt. He wasn't happy I had taken over his inquisition.

"California," Ebbie said.

"Left coast, huh? I'm a New England man myself," I said. "I mean I'm in Chicago now, but I always wanted to make it out to California. Kind of my own manifest destiny."

"What did those men want with you?" Grady interrupted. He was balling and twisting the end of the bedspread between his beefy paws.

"It's a little embarrassing. I don't even know you guys," Milch said.

"We promise not to laugh," Grady said, and the look on his face guaranteed it.

"I owe them money," Milch said.

"Gambling?" Grady said. Milch nodded. Grady stood up and threw his orange crate against the wall, cracking the plaster. Milch crawled up against the headboard and held his hands out defensively, but Grady kept his back to him and seemed to focus on the shadows on the wall. He wiped his hand over his face, marched the five paces to the wall, and retrieved his orange crate. He set it down back where it had been and took a seat.

"Ok," he said, once again in control. "Tell me about the manuscript." Milch flinched. His eye shot to his overturned suitcase and the clothes littered around it.

"You went through my stuff?" he said. Grady nodded. Milch's mouth curled into an indignant snarl. "You had no right."

"Bullshit," Grady spat. "I saved your life. A man is dead because of it."

"In all fairness, he was kind of an asshole, though," I said.

"Who's dead?" Milch asked.

"Dell," I said, and when Milch looked at me like I was speaking Klingon I added, "The one in the suit. The other one, the Texan, the one that kicked your ass, is in a hospital up the road."

"What killed him?" Milch said. He was looking at Grady now.

"Lack of situational awareness," Grady answered. "Tell me about the manuscript." Milch nodded, taking it in stride.

"Have you read it?" Milch said, and it took me a moment to realize he was talking to me.

"Enough to know it's worth something," I said. "If it's real." I kept my place by the door as if my proximity to Milch equaled my involvement in his problems.

"It's real," Milch said. He grimaced and scratched his bandage again. "I took it to a rare book dealer in Modesto. Guy looked at it with a magnifying glass had a little light on it and everything. Tells me he thinks it might be some lost chapters from the other book."

"*A Moveable Feast*?" I said. "Your guy said this was Hemingway's work?" I remembered I had left the portfolio in Grady's bag under my chair by the bluff. Never-before-seen work from the most famous American writer ever, and I left it in a pile of sand. "How the hell did you get something like that?"

"An auction," Milch said, focusing his attention on me like a field mouse eyeing a hawk. "I went there with this girl and I tried to impress her. Bid on a cheap little trunk and won. Bought the case for like twenty bucks, and this chick, you know, she thinks I know something about art or whatever. Nothing in it 'cept some old stationary and those pages." Doc gave an impressed whistle. I had forgotten he was even there. I turned to look at him, and he adjusted his glasses on his long nose.

Doc was a British surgeon who had lived at the Hotel Baja for the last two years. He claimed he used to fix bullet wounds for the London Mob. He also claimed that he had been on the run ever since stealing seven hundred thousand pounds from them and absconding with the boss's wife. The wife had taken the money and left him when they reached Los Angeles, and now he was stuck in Pendira with nothing but his hands. Butch had let him stay as a concierge doctor for the hotel in exchange for free room and board. His booze he had to pay for himself.

"I was an amateur collector once," Doc said. "Long time ago, so I don't know as much as I used to. Still, I imagine lost chapters from an original draft of *A Moveable Feast* would be a hot item. Chapters that no one has ever seen may be worth a lot of money."

"How much do you think it would be worth, Doc?" Grady said. Doc looked up at the ceiling, his eyes ticked back and forth in their sockets like twin metronomes.

"Oh, I don't know. Depends on what's in it. Literary scholars have enjoyed arguing about that book since it was written. Posthumous publication, you know. Lots of back-and-forth about the editing process. I imagine a new draft, *if* it can be authenticated, mind you, would cause quite a stir among the book set. I can think of only one other Hemingway item that would cause a bigger stir in the community."

"Guy I took it to said it was worth maybe five K," Milch interrupted.

"Sounds low," Doc said. "Then again, I imagine he was hoping to get it cheap. He wouldn't want to put out too much money unless he knew what he was getting." He took off his glasses and cleaned them. While he wiped the glass with his hanky he glanced around the room at us. I liked Doc, though most of this affection was born from pity. He had been an important man once. Someone the Caesars of the London underworld had come to for advice and succor. He had been a man of letters and science and, if his story was true, of women. Going from there to sometime nurse for drunks and drugged-up surfers was a long way to fall. And so I didn't blame him for reveling in our attention; for taking a long drink from that fountain. Grady, on the other hand, did not suffer such things.

"Come on Doc, for chrissakes," he growled, "what makes you say that?"

"Would you buy a car without checking to see if it ran?" Doc said with a light chuckle. He placed his spectacles back onto his bony nose.

"You see the problem is there is no way of telling if the manuscript is real or not just by looking at it. At least not at first blush. I imagine the initials on the portfolio are for Harry Brague, the original editor who helped Hemingway's last wife put the book together. If that's the case, then I would love to know how it came to be in a random trunk at an auction, selling for twenty dollars."

"How the hell should I know?" Milch said, and it came off more defensively than Doc's statement had warranted. Doc gave a solemn nod.

"Yes, of course," he said. "But you have to understand it would take a team of scholars from several disciplines to determine its authenticity. You'd need a literary scholar, at the very least. Preferably someone with a heavy background in Hemingway. There are chemical tests to determine the age of the paper. You could get access to Hemingway's typewriters and compare the ink and typing structure to determine if the pages came from one of them. There are ways, gentlemen, indeed there are ways, to determine if this is truly the work of Ernest Hemingway; but I assure you, taking a look through a magnifying glass, even one with a little light on it, is not one of them."

"Well, someone thinks it's real," Milch spat. "I got a guy lined up in Ensenada to buy it."

"Is that N. Thandy from Atlanta?" I asked.

Milch flinched again, this time almost imperceptibly. His visible eye narrowed, and he looked at me down along the line of his nose.

"How do you know that name?" he asked. I took the business card out of my pocket and tossed it at him like throwing a playing card into a hat. Milch looked at it for a moment, checking both sides.

"It was in the portfolio," I said.

"Yeah, well, he was the first guy I brought the manuscript to," Milch said, sticking the card in his shirt pocket.

"And you went all the way to Atlanta to meet him?" I said with a raised eyebrow.

"No, smart guy. In California. I found him on the Internet and he was already in Cali on a thing. So I met him up in Modesto. That's where he did his thing with the magnifying glass and the little light.

Told me he thought it was real, offered the five grand, but, see, the guy I'm meeting up in Ensenada is named Norwood, Philip Norwood. Seventy grand he's offering. That's why I'm down here. I figured I could use the money to pay off my debt."

"But Dell and Andy thought you were lamming it, right?" Grady said.

"'Lamming it'?" Milch said. "Who are you? James Cagney? Yeah, they thought I'd rabbited, but I'd told them about the manuscript and how I was going to get the money to pay them. I owed them thirty grand. I guess they wanted the whole thing."

"Seventy thousand?" Grady said. He adjusted his weight on the orange crate with a series of clicks. "That sound right to you, Doc?"

"Who knows," Doc said, and pulled on the end of his nose as he thought about it. "Of course, I'd be suspicious of anybody offering money for it at this stage, especially that kind of money."

"Look, I need the money," Milch said. He bent his head in that aw-shucks way again and pointed to his bandages. "I can't make the deal myself. Not in the shape I'm in. I need someone who knows how to take care of himself. Someone like you, Grady. You go up there and make the deal for me and I'll cut you in for thirty percent." Grady sucked his back teeth and said nothing. Milch relented. "Ok, forty percent."

≡

We left Doc to tend to his patient and closed the door behind us.

"You believe him?" I whispered, and patted my pockets for cigarettes. Grady recognized it as the signal that I wanted to bum one of his. No one actually looks for anything in their pockets by patting the outsides. He offered me one from his pack and fished one out for himself.

"I believe that manuscript is worth something," Grady said, leaning in to use my lighter. "But I'm not sure we got the straight dope on why he got his ass handed to him yesterday. I say we go up tomorrow and check it out."

"We?" I pinched my nose and leaned back against the adobe wall. I felt a terrible headache rising. The sweat on the back of my shirt had cooled, and it felt like a long, icy finger down my spine. "Look, Grady, I consider us friends and all, and the last month's been great, but I think this seems beyond me. I think I'm done."

"Are you breaking up with me?" Grady said, affecting a puppy-dog look.

"I'm just saying we don't know for sure if Andy and Dell were the only ones after Milch. There could be others waiting up the road, you know?"

"They'll be looking for Milch, not us," Grady said with a condescending sniff. "All we have to do is get to Ensenada and make an exchange with some book nerd. It'll be a cake walk."

"I already shot a guy, Grady."

"In the foot. Come on, you're not going to make the drop with me?" Grady asked.

"No," I said. "And don't say 'drop.' It's a manuscript, not microfilm of Soviet tank placements."

"There's money in it for you."

"I got money. So do you."

Grady ran his hand through his hair and looked at the ceiling. "Yeah, um, as it turns out, buying a hotel in Baja cash on the barrelhead may not have been the soundest of investments," he said.

"You paid cash?"

"Yeah." Grady picked at a tear in his sleeve. "And apparently there are some back taxes."

"How much money do you have left?" I asked.

"That's kind of a personal question, Coop," Grady said, putting his hand on my shoulder. "Forget about that. Come on, it'll be fun. You're not going to let me go up there by myself, are you?"

"You just said it wasn't going to be dangerous," I said.

"No, I said it would be a cake walk. No one wants to do a cake walk by themselves, right?" I knew trying to talk him out of going at all was a nonstarter. I saw the junky gleam in his eye. He was an ex-cop or agent or whatever. Movies and TV taught me these guys couldn't give up the action. They needed it as bad as the crackheads they busted needed their rocks. The best I could hope for was that he wouldn't make me go too.

"What the hell is a cake walk," I said, trying to change the subject. "I hear that phrase all the time and I have no idea what it means."

"Look, the manuscript is worth something," Grady said. He took a long drag on his cigarette. "You see how pissed Milch was when he found out we had it?"

"We don't have it. I left it up by our lawn chairs."

"Where do you think I sent Digby?" he said, and waved his hand absently. "And to take care of the other thing. Can't leave a body up on the side of the road, you know?"

"Yeah, the dead man isn't exactly sweetening the pot here, Grady. And if he is, um, being taken care of, and the Texan is in the hospital, then why does Milch need to make the deal? And if it's so valuable, then why is he letting us do it? He doesn't know us," I said.

"He doesn't have a choice. Doc says he can't go anywhere for a couple of days. He needs to make the deal now. Besides mine is not to reason why."

"There's a second line to that quote you might want to think about, pal."

"You wanted a chance to write something gritty, right? You been bitching about that since you got here." He put on a high-pitched voice and flailed his arms. "*I want to write something dark, Grady. Oh, Grady I want to be a real man and write something gritty.* This is it, buddy boy. This is the gritty train. Get on board. In order to write life, you need to live life. You know who said that?"

"No idea." I wasn't falling for his line. "You really need the money, huh?"

"You ever deal with Mexican tax collectors?" he said with a grin. "Hey, look, if it's all bullshit, I'll owe you a soda." He laughed and slapped me on the back, not giving me a chance to reply. "Meet me downstairs," He rubbed his hands together like a greedy poker player about to collect his pot and was gone before I could say no again.

I was going to go with him. I knew it. He knew it. The wind made the moth-eaten curtains on the window at the end of the hall swirl and dance like the maenad at festival time. I stared at it for a long time and I couldn't help but think this business would go poorly.

It would.

Chapter Six

Digby returned from the bluff while I was on the phone with Ox. He'd been able to convince the VW driver that Dell was involved with the cartels and was trying to shake us down. Digby gave him a bag of weed and some of the money out of petty cash for his troubles. He also made sure poor Glenn knew exactly what happens to gringos who cross the law in this part of Old Mexico. Digby had rolled Dell's body over the side of the cliff and down to the raging surf below. He'd wash up somewhere else where there wouldn't be much of an investigation. With the cartel wars raging, it was an odd day when a body didn't show up someplace.

"I need you to do me a favor," I said when Ox picked up the phone.

"Get back to Chicago and I'll do any favor you want," Ox said. He had the usual twang of irritation in his voice that was oddly comforting.

"You're the one who suggested I come down here, remember?"

"For a week, maybe two," Ox sighed. "You've been there for over a month."

"Are you going to do me this favor?" I said. I pressed my hand against the phone-booth wall and pushed my back into the opposite one, trying to stretch it out. I was still hurting from the ride in the VW.

"We need to talk about your plans for Toulouse, Coop," Ox said. I could hear his two-day stubble rubbing against the receiver. "You are killing the proverbial golden goose."

"Which proverb was that, Ox?"

"The one where God came down from the mountain and told the Israelites not to kill off a lucrative brand so they can pursue some bullshit artistic flight of fancy. Don't you know that a brand, a solid brand, is a gift from God?"

Oxblood had been my agent from the beginning, almost ten years, ever since he'd judged a short-story contest I had entered just after college. I'd come in third place, but Ox had championed my story about a once-ambidextrous amputee trying to make it on the professional jai alai circuit. It wasn't long before he became one of my closest friends, which put him at the top of a very short list.

"There's a precedent for killing off a pen name," I said. "Stephen King did it."

"You're not Stephen King," Ox said. "And he killed off Bachman years after everyone was in on the joke. He was also already successful under his real name. No one knows who the fuck you are."

"That's what I want to change." I looked out the window and saw Grady standing next to my rental. It was a nice ostentatious yellow Hummer, the perfect vehicle for a covert operation in Ensenada. Grady was giving some last-minute instructions to Digby, who was nodding enthusiastically while trying to light a joint in the stiff wind coming off the sea.

"You want people to buy you drinks, is that it? Don't I buy you enough drinks?"

"I'm tired of people thinking I have a vagina," I said.

"You whine like you do. There are more people who depend on Toulouse than just you, you know." This was the umpteenth permutation of the same conversation we'd been having for the last month and a half. The hardest thing to achieve in publishing is a recognizable brand. There are only so many authors out there whom the average reader has time to give a shit about. To most readers, books are like potato chips; you go with the brand you like. It's why new writers clamor all over themselves to get a blurb from a recognizable author. It's why Toulouse Velour gets six-figure book deals and Henry Cooper does not. It matters not that we're the same person.

The idea to bump off Toulouse Velour had germinated last year when I was reading Klosterman's *Killing Yourself to Live*. He posited that one of the best things that could happen to a musician's career was dying. The artist's death makes his art more valuable because there won't be any more produced. Rarer is more valuable. This coupled with our species' overwhelming obsession with death and all its connotations makes shuffling off the mortal coil one hell of a marketing scheme. Look at Michael Jackson. The King of Pop was always a big seller, astronomical even, but after decades of weird scandals his sales had begun to slide into oblivion. It was his ignominious death, however, not his overhyped comeback tour, that rocketed him back into the stratosphere. Consumers are like the Irish. To them everybody is a saint after they die.

This phenomenon is not limited to the music industry. In fact, it had already been perfected by the publishing world. Take J. D. Salinger, who was already using the old marketing trope of lunatic isolation to garner respect and adulation. The day he died, bookstores were inundated with people clamoring for Holden Caulfield as if they hadn't stuffed *Catcher in the Rye* in the bottom of their lockers when they were in high school. It was this example that I used to approach Ox with my plan to kill Toulouse. I brought up the multitude of manuscripts that Salinger had squirreled away in a desk drawer. Now they could be posthumously published and would fly off the shelf regardless of their quality. Hell, if they found a collection of grocery lists in his closet they'd try to publish it.

Ox was right on board with the idea at first. His eyes glazed over, and a touch of drool congealed at the corner of his mouth as he thought of the swarming mass of MacMerkin fans beating their breasts and tearing their sleeves over the loss of their beloved Toulouse. He conjured up a picture of them descending on Barnes and Noble like ants on a discarded Snickers bar, consuming every last MacMerkin crumb. He imagined parceling out Toulouse's posthumous works as each one was "found" in a fictitious attic, like a literary Tupac.

Ox's excitement lasted for two days, until he met with his mentor and former boss, Stu Weingold. Weingold had tutored Ox in the immutable laws of agency. The first rule, or one that was right up there, was "Thou shalt not fuck with a brand." Ox, properly chastised, had been dead set against Toulouse's death ever since.

"You're a murderer, Coop. I don't know how else to characterize it," Ox said. We had been referring to Toulouse's impending doom with such casual hyperboles for a while now. I knew he only meant it as a joke, but in the light of the last two hours it wasn't funny anymore. The phone became cold and clammy in my hand.

"Listen, Ox," I said as calmly as I could. "Help me out with some research."

"You think I have the time to do your research for you? You think I've got all day?" Ox said. He probably did have all day, and most of the next as well. His agency had three clients, and two of them hadn't written anything in five years. While Ox was an unabashed bibliophile, he had zero feel and even less ambition for literary-agenting. It was more of a hobby than a profession for a man whose personal wealth rivaled that of small nations. The money had been passed down for so many generations that not an Oxblood alive could remember how it was made in the first place. The most popular rumor was that an ancient Oxblood had invested in the original East India Trading Company.

Ordinarily I'm not the type to consort with a man so deeply embedded in the upper crust, but Ox had three things that appealed to me. The first is that he actually thought I was a decent writer. He liked my early work on its merits as much as my latest work for its profitability. The second was that he was also a Notre Dame alumnus, which always buys someone a place in my heart. The third reason was that the upper crust, what would otherwise be his birthright, had thoroughly rejected Ox from the time he was in diapers. They just didn't like him. He had as much insight and understanding into the mercurial world known as Society as I had, and far less interest in it. For reasons unknown to either Ox or his parents, he simply did not get it. He moved through that world with all the grace of a mule in an evening dress. On the other hand, in a twist that would make O. Henry groan, his breeding, education, and money made it nearly impossible for him to relate to anyone who's net worth was less than on par with Bill Gates.

"Do you know anybody into rare books?" I said, pressing on.

"Maybe," he grumbled.

"Can you ask around about a guy named N. Thandy? Rare book dealer, maybe out of Atlanta."

"I want the first draft of the new *MacMerkin* by the end of the month, and I want you to do that anthology I asked you about."

"Those are your terms?"

"Yes."

"Oh come on, Ox," I said, aware of the whine in my voice. "An anthology of stories set around a celebrity reality-show contest? You really want me to do that?"

"*Dancing with the Dead* has a lot of great writers attached to it," Oxblood said. "And they're offering a lot of money to do it. But, if you think it's beneath you, then maybe I don't have the energy to poke around about this Thandy fellow."

"Fine," I said. "When did you suddenly learn how to negotiate?"

"That hurts, but I'll let it go," he said, almost giddy. "Why do you need to know about this guy?"

"Research," I said. "For a new novel."

"Uh-huh."

I said good-bye and hung up. The thing to do with Ox was to get off the phone as soon as you got what you wanted.

Chapter Seven

We took the Hummer I'd been renting for the last four weeks. The road to Ensenada was a sidewinding, potholed business cut into the side of the Sierra de San Pedro Mártir. The edge of each precarious turn was decorated with prismatic flurries of flowers and wooden crosses, memorials for those who didn't have the dexterity or the sobriety to safely complete it. Graveyards of Detroit's finest scrap metal decorated the mountainside below. These harbingers hadn't any effect on Grady, who took each turn as if we were on the Bonneville Salt Flats. I did my best to concentrate on the Hemingway pages while blocking out that I was probably going to die before we reached Ensenada.

I tried to reconcile my memory of *A Moveable Feast* with Milch's new pages. It had been ten years since I'd read Hemingway's Parisian memoir, and the only snippets I could conjure were veiled references to Gertrude Stein's sexuality and a brief appearance by Aleister Crowley. I had read it in college while taking a class on the lives of American novelists. Hemingway had finished the book just before his death in 1961, but it wasn't published until three years and several extensive edits later. His third and final wife, Mary, had edited the book, rearranging the order of the chapters and leaving out an apology to Hemingway's first wife, Hadley. My professor had made a crass joke about catty women that didn't go over too well with the ladies in class.

I looked for the apology first and found it toward the end, written, not typed, in Hemingway's looping, somewhat-feminine handwriting. It was short and the notes on it were sparse with only a few red circles and an occasional *(sp?)*. As expected, Papa didn't lay his soul bare or beg forgiveness from a woman long gone from his life. It read more like regret than redemption. I was about to move on when I spotted a cryptic line that the editor had furiously crossed out: *And I should have never involved her in the business with the man from Auteuil.*

"Anything good in there?" Grady said over the dying cigarette in his teeth. His bare elbow dangled out the open window, and his Wayfarers hung off the tip of his nose. He looked like he was on a weekend road trip to catch some waves.

"There's an interesting note here about the Auteuil Hippodrome," I said, flipping through pages. When an editor goes through a first draft with her red pen, the result usually looks like the aftermath of a grisly battlefield. Two of the chapters in the collection of pages looked like Gettysburg and Antietam respectively. The first was Hemingway's description of the suitcase Hadley lost at the Gare de Lyon, and the second was an extended chapter on his time at the Auteuil.

"Never heard of it," Grady said, and swerved to avoid some dead animal in the road.

"It's a racetrack in Paris," I said. My thumb found the chapter heading "End of a Vocation," and I pulled the pages close to my eyes. The red pen had swept over it with the sanguine focus of Sam Peckinpah. "Hemingway spent a lot of time there when he was in Paris."

"Is it something new?" Grady said.

"There was a chapter on it in the original," I said, trying to talk and read at the same time. This Auteuil chapter was much longer than I remembered. "There's a note in here about involving Hadley in something, maybe something bad. It has something to do with someone he knew from the track."

Grady peered over his Wayfarers. We had crested over a mountain, and the valley flowed out below us like a sandy-green Persian carpet. Grady pointed at a small group of buildings set in the shadow of the next mountain. I could see a red-and-white strip stretched across the road and several people milling around it.

"Checkpoint up ahead. Hide the drugs."

"You didn't bring any, did you?" I said, snapping my head up from the manuscript. Grady laughed and shook his head but checked his breast pocket anyway.

"You think Hemingway got himself in trouble with gamblers?"

"Maybe," I said. "It seems like something he'd do." While the idea of holding the raw material of one of America's greatest writers in my hands was exciting, the only thing I could think of was the note the editor had scrawled on the last page. Something in these pages could have, in the mind of the editor, destroyed Hemingway even after his death. I scanned each sentence with a voracious need to find clues to what that something could be. I began to suspect it was connected with Hadley and the unidentified man from Auteuil.

Auteuil had been a place where the Parisian elite mingled with the lower classes of the day. Rich men of industry rubbed elbows with starving artists and shifty criminals. Hemingway loved watching the people interact as much as he loved watching the horses race. The racetrack was a cornucopia of humanity, and the budding author had soaked it up with gusto.

"It seems he was close with an American thief," I said. "They were drinking and gambling buddies. I don't remember anything like that from the published book."

"A thief?"

"Yeah, story says the guy had come over with General Pershing during the war and just stayed in Paris after it was over."

"Which war was that?"

"World War I," I said. "The one we never seem to talk about anymore. Apparently the guy was an accomplished cat burglar in the States."

"No wonder he stayed in Paris. A lot more good shit to steal," Grady said.

Grady was half right. World War I had been a depressing awakening for a lot of Americans. It had been their first chance to see the world, and it turned out to be a sewer. The leaders of the world had mined humanity's darkest depths for four long years of blood and destruction and never deigned to explain why to the people who had plumbed those depths.

But how could they? How could they apply reason to madness? Many of the American soldiers who had fought in the trenches stayed in Europe after the fighting was done. They chose a foreign land over a home that would look just as foreign when they returned. Hemingway had been one of these men. He had turned his angst to the written word and to drink. While one ventured to save him, the other worked its subtle destruction on him for the rest of his life.

"Why would a smart guy like Hemingway hang out with a crook?"

"I suppose he found the guy interesting," I said. "You gotta remember, everyone he knew in Paris was famous or on their way to being famous. It must have been nice to chat with a guy who didn't give a shit if you were published."

"Hemingway wasn't famous then?"

"No, he was a nobody reporter with the *Toronto Star*." It was this fact, the pages illuminated, that attracted Hemingway to the thief. He was the only one with whom Hemingway could share his true fears, chief among them was the idea that he would fail as a writer. It was a frequent topic of conversation between them at the track. One anecdote in particular, one that had been scrubbed by the editor's red brush, demonstrated Hemingway's supreme angst and the thief's singular advice as Hemingway was about to give up on fiction and accept a life as a correspondent.

"It seems to me that art isn't nearly as important as the artist," the thief told him one day over a café au lait. "What you need, Ernie, is a story."

"I got stories," Hemingway told him and waved a heavy Moleskine notebook in the thief's face.

"No one gives a damn about those," the thief said. "*You* need a story to tell the editors. Like when you got shot up driving that ambulance. What you need is a story to impress all your friends who are so damn impressed with themselves. And you know what impresses people these days?"

"What?" Grady asked. He was listening to me read the story out loud. Only a handful of people had ever heard it before.

"Suffering and loss," I said.

"'Suffering and loss'?" Grady said.

"That's what the story says."

"Who was this fucking guy?"

"The name's covered with black ink," I said. We pulled to a stop, and several soldiers came running to the car, a few more than usual, but mostly routine in this region.

"Hold the page up to the sunlight, dumbass," Grady said, reaching for his license. I held the sheet of paper against the window, and the sunlight illuminated the thief's name. One of the soldiers racked his weapon, but it sounded like a dull echo somewhere far away as all of my senses screwed together to focus on the name outlined in a black-red halo.

"Holy shit, Grady," I whispered.

"Uh, Coop," Grady said.

"You're never going to fucking believe this," I said. "The thief. Holy fucking shit."

"Coop," Grady said. "We have bigger problems at the moment." I turned to see Grady with his hands in the air and the barrel of a machine gun pressed against his cheek. I turned back to the window and let the manuscript page drop. A serious-looking Mexican soldier was pointing his rifle at my head, and he beckoned me out of the car with a nod. I put my hands up and stepped out of the car. Grady got out on the other side and looked apologetically at me over the Hummer's roof.

I would have to wait to tell him the name that had been so determinedly crossed out with black ink, the name of the thief that had been Ernest Hemingway's confidant:

Ebenezer Milch.

⌇

They put us in a windowless room in a hut about the size of a Dunkin' Donuts. It smelled of sweat and moldy paper, and we sat in wooden folding chairs that felt like they could collapse under our weight at any moment. The guards had been silent as they shoved us over the narrow footbridge spanning the ditch between the road and the compound. One of them, a stumpy-looking man with splotches of facial hair on his craggy face, tore my wallet from my back pocket. He took my license and my cash, a little under a hundred dollars, and tossed the eviscerated leather back to me. They did the same with Grady, though there wasn't any cash. The stumpy guard pointed to the chairs, and we sat down without further prompting. They didn't tie us up, which I found encouraging, but only a little.

"It's Mexico, Coop," Grady said, more annoyed than scared. "They expect us to pay them their bribe and be on our way."

"They already took my money. You got any?"

"In my shoe. Should be enough."

After an hour, the plywood door shuddered open and a stooped young soldier came in with two cold Jive Cola bottles on a cardboard lunch tray.

"Do you have rum? With or without lime. I'm not picky," I said. The soldier scuttled out the door without a word, and we were left in the stifling heat. We sat and drank our colas. Mine was flat and had an acidic aftertaste, but I supposed that was what a Mexican Jive Cola tasted like.

When the bottles were empty, a middle-aged Mexican in fatigues stomped into the room and stood in front of us like a teacher about to discipline a pair of unruly boys. He had the hefty well-fed look of a man who had been in charge for quite some time. He held three manila folders in one hand and pushed his slick black hair back across his head with the other.

"*Te llamas Grady Doyle?*" he barked. "*Por que estás en Mexico?*" Grady blinked a few times and shook his head. "*Yo sé que hablas español.*"

"*No sé,*" Grady said. They stared at each other until Grady cracked a smile. Then the Mexican shook his head, held up his hands, and walked back to the open door. He waved his hand at someone outside and waited in the doorway, looking back at us.

The shadow of an ambling, slight man walking with obvious difficulty loomed over the threshold. The shadow stopped and its owner exchanged a few words with the Mexican at the door. The shadow's voice was raised, but not loud enough for me to make out the words. It was clear, however, that he was in charge. The Mexican spoke quickly, shaking his head and shrugging his shoulders until eventually he threw up his hands and marched back to the far corner of the room, where he stood with his arms crossed like a petulant child. The shadow took a moment to compose himself before coming in.

He wore a tobacco-colored linen suit, a matching fedora, and round, wire-rimmed spectacles perched precariously on the end of his bony nose. A gold watch fob completed the dandy-on-safari look. He moved across the room with a delicate, waspish grace that belied his tall, gawky frame. He waved the leather portfolio containing the manuscript, dropped it on the metal desk in the center of the room, and leaned against the desktop. There was a moment when the desk threatened to slide across the floor and dump him on his ass, but he adjusted his weight and folded his hands in his lap. He had a thin, Clark Gable–style mustache that made me hate him at once.

His skeletal hand took a bottle of Walgreens-brand pink bismuth from his inside jacket pocket. He slit the thin plastic seal with a manicured thumbnail and tossed the scrap on the ground. Eschewing the dosage cup, he chugged directly from the bottle. There was less than a third of the bottle left when he was done.

"Mexico," he said with a pained grimace and a commiserating nod. Apparently just invoking the name of the country was enough to explain his gastric distress. "Gentlemen, my name is Newton Thandy," The name didn't register right away. For starters, I had only previously known the first initial. Secondly, the pronunciation of his last name dripped from his mouth in a southern drawl that turned the two syllables it should have been into something along the lines of seven or eight. When my brain finally did make the connection, it came with the realization that the chances of this encounter being about a bribe were now quite slim.

"Newton Thandy, rare books and antiquities?" I said with raised eyebrows. Thandy pointed at me like a game-show host congratulating a contestant on a particularly difficult piece of mundane trivia.

"Exactly, Mr. Cooper," he said, and took a sip of the pink stuff. "The one and only."

"He work for you?" Grady said, nodding at the uniformed man.

"Colonel Ramirez?" Thandy said. "Today he does, yes."

"You see this, Coop?" Grady said with a sardonic smile. "A white guy in charge of a Mexican military operation. That's the problem with this country. Too many white Americans coming down here, taking all the jobs."

"Don't see a lot of rare book dealers with that sort of clout," I said, ignoring Grady. He hadn't sensed the danger we were in. I had only the barest wisp of it myself, and it was only because of the absolute wrongness of a man like Thandy being in a place like this. All I knew was that something was off and it raised the hairs on my arms.

Thandy gave a shrill, polite laugh and clapped his hands together.

"Very good, Mr. Cooper, very good." Thandy said, smoothing his mustache. "As it happens, book dealing is my second career. Actually, to be more accurate, it is my second life. This life, my new one, is far more, um, civilized than my last one, but I have to tell you that I am astounded on an almost daily basis by how much my old life keeps bleeding in." He chuckled at this, not with the pantomimed gaiety he previously displayed, but with something more genuine and dark. "Bleeds," he said, as if this offered enough of an explanation to let us in on the joke. "For instance, I am aware of who would and who would not be sympathetic enough to help me with my, well, I guess you would call it my mission down here in Old Mexico".

"Your mission to steal Milch's manuscript?" I said. Grady looked at me as if I was the biggest fool he'd ever seen. I flipped him the bird. "You think there's any chance he doesn't know we know about it?"

"Mr. Cooper is indeed correct," Thandy said, and took another swig. "But not entirely. I'm not stealing it. I am reclaiming it. You see, the Ebenezer Milch you know stole it from me less than a week ago."

"That's not the story he told us," Grady said. He spat the words with some bravado, but I knew as well as he did that Milch had been lying. Doc had been suspicious of the story of discovering the manuscript in a random trunk, and a person of Thandy's obvious means finding and purchasing it made much more sense. Still, Milch's name *was* hidden in the manuscript. That couldn't have been a coincidence, and I wasn't ready to jump on the Newton Thandy train so quickly. After all, he had made his introductions via gunpoint.

"I'm sure Mr. Milch told you all sorts of wild tales," Thandy said. "He is a career criminal. That's what the police told me, at least. A career criminal with a violent streak. A dangerous man is what I'm saying." He snapped his skeletal fingers and the colonel handed him the manila folders. He handed one to me. I took it and flipped through the thin copy paper as if I were handed dossiers like it every day. There was a mug shot of our Mr. Milch along with what I can only assume was a police record, at least it looked like the ones I'd seen on TV. I closed the folder and handed it to Grady.

"Con man," Grady said, more to himself than me. "Thief, too."

"It's all here in the files, gentlemen," Thandy said, rubbing his hands together again. "I have men on my payroll who can find out anything about anybody." He opened another folder. "For instance, Mr. Doyle, the file we've compiled on you is especially interesting. This file suggests you are a man who is no stranger to criminal enterprises." He closed the folder and a reptilian smile slithered across his face.

"Well, yeah, I was in the DEA," Grady said with a sniff.

"Yes, well, it also says you are the type of man who worked both sides of the street."

"It says that?" Grady said. He gave me a quick glance as if to assess my reaction to this news.

"Not in so many words."

"Then how many words did it use?"

"It says you were a DEA agent assigned to New Orleans," Thandy said. He put the bottle to his lips again and grimaced when he realized it was empty. He tossed the bottle onto the desk and pulled a fresh one from his inside pocket. I had an uncle who used to pull the same trick with rum bottles he would swipe from airplanes. "It goes on to say that you were under investigation for corruption; bribery, to be specific. You chose to leave the agency on your own, and then two witnesses disappeared. The case was closed due to lack of evidence."

"And you think that means what? I was dirty?"

"It suggests that other people saw you that way. There must have been a reason for them to think you're that sort of man. I'm simply appealing to that part of your nature. The part that might be willing to hear my offer."

"You know, for a bookseller you're not too good at reading between the lines, are you, Thandy?" Grady said. Thandy closed Grady's folder, placed it in on the desk, and picked up the last one. He checked his watch.

"And that means?"

"It means fuck you," Grady said.

Thandy took a swig of the pink stuff and turned to me.

"Your turn, Mr. Cooper."

"For what?"

"It says here you're from Chicago," he said. "I have your occupation as author?"

"Novelist," I said. I could feel my face reddening. I knew what was coming next.

"I've never heard of you," he said, as if that were the definitive word on my career. "But that might be because you write under the name Toulouse Velour. I don't blame you. If I wrote that crap, I'd hide under a woman's name too."

"Toulouse is a guy's name," I mumbled, but Thandy had already closed the file and dropped it on top of Grady's. He sat quietly for a moment, maybe to let it sink in that he had attained all this information, including my pen name, in the short amount of time we had been in the shack.

"I've been trying to understand how you two came to be involved in this. I can't imagine it was simply happenstance. A former corrupt

Fed and a writer? Why did Milch come to you? What is your involvement? How do you know him?"

"I never saw him before yesterday," Grady said. Thandy looked at me and I nodded. Thandy sighed and pulled the gold watch from his pocket. It had his initials on the back.

"What time is it?" Grady asked. "We have an appointment we're late for."

"Ah, yes," Thandy said, and clapped his hands. "With Mr. Philip Norwood, owner and operator of City of Angels Books, correct?" Grady looked back at Thandy with insouciant ease, not letting on that Norwood was, in fact, the rare book dealer we were meeting in Ensenada. I, on the other hand, swore under my breath. "Unfortunately, Mr. Norwood was arrested in Ensenada for something or other about an hour ago. He'll be detained for quite some time."

"You got him arrested," Grady said, nodding at the colonel. Thandy nodded back with smug satisfaction.

"How did you even know?" I asked.

"News travels very fast in the rare book business," Thandy said. "Norwood asked an interesting question about Ernest Hemingway in a chatroom Mr. Costas and Mr. Daniels were monitoring. After that, it was easy to track him.

"Who the hell are Costas and Daniels?" I asked.

"Good question," Thandy said, and held up the watch for the colonel to see. "It's time." The colonel gave an indifferent nod and opened the shack's door. Pale purple light poured in along with a familiar face.

"Did you fellas miss me?" Andy said in his Texas drawl. He walked with the use of a cane, and his foot was wrapped in a comically large cast, making it look like something a child would draw. He was dressed in fatigues like the soldiers, except one leg of his trousers was cut off to accommodate the cast.

"Aw, shit," Grady said.

"This is Mr. Andy Daniels. You also know his partner, Dell Costas."

"I thought you were in the hospital," I said.

"You think I'm gonna let some spic operate on me?" Andy said. "You should see my fucking foot. Swelled up so big it looks like a fucking pig's foot."

"It was an accident," I said.

"Boss?" Andy Daniels said to Thandy with a hungry look.

"Yes, it's time to begin, Mr. Daniels," Thandy said, and snapped his fingers. Andy uncrossed his arms and walked a few paces to stand in front of me. He unholstered his .45 with the casualness of a mailman pulling a letter from his bag, aimed it with the same nonchalance, and fired a bullet between my legs. I let out a noise like a wounded puppy, jumped up, and stared at the smoking splintered wood that had been just inches from my crotch.

"What the fuck!" I yelled. Andy balled my T-shirt in his fist and shoved me back in my seat. The gun was still out of the holster.

"I have found you two with my stolen property," Thandy said, holding up the leather portfolio that held the manuscript. "I'm sorry if my demeanor gave you the impression this was going to go civilly."

"Look, Mr. Thandy," I stammered. "You got this all wrong."

"I do?" Thandy said, and tilted his head quizzically. "You're ready to tell me your tale, is that it?"

"Sure," I said, talking fast. "We got this guy, comes into the hotel. He gets in a fight and we help him out. Just trying to do the right thing, you know? Then we find he has this manuscript. We haven't even read it. So this guy, Milch, asks us to bring it up to Ensenada for him. We didn't know it was stolen. You say it's yours. It's yours. No skin off my nose. I was going to ask for a finder's fee, maybe, but at this point I'd just like to go home."

"I see," Thandy said. "So you're just trying to do the right thing? Is that it?"

"Of course," I said.

"Of course," Thandy repeated. He nodded along with the words and ran his bony hand through his hair. "Is this the truth, Doyle?"

"He forgot to mention Mr. Costas had a bad meeting with the grille of a VW truck, but yeah, that's the sum of it." Andy took a swipe at my head and I saw stars.

"What the hell," I said. "He's the one who said it." I felt a strange tingling in my stomach. Something turned over and my head felt fuzzy as I became completely aware of each hair standing on end. Andy either had a hell of a right cross or something was seriously wrong.

"That's no longer necessary, Mr. Daniels," Thandy said, and checked his watch again. I felt a cool rush in my system as if ice water had been injected into my veins. My head swooned and the edges of the desk began to blur.

"I don't feel so good," Grady said. He put his head between his knees. I did the same.

"That would be the sodium pentothal I put in your Jive Cola," Thandy said. "It's a proprietary solution a friend of mine in Guatemala came up with. It can be ingested rather than injected, and it works much better than the chemical solutions the CIA use. You didn't taste it?"

"I just figured that's what Mexican Jive Cola tastes like," I said. There was a lurch in my stomach and I started to see double.

"The only drawback is that it takes some time to take effect," Thandy continued. His voice sounded deep and distant, like Lou Rawls at the bottom of a well. "So I thought, why waste the time, why not see what you had to say for yourselves on your own. I think it will be fun separating the lies from the truth, don't you think? For instance, have you read the manuscript?"

My brain told me to say no, but when I opened my mouth I gave a slurred yes along with a vigorous nod.

"And do you know what it is?" Thandy asked. He rubbed his hands on his pants and leaned toward me in an almost-paternal gesture.

"Theories," I mumbled. There was a loud ringing in my ears. "Missing chapters. *A Moveable Feast.*"

"Nothing else?"

"Milch," I said. Grady vomited on his shoes. Thandy frowned and said something to the colonel. The colonel shrugged his response.

"We may have given Mr. Doyle too much," Thandy said. "Now, I want you to pay attention when I ask you this next question, yes?"

"Yes," I said. My gut clenched and bolt of bile traveled up my throat, but I was able to swallow it again. Thandy lifted my chin with his delicate spider web of a hand. He held my face so that I looked right into his blue-green eyes. Eyes like a raging sea. Confident eyes, yes, but there was something else. If I was honest with myself, and the sodium pentothal made sure that I was, I would say they were the eyes of a madman.

"What did Milch tell you about Hemingway's suitcase," the madman asked.

Chapter Eight

It was late in the day, and the sun was making its descent behind the mountains as we finished digging our graves. A few harsh rays lit up what would be our final resting place, a couple of plots scraped out of the dusty, hard pan. The soldiers had watched us for about half an hour until the scene of the two gringos digging in the dirt lost its entertainment value. They shuffled off to the large hut on the other side of the road. It was dinnertime and we could see their shadows through the closed windows as they lined up for their chow.

The interrogation had been quick. Thandy realized, around the same time I did, that we didn't really know anything. We told him where Milch could be found and who was with him. I told him I had found Milch's name in the manuscript, but I hadn't figured out why it was there. When Thandy decided we had nothing more to offer him, we were brought outside and given shovels. With our final resting places complete, we dropped our shovels in the dirt and fell to our knees next to them. I am not a man who is used to manual labor, but I was proud of the hole I had dug. Looking at it, one would never know it hadn't been done by a professional gravedigger.

Thandy stood over us as we knelt in the dirt. His thin silhouette, tinged purple in the gloaming dusk-light, gave him a ghoulish character. He examined our graves, and when he was satisfied, he clapped his hands and rubbed them together with the vigor of a man scraping difficult blood stains from his flesh. His grin had gone from gleeful to lascivious.

"Boys," he said, and I wondered what happened to "gentlemen." "I have to apologize. My good cheer has nothing to do with your incipient demise. I assure you the look on my face is excitement not joy, and, I'm sure as a writer, Mr. Cooper, you know the difference."

"This look, though," Andy said, pointing to his own thick face, "is joy. I'm fucking ecstatic." He had been quiet during the grave-digging process except for an occasional word with the colonel. He sat in a dilapidated beach chair, and every now and then when I lifted a clump of dry dirt from the earth I caught him looking at me while rubbing his hand over his ridiculous cast.

"Yes, thank you, Mr. Daniels," Thandy said, and fancied him with a look that said he was not at all grateful for the interruption. "You see, boys, whenever I travel I try to learn as much about the local culture as possible and to experience it whenever I can. And I am learning so much on this trip. So, as I'm told, the Mexican government, at least the part where the rubber meets the road, does not hold due process in very high regard. The colonel here has a particular disdain for it. For instance, in this part of Mexico—well not exactly here, it's usually found more in the Sierra Madres, but we're close enough for government work—anyway, there is a time-honored tradition for when a criminal is taken into custody away from civilian witnesses. Basically the very situation we have here. The tradition is called *La Bota, la Lena, y el Plomo*."

He waited for us to ask him what that was. We kept silent. Grady was most likely being obstinate. I was just too damned exhausted to make my tongue work. Time mixed with profuse perspiration had exorcized the sodium pentothal from my system, but it had left me in the throes of a profoundly weird hangover. When it was clear he wasn't going to get any audience participation, Thandy raised his hands like a pastor about to give a benediction.

"*La Bota*, Mr. Cooper and Mr. Doyle, is 'the boot.' It means, simply, that you are sent to prison. At first this seems like the logical choice, especially compared with the other two, but one must consider the nature of the prisons in Mexico. I understand that the only uncertainty in regard to dying in a Mexican prison is the method in which it will occur. A dull knife to the abdomen coupled with infection is the most common way, but the colonel tells me there are a number of sexual, microbial, and nutritional methods that are much more terrifying. So that's the first option, *la Bota*."

He paused again as if imagining the scenarios in his head and admiring each one as they passed before his mind's eye. He looked at me, and while his eyes made me doubt his sanity, they also gave me no illusions about his sincerity.

"*La Lena* is 'the wood,'" he continued, like a museum docent. "That is, they find a long, solid piece of wood, a two-by-four, or in some instances a lead pipe; these people are not ones to stand on ceremony or get caught up in semantics. They tie you to a stake or a chair, and they beat you until every inch of your body looks like a bunch of ripe grapes. It's not pleasant, and it goes on forever, but at least you'll be alive. Which brings us to the next option."

"Thunderdome?" I said.

"*El Plomo*, I think, is the most interesting. It means 'the lead.' It's a kind of contest for your life, like playing chess with the Grim Reaper. They stand you about fifty yards away from the woods or brush or whatever cover is around. You get a ten count. After ten, they open fire. If you make it to the tree line, you live and you go free. Some live and some don't. I suspect it depends less on how fast you are and more on what type of weapon the shooter has, automatic versus revolver and all that."

"You made that up, right?" I said. There's a sort of courage that comes with knowing, absolutely, that you are going to die. *Courage* may not be the right word, perhaps *foolhardy disregard* would suit it better, but really it's just a realignment of priorities. Up until then I had been preoccupied with living to see tomorrow. When that ceased to be a viable option, I shifted to just wanting one last tumbler of rum. When that also seemed not to be an option, I shifted again. Now, all I wanted was to wipe that fucking smirk off the old bastard's face.

"I did not make it up," Thandy said with a hint of offense.

"Come on, there's no way that's a real thing."

"It is too a real thing, Mr. Cooper," Thandy said. I glanced at Grady. He had gotten to his feet and was standing tall as a courthouse statue, fists clenched, staring down Andy and the colonel, who stood behind the old man. Silent grit was an admirable way to go down, I suppose. I, on the other hand, did not possess that level of self-control.

"You made it up."

"I certainly did not." The first crack in Thandy's gentleman facade began to show. It wasn't much, only a slightly higher note in his voice, but it was there, and it was satisfying.

"I'm just saying it reeks of bullshit," I said.

"They do it all the time," Thandy said, losing more of his dandified comportment. He looked up at the penumbral twilight climbing down the mountain, and when he looked back at me he was calm again. "I appreciate your spunk, Mr. Cooper."

"What the fuck is spunk?" I asked Grady with a stage whisper out of the side of my mouth.

"It's a polite word for 'balls,'" he whispered back.

"Just say 'balls,' then, man," I said to Thandy. "We're all adults here."

"Just fucking pick something," Grady said, sounding more annoyed than frightened.

"There are a lot variables, you know?" I said, turning to face Grady, showing the rest of them my back. "I mean, how big is the wood? How far do I have to run? Are they good shots? Will they be using automatics? Semiautomatics? Machine guns, for shit's sake? And will there be more than one shooter? And who will be swinging the wood? Will it be wood? He said something about a pipe. There's just too many questions to make an informed decision."

"Do you ever just shut the fuck up?" Grady said. The sudden change in his voice and the disgusted look on his face hit me harder than anything Andy had dished out thus far. "They're going to kill us. There's nothing else to it. Be a man and die." He turned to Andy. "Hey, do me a favor and kill us separately. I don't want to have to die with this pussy piece of shit."

"I don't take requests, asshole," Andy said, drawing his gun. He stuck it in my back hard enough for me to feel it pressing against my navel. I looked at him over my shoulder.

"You know bullets come out of that thing, right?" I said. "You don't have to stab me with it."

"Newton, I'm just gonna pistol whip the little shit-bird to death, okay?"

"No, I want him to choose," Thandy said, stepping up close to hiss in Andy's face.

"I don't care what you do," Grady said, sneering at me. "Just as long as you don't do it with me. Shoot me if you want, but take this gutless fuck and kill him out back by the trash cans like the bitch he is. I don't want to die with him."

"Hey, Grady" I said, more than a little nonplussed, "You know they're going to kill us right? This isn't something you can take back later."

"Fuck you," Grady said, and hocked a wet hunk on phlegm the size of a man o' war jellyfish onto my chest. I looked down more surprised than angry. The day had taken many twists and turns, but somehow digging my own grave had been less mystifying than the fact that my friend's loogie was soaking into my shirt.

"Jesus, Grady," I said.

"You see this shit," Grady said, looking past me at Andy. "Man spits on him and he just takes it. That, friends, is what you call a pussy."

"That's enough out of you," Thandy said. He grabbed Andy's shoulder and shook him with all the force his rangy frame could manage. "I've had enough of this nonsense, Mr. Daniels."

"You've had enough?" Grady bellowed. "I've been putting up with this fucking romance author for the last month. You ever meet a man writes romance novels? I never have. He's the first. You know who would have been cool to die with? You know who would have gone out like a man?"

"Don't say it," I growled. Grady narrowed his eyes and pursed his lips like the barrel of a gun.

"John. Fucking. Grisham."

"Fuck you," I screamed and launched myself at him. I hit him in the gut with my shoulder and we spun around, my legs twirling in the air. We landed hard in one of the graves, I think it was mine, and the air was pressed out of my lungs with an audible "Oof." I swung with wild abandon, my eyes closed. Occasionally, my fist would connect with Grady, but with what part of him and to what effect I did not know. Two boots landed next to my head with a heavy thud. There was shouting and I felt another pair of hands grabbing at me. A boot connected with my face, and bright white lights flashed inside my head.

I rolled over onto my stomach and realized I was no longer actually in a fight.

The sun had gone completely behind the mountains during our scuffle, and when I opened my eyes they had to adjust to the darkness. It became clear that a face was very close to mine in the dirt. The eyes were open and unblinking; a small rivulet of blood trickled from a tear duct and over the bridge of the nose. It was Andy.

"You don't look so good," I groaned.

"He's dead, Coop," Grady said. He was out of the grave, silhouetted by the moonlight. He had a gun—it looked like Andy's—and held it on the colonel and the old man. The colonel was unstrapping his gun belt. Thandy was pulling the leather portfolio containing the manuscript out of a satchel. They tossed both down onto the ground at Grady's feet. "Get those, would you, Coop?"

"Did we win?" I said. There was a dull ache growing on the side of my head where the unknown boot had kicked me. I wondered if maybe I had been knocked unconscious for a moment or two. Everything, it seemed, had changed.

"If we can get out of here before dinner's over, yeah," Grady said, grinning at me. He turned to Thandy. "That's why you hire pros, schmucko. First thing you learn when transporting prisoners is to secure your gun when you break up a fight."

I almost tripped over Andy's corpse as I moved to gather the gun belt and portfolio in my arms. He was lying on his stomach, the head twisted around to face the sky. Broke his damn neck. It took a lot of strength, a lot of anger, and a lot of mean to kill a man that way. I clutched the items to my chest and climbed out of the grave.

"Now, gentlemen," Grady said, putting emphasis on the formal address. "If you would be so kind as to accompany us to our Hummer."

The keys were in the ignition. I drove. Grady sat beside me with his gun trained on our prisoners in the backseat. As I pulled onto the road, I caught Grady's smile in the moonlight reflecting off the rear-view mirror.

"Ok, boys. One last thing," he said as he cocked the gun. "Take your pants off."

Chapter Nine

We dumped them over the side of a gravel incline a dozen or so miles from the roadblock.

I had never tied anyone up before, either for professional or recreational purposes. I was learning all sorts of new skills out there in the field. I followed Grady's instructions as best I could, but I'm sure I left both Thandy's and the colonel's wrists and ankles cramped and raw. We were without rope so I used their belts and pant legs. We had left them there, gagged with their own socks, staring at us with bitter, hateful contempt. I was back behind the wheel when Grady kicked them over the side. When he returned to the car, he dropped Andy's gun on the dashboard and grunted.

"You got a problem?"

"We're just leaving them out here?"

"What should we do, then?"

"I don't know," I said, and put the Hummer in gear.

It was past midnight when we got back to the hotel. The parking lot was empty, save for Grady's ancient pickup and the rusted compact Milch had arrived in. The wind kicked dust up over the Hummer's windshield, and the only sounds were the waves crashing against the shore and the birds wailing. The parking lot used to be a courtyard, and in the middle of it stood a three-tiered fountain, long since gone dry. Digby sat on the second tier's ledge, with his feet crossed at the ankle.

It was a different Digby than I was used to seeing. He wore a brown twill sports jacket worn at the elbows over a dingy oxford shirt with a torn collar. A straw fedora lay next to him on the stone ledge. A beat-to-hell leather gun belt holding a Colt automatic sat next to the hat. He was reading a book by an electric lantern, and he held the pages close to his nose in the small light. The cover was familiar.

"Keeping watch?" I asked, hobbling up to him. The last day and half had left my body functioning, but in protest. Digby looked up from the book.

"Seemed prudent," he said. Grady slammed the car door. He nodded at Digby and started walking. Digby hopped off the fountain and followed. When they were out of earshot Digby nodded as Grady spoke, but he gave no emotional hint as to their conversation. When Grady was done, he stalked off to the lobby. Digby fiddled with his watch as he came back to the fountain.

"Where did you find that?" I asked, pointing to the copy of *MacMerkin's Folly* under his arm.

"It was next to your fingernail clippers," he said.

"Like it?"

"I remember when vampires used to kill people," he said, and slid the paperback into his jacket's frayed pocket.

"He kills people," I said, wounded by the slight criticism. I was done with MacMerkin, but he was still my darling, my baby. "He kills people who deserve it."

"The bad guys, huh," Digby said, and scooped up the holster.

"That's right."

"I remember when vampires *were* the bad guys." He grinned, tucked his hat onto his head, and touched his thumb and forefinger to the brim. He sauntered back to the hotel and I waited a few minutes, soaking up the ghost-town atmosphere before wandering inside to call Ox.

≋

"N. Thandy is Newton Thandy, and he is what we call in polite society a real motherfucker," Ox said when I reached him.

"Yeah, no shit," I said. I'd been using a handkerchief to clean up the wound on my forehead. Disgusted by the blood and grime, I threw it on the bench, where it landed with a sickening squelch. The cut had been minor, but it bled like a bitch. *The head bleeds*, Grady had said philosophically. I cradled the phone against my shoulder and searched my pockets for a notebook and pencil. For the first time in a decade I had neither.

"I had to do some digging." Ox said, almost giggling with excitement. He was still in his office. He told me he was working late trying to land a new client, but I knew better. He had a complete set of first edition Hardy Boys novels on the bookshelf behind his desk. An original copy of *Beeton's Christmas Annual* in which Sir Arthur Conan Doyle's *A Study in Scarlet* first appeared. He kept an extensive file on the Black Dahlia case in a locked drawer. Ox was a mystery junky, and the assignment I gave him was just too irresistible. "On the surface Thandy comes off as just kind of an asshole, but they're common enough in the rare book business."

"Which you know all about, right?"

"I have friends who collect," Ox said. For as long as I'd known him Ox had never once told me he didn't know someone in whatever business we were talking about. "So, alright, Thandy comes from old money. Old South money too, but the kind that's more status than actual bank accounts. The Thandy name is on a lot of buildings in their town. His father owned the local branch of the bank, but they're not the Rockefellers. Most of the family money ran out during the Depression. Newton went to UGA, no military, too young to fight the Nazis, and he was in college for Korea. After UGA he fumbled around in a few businesses and then he went to work for the Jive Cola Company in '64. He worked there for thirty years. Worked his way up to vice president. Retired about twenty years ago and started collecting books and antiques. I guess he did pretty well with Jive because he's listed as one of the richest private citizens in the South. He owns a shop on Peach Tree Street."

"Doesn't sound too shady," I said, and leaned my head back against the booth's cracked plaster wall. Sweat dripped down my neck and the hollow of my back. Thandy had said his previous life and career had been "uncivilized," even bloody. I doubted running Jive's bottling company in East Bumblefuck, Arkansas, would qualify as either.

"Personal life was kind of a mess," Ox said. "Failed marriage. Rumors of an affair, wife supposedly fucked a cousin. I'm not sure if it's a cousin of his or hers."

"Jesus, Ox, where'd you get that?"

"I told you, I know people, and Thandy is well-known and not liked. You remember Wanda Coulter over at Hampton House? She remembers everybody. Said he was a real cocksucker."

"Wanda said that?" I had met Wanda a few times at various writing conventions. She wore a shawl and spoke in hushed tones that would make a dormouse sound like an air horn.

"Her words," Ox said. "A few other people remembered him too. He's got a bad rep. He uses his money to bully people out of his way. His specialty is buying up high-profile estate sales and scrounging their collections. There have been rumors of intimidation, but I couldn't get anybody to give me any specific instances."

"Has he ever done anything..." I searched for a word describing the malevolent and certainly insane man I had met earlier. I arrived at the weak and insufficient, "criminal?"

"Criminal?" Ox said. I heard papers rustling on the other end of the line. "Well, I'll tell you this. Jive Cola execs do pretty well, but the money he shells out is ridiculous. Mary Spinnaker—you know Mary, she runs a small imprint over in Brooklyn—she says the guy has a yacht that would make an Arab prince jealous. Nobody knows how he made all of his money. "

"But I'm sure there are theories, right?" I heard pages flapping on the other end of the line. My head ached something fierce, and all I wanted to do was go to bed. I doubted that was in the cards for a good long while.

"Alright," Ox said. "You've heard about Jive Cola in South America, right?"

"Let's assume I did," I said. Ox gave a dramatic sigh. He was always chastising me for my lack of interest in the world around me.

"Suffice it to say there have been some labor disputes in South America," he said. "And there have been stories about the Jive Cola Company getting involved with some paramilitary types to put down the unions."

"No shit," I said. "Good thing I only put lime in my rum. What's it got to do with Thandy?"

"The rumor is he was the go-between for Jive and the paramilitary guys." I smiled to myself and almost laughed out loud. This was more in line with the man I had met at the roadblock. Still it didn't completely add up.

"I can see him making some side cabbage on something like that. But yachts?"

"Yeah, I said the same thing," Ox said with a chortle. "The prevailing theory, and mind you I got this from Phil Yancy, is that he went into business for himself. He brokered a bunch of arms deals with groups like FARC, ELN, things like that. Now that would get you yacht money."

I'd heard of FARC, but my knowledge of violent groups in South America was limited to plot points from Call of Duty. A shiver ran up my spine.

"Fuck me. He's a gunrunner," I said. "Who's Phil Yancy?"

"Guy owns a bookstore over on Halstead. Conspiracy nut. Thinks 9/11 was engineered by the National Parks Department to get more funding for Yellowstone."

"I don't know about that, but he might be on to something as far as Thandy goes."

"How do you know Thandy?"

"You did good, Ox," I said. I didn't think he'd find what happened to me out on the road to be amusing, at least not until it was written and sellable. "I'm going to be stuck here for at least a couple more days." I expected a tirade, but instead there was a soft plaintive sigh.

"What are you into down there?" Ox asked. He sounded more curious than concerned. I had the tiniest barbed hook in him.

"A new book," I said. It was only half a lie. I did think there was a story, and I knew I wanted to write it, but that wasn't the only reason I wanted to stay.

"*MacMerkin in Mexico?*" Ox asked with an excited lilt.

"No."

"You're not still thinking about ending the franchise, right?" Ox said. If I didn't give him something, I was going to get dragged into another Ox vortex.

"I got something going down here," I said. "Look, this is the type of thing that makes a career."

"You have a career."

"I have Toulouse's career, Ox. I'm talking about my own thing. I'm thinking of it as a nonfiction novel, like *In Cold Blood*."

"You're no Truman Capote, Coop," Ox said.

"Why are you always telling me how not great I am?"

"What about the posthumous works of Toulouse Velour," he said. "I was starting to come around to that."

"It'll have to go on the back burner."

"I want you to come home," Ox said. "Come home and we'll sort this out."

"Not yet," I said. "The book's not finished."

"Can't you just make it all up?"

"Seems a little dishonest."

"You're a novelist," Ox said. "Your whole job is dishonesty."

"Still," I said. There was a sucking sound on the other end of the line. Ox was a nail biter.

"You really think it's a bestseller?" he said through a mouthful of cuticle. I told him I did. "And you won't tell me about it?"

"If I told you now, you'd have to up your Xanax prescription," I said, and hung up. I looked down at the small puddle of blood that had formed on the bench. Jesus, how the head bleeds.

Chapter Ten

Grady was sitting at the bottom of the stairs with a bottle of Patrón. A shot glass, filled to the brim, sat next to him on the uneven wooden step.

"I thought we were out of Patrón?" I said.

"Private stash," Grady said, and took a swig out of the bottle.

"Is that shot for me?"

"No. That's the reserve. So I don't drink the whole bottle."

"Maybe you should keep yourself straight, seeing as though there's a lot of shit going on right now," I said.

"So Thandy was a gunrunner?" he said. He had been listening to the whole conversation. It was my own fault for not securing the booth's door, letting it hang open an inch or two. Maybe it was an invasion of privacy, but on the bright side I wouldn't have to repeat the whole conversation for Grady. He stood up and leaned against the wall, tipping his head against the plaster. The tequila was working its agave magic on him. "Come on. Let's get some answers."

"You think Milch'll tell us the truth?" I said. Grady blinked slowly; so slowly he may have taken a nap.

"I do," he said. He turned on the step, using the back of his head as a pivot against the wall.

"What are you going to do?"

"Couple of things the ACLU probably wouldn't approve of," he said. He marched up the stairs with inebriated determination.

Digby waited for us at the top of the stairs. His gun belt was on and the large revolver hung at his hip.

"Doc's gone into town to visit his girlfriend. I don't think he'll be back tonight," he said. Doc had never mentioned a girl-friend before, and the "town" he spoke of was really just a col-lection of trailers huddled around a church. I didn't blame him. If I had stopped and thought about it, which is something I had seldom done on this adventure, I would have been looking for an exit as well.

"OK," Grady said, and started for the door. Digby stopped him with a hand on his shoulder.

"And Milch tried to leave," Digby said.

"When was this?" Grady asked. He pulled a handkerchief out of his pocket and dabbed at the cut that ran under his jawline.

"Just after you left," Digby said. "Thought it was odd, seeing as though he was supposed to be too banged up to travel. I mean that was the whole reason you went instead, right?"

"Yeah," Grady said. He used the bloody handkerchief to wipe the sweat off of his face. "What stopped him?"

"Apparently his distributor cap went missing," Digby said.

"What the hell is a distributor cap?" I asked. Digby brought his hand from behind his back. In a red-and-white striped handkerchief, he was holding a black metal cylinder with five small metal tubes jutting out on one side.

"This is a distributor cap," he said with a wink, and stepped inside Milch's room.

"Doesn't that concern you?" I whispered to Grady, pointing out the leviathan-like pistol that clanked behind Digby like tin cans off the back of a newlywed's car.

"What? The gun?" Grady asked.

"Yeah, the gun."

"The Digby mystery deepens, doesn't it," Grady said. He saw the look on my face and feigned sympathy. "Hey, at least he's on our side." He drifted into the room and I followed.

Digby was already stretched out on the bed like a lounging cat. His legs hung over the footboard, his toes clicking together merrily. He was reading my book again and didn't bother to look up when Grady and

I came inside. Milch sat in the desk chair. Doc must have changed his bandage. It looked crisp and clean against his grimy skin.

"Surprised to see us?" I said.

"Not really," Milch said. "What's this shit about no showers 'til tomorrow?"

"We met a friend of yours," Grady said. He took another swig of tequila and rested the square bottle in the crook of his arm. "Newton Thandy."

"Him?" Milch said, scratching at the bruise on his neck. "Does that mean you didn't get the money?" Grady crossed the room in three long strides, grabbed the section of the seat between Milch's legs, and heaved the chair backward. Milch's head struck the wall, but Grady put his boot heel on the seat, keeping the chair tilted on the back legs. Milch waved his arms, trying to keep his balance.

"You set us up," Grady said.

"Easy," I said, and put a hand on his shoulder.

"I am easy, Coop," he said, but didn't look at me. I gave up, pushed Digby's legs out of the way, and sat down on the bed. I hoped Grady was only trying to scare the kid. If not, there wasn't much I could do to stop him.

"Set up?" Milch sputtered. "What?"

"Ebbie, things have gone a bit sideways," I said. I supposed I was falling into the role of good cop to Grady's bad cop. That was fine with me. I was too exhausted to play anything else. "Thandy told us you stole the manuscript from him, and, to be honest, we're leaning toward believing him."

"That's bullshit," Milch said. "It happened just like I told you."

"I don't believe you, dipshit," Grady said, and shook Milch's chair with his foot.

"The problem, Ebbie, is that Thandy wasn't in a position where he had to lie to us," I said. "Also, it seems you were trying to split on us even though you were supposed to be so hurt you couldn't move."

"Wait, I—" Milch said. Digby looked up briefly from his book and marked his place with his thumb. He picked up the distributor cap, which had been next to him, and tossed it to Milch. It landed in his lap, smearing grease on his T-shirt. A murderous look came over Milch as he realized what it was. The look was there for a flash, and it may have only been a trick of the light. Just as quickly, the worried boyishness came back to his face.

"So you see, we've already caught you in one lie," I said.

"What happened with Thandy?" Milch's voiced cracked. His eyes whipped back and forth from me to Grady.

"He tried to kill us, you little shit," Grady said.

"Kill you," Milch said, almost in tears now. "Oh God, I'm sorry, I never thought . . ."

"Got out by the hair on our asses," Grady growled.

"Where's the manuscript?" Milch whimpered.

"Really, Milch?" I said, nodding at Grady. "Is that your biggest concern right now?"

"Where is it?"

"I have it," I said. I had left it downstairs in the phone booth.

"And Thandy?"

"On the side of the road tied to a colonel," Grady said, and he let the chair come down on its front legs with a loud bang. He pulled the orange crate from under the pile of clothes and took a seat.

Milch scratched at the bandage on his head and took a deep breath. A wide smile came over his face. The whimpering was gone, along with the tears I could have sworn had been rimming in his eyes.

"Then what's the fucking problem, guys?" he said, shaking his head with a laugh. Grady and I looked at each other with confusion.

"Are you seriously . . . ?" Grady started, but he was cut off by more of Milch's laughter.

"Yeah, yeah," he said. "I get it and, yeah, I kind of set you up, but you have to believe me; I wasn't a hundred percent sure Thandy would have anybody other than the first guys out here looking for me. And, I really mean this, I really didn't think the son-of-a-bitch would try to kill you."

"Was that an apology?" I said to Grady. He looked back at me, bewildered.

"Guys, focus here," Milch said, and stood up. He opened his hands out to us, and it reminded me of a magician showing how he had nothing up his sleeves. "We got the manuscript and Thandy is out of the picture, right? We're in the pink as far as I'm concerned."

"'We'?" I said.

"Of course," Milch said. He patted me hard on the shoulder and tossed the distributor cap back to Digby. Digby let it fall from the bed to the floor without looking. He kept his eyes on my novel and turned the page.

Milch was unfazed. Indeed, if I had not been there, I would be hard-pressed to believe that we had been interrogating the man just half a minute before. He appeared to us now not only uninjured, but vigorous and high-spirited. He filled the room with his voice and stood over us like the archangel Gabriel delivering the Good News, or maybe just a carnival barker offering to guess my weight.

"We're in this together," he said, snapping his fingers to count the beat of his words. I have to admit I was mesmerized by it. "We're bound by this thing and there's no way around it. Me, I'm bound by history. You, you're bound by providence. Yes, sir, we're in this together."

"Together in what?" I said before I realized I was even talking.

"Hold on there, Coop," Grady said. "I'm still not over the part where he set us up."

"Well, you best get over it, Grady," Milch said. He grabbed Grady by the shoulders and gave them a vigorous rub. Grady returned the gesture with a glare that almost made *me* piss my pants. Milch didn't even flinch. "If you don't, you're going to miss out on the big prize."

"We've already got the manuscript pages," I said. Milch's expansive smile curved into a grin like a knife slashed across his mouth.

"The manuscript?" he said. "Guys, this is about so much more than the manuscript."

Then he told us another story.

Chapter Eleven

*G*rifter was the proper term. In the parlance of the uninitiated he would be called a "con man," but *grifter* was the nomenclature Ebbie Milch preferred. It was a family business started by his great-grandfather, Oliver, who traveled around the Southwest in a buckboard, selling a concoction of river water, cod-liver oil, and camphor dubbed "Doc Saturn's Cure-all Liniment Oil." The tradition continued with his sons, Joseph, who peddled bogus land deals around Southern California, and Ebenezer, who branched out into the more labor-intensive field of pickpocketing and second-story work. When the Great War erupted, Ebenezer went off to fight the Hun in France, and Joseph went off to do a nickel in Folsom. Oliver died before either of his boys returned home.

When Joseph got out, he tried to go straight, and this lasted until the fifties, when the real-estate boom was too damn tasty for a clever man to resist the possibility of illicit profits. He had time to get married and have a son before he went down for a second fall and died on the inside.

Joseph's son, Ebenezer Oliver Milch II, named after his uncle, followed in his father's footsteps and kited bad checks around his father and grandfather's old territory. He enjoyed a certain amount of notoriety in the seventies when he briefly became the most wanted paper hanger in the state of California. He took a fall and, like his father, did a nickel in Folsom. He got out went back in, rinse, wash, and repeat. In the nineties, the aging bunko artist fathered a son, Ebenezer Milch III. When young Ebbie was old enough he was taught the family business, getting his start as a roper. The grifts ranged from long to short, from the Spanish Prisoner to the Pigeon Drop, from skillful and brilliant to clumsy and stupid. It was during one of these last swindles that the mark turned out to be an undercover cop. Milch the elder was shot fleeing from the police, and the son, only nineteen at the time, continued the time-honored Milch family tradition of time well spent in Folsom State Prison. He did the usual nickel.

Which is how Ebenezer Oliver Milch III came to be sitting in the kitchen of the family homestead, wondering what the hell he was going to do with his life. He had been paroled three weeks earlier. His mother had died while he was on the inside. The house had been left to him, which would have been great news if he'd had the money to turn on the electricity and the gas. He had a line on a few grifts friends were setting up, but it was looking more and more like he might have to do something drastic, like look for a straight job.

That was when Newton Thandy knocked on his back door. Newton presented himself as an old academic—shawl-collar cardigan, wooden cane, the whole business. Milch wasn't fooled. First lesson his father ever taught him was how to spot a fellow grifter. Thandy reeked of the con, maybe not a pro, but he was running some kind of scam. The only thing genuine about him was the leather on the portfolio he carried under his arm—the one with the brass nameplate with the initials *HB*. The old man offered Milch a hundred dollars for an hour of his time, cash up front. Milch stepped aside and let him into his kitchen. He was curious as to the game this guy was playing, and a hundred dollars was a hundred dollars.

The old man sat down at the cracked Formica table and pulled from the portfolio a sheaf of aged and battered typewritten pages held together by a piece of string tied in an elegant bow. He patted the top sheet with one wrinkled, blue-veined hand.

"What's that?" Milch had asked, pouring himself a glass of Johnnie Walker without offering any to his guest.

"This, Mr. Ebenezer Milch III, is a portfolio that I bought at auction," the old man had said. "It was a blind auction. Nothing more than a trunk belonging not to a famous man, but to the acquaintance of a famous man."

"There a lot of money in that?" Milch had said. He wasn't really interested, just being polite, letting the man work his con. So far it seemed like a variation on the fiddle game. A classic, and one of Milch's father's favorites.

"Normally no," Thandy had said. "And in this case it's actually worth less than a hundred grand."

"Chicken feed," Milch had said. He liked the rope. The way the man said *a hundred grand* like most people would say *fifty bucks*. Thandy knew to make Milch ask the questions. Information offered is not as trusted as information solicited. Milch was bored, so he kept it going. It was better than searching the want ads. "So what is it?"

"It's a manuscript. Well, part of one. It's not very old, but it is rare. I've had it looked at. Authenticated by my people. People who know to keep it a secret. It's real."

"I don't deal in books," Milch had said. His drink was done and he dropped the plastic cup in the sink. He dug the man's patter, the stuff about secrets and authenticity, but he wanted to cut to the chase. "What's your pitch?"

"I am prepared to offer you five thousand dollars for your help," Thandy had said.

"Help with what?"

"This manuscript is a window into an incomplete history, Mr. Milch," the old man had said, and tossed an envelope full of hundreds onto the table. "I want you to help me complete it."

"I ain't no historian," Milch had said, picking up the envelope. If the bills were bogus, someone had done very good work on them.

"But you are," Thandy had said. The old man leaned across the stained, cracked kitchen table and said in a clear, deep melody, "Tell me about your Uncle Ebenezer. Tell me about Paris, 1922."

That was when Milch knew this was no fiddle game.

Chapter Twelve

"**S**o you did steal the manuscript," Grady said.

The conversation had moved from Milch's room down to the cantina. Grady was stretched out on top of the bar with a cigarette extending up from his mouth like a smoldering antennae and his hands crossed over his chest like a corpse. Milch had changed clothes, opting for a pair of jeans and a brown chambray shirt unbuttoned to the navel. He had replaced his bandage with a blue-and-green paisley bandana, which gave him the look of someone who shops the Keith Richards collection at Urban Outfitters.

"Sure. I followed Thandy after he left my house," Milch said. He reached for the pot of Maxwell House, and Digby, who had been brewing it, slapped his hand away. Milch put up his hands defensively and took a seat on top of the broken cooler. "He was having dinner at this swanky place down the beach. Kept the manuscript with him while he ate. Easy pull. Called the hostess and asked for Thandy. Swiped the case when he went to answer the phone."

"What about Andy and Dell?" I said from my usual spot on the stool at the end of the bar. Milch looked confused so I clarified. "The guys who beat the shit out of you? You said they were here about a gambling debt?"

"Oh, yeah, I may have told a little fibber there," Milch said with a sheepish grin. "I never saw those guys before yesterday. Thandy must have hired them to track me down."

"Is it wrong that I think I trust the guy who tried to kill us more than you?" I said only half joking.

"Come on," Milch said with a mock frown. "The only way to trust a man is to trust him. You know who said that?"

"Not a clue," I said. "And we already trusted you, and it bit us on the ass."

"*Touché*," Milch said, and gave another one of his winks. "But you have to understand, in my world trust is a matter of degrees. Sure, I lied. Sure, I do it for a living, but I never killed no one. And let me tell you this, those pages belonged to me before Thandy ever got his bony hands on them."

"You're saying Thandy stole the manuscript from you first?" Grady said. Digby poured a cup of black coffee that looked like motor oil into a steel mug and passed it to Grady. Grady held it with both hands on his stomach but made no move to drink it.

"No, I'm saying I stole it, but I had my reasons," Milch said. He got up from the cooler and ambled to the door, favoring his right leg so that his walk was like a stilted shuffle. The limp, along with his other aches and pains, seemed to come and go, summoned by his own will. He stepped outside and returned with three plump limes from the tree.

"So my uncle, my granduncle, met Hemingway in Paris after the war." Milch smiled and juggled the limes as he spoke, keeping his eyes on us rather than the fruit. "They were track buddies, you know, but real good friends. *Confidants* is what the bridge club would call them. That's why he's in the book. More than once too. The chapter about Fitzgerald. Take a look."

I had the portfolio and Milch's dog-eared copy of *A Moveable Feast* bookending my bottle of rum—I had given up on limes and tumblers for the moment. I thumbed through the book until I found the chapter aptly titled "Scott Fitzgerald." I read aloud for the benefit of Grady and Digby. After a brief introduction comparing Fitzgerald's talent to the dust on a butterfly's wings, the chapter moved into the story of the first time Hemingway had met the man. I had gotten through three sentences of this before Milch stomped his foot and gave an honest to goodness "Huzzah."

"See, right there," he said. "Hemingway writes 'He had come into the Dingo bar in the Rue Delambre where I was sitting with some completely worthless characters.' That's him. That's my uncle."

"One of the completely worthless characters," I said, not caring about the skepticism in my tone or on my face. Milch caught the limes in one hand and dropped them on the bar. He flipped open the latch on the portfolio with one deft hand and pulled out the manuscript pages. He flicked through them with nimble fingers until he found the passage he wanted. He handed it to me. The top of the page read "Fitzgerald," and it was written in the looping, sprawling handwriting.

"I've done my research, Coop," Milch said. "There are a couple of different versions of this chapter. They think the original's at the JFK Library, but it's not. You're holding it." He pointed to the middle of the page and read aloud. "He had come into the Dingo bar in the Rue Delambre where I was sitting with the thief, Ebbie, and another completely worthless character."

He was right. The sentence was there, scrawled out and unmistakable. Milch picked up the limes again and continued his routine, juggling them with a casual ease and punctuating his words with the occasional toss behind his back or through a raised leg.

"He's in there a couple more times, but there's only one that matters. The one Thandy came to see me about. Did you read the chapter about Auteuil?" I nodded, and Milch flashed his knowing smile again. "Right, so, Thandy reads about Hemingway's thief friend in the same chapter as the suitcase and he puts two and two together."

"So did I," I said. "Especially when Thandy asked about the suitcase." I'd had my suspicions about the significance of the thief in Hemingway's story since reading it on the way to Ensenada. It had been more of an idea than a theory. The type of thing a reader would imagine about a twist ending while they were still in the first act of the book. It seemed too fantastic to take seriously, but that was before a rare book dealer had tried to make me choose which way I wanted to die after digging my own grave. Now the fantastic seemed quite ordinary.

"How 'bout you let the rest of us in on what seems to be so obvious," Grady growled. "What suitcase?"

"1922," I said. Milch's smile widened, and he began to nod as I told one of the most famous stories in American literature. "Hemingway was the Parisian correspondent for the *Toronto Star*, but he moved in some high-flying circles. He was friends with some of the bigger names in art and literature but still couldn't get published. He was on assignment somewhere, I don't know . . ."

"Lausanne," Milch helped. "Switzerland."

"Right, Lausanne," I continued, impressed that Milch knew the story as well, but then he had been, as he said, doing research. "So he's in Geneva and he suddenly wants everything he's ever written, first drafts, final drafts, onion skins, everything. Ostensibly it's because an editor is impressed with his work and wants to see it. So, Hemingway cables his wife and tells her to pack everything up and get her ass on a train. She does, and while she's waiting for her train in Paris, somebody swipes the suitcase. Almost every piece Hemingway'd been working on since the end of the war. No one knows what happened to it."

"Crook probably looked inside, found a bunch of worthless paper, and tossed the whole thing in a river," Grady said.

"Probably," Milch said, "Or he left France, came home to the States, and took the case with him."

"Jesus," Grady said, and his cigarette fell out of his mouth and onto his T-shirt. He brushed it away with a curse. "So, Thandy thought your uncle stole this suitcase?"

"He didn't come right out and say that," Milch said, and began to juggle the limes one-handed. "But it seemed to be what he was driving at."

"What'd you tell him," I said.

"Told him my uncle never returned from the war and we never heard from him again."

"But that's not the truth, is it?"

"No," Milch said. He put the limes down and held up his hands to show they were empty. He spread his arms out wide and clapped his hands together twice in quick succession. After the second clap, he held a postcard in his hand, and he laid it on the bar like a winning poker hand. I picked it up and ran my thumb over the rough, pulpy paper. It had been folded in half several times, and the creases looked like they could split any moment. The sepia-toned picture was of a nondescript Mexican mission, and the words "Greetings from Tequilero" were scrawled in gaudy technicolor across the top. I flipped it over. No message, just a signature reading *Fred C. Dobbs* and a red-brown stain in the corner.

"This is supposed to be from your uncle?" I said. Milch nodded. "Was he a big *Treasure of the Sierra Madre* fan?"

"Obsessed, according to my dad," Milch said. "You see, Ebenezer did return to the States, but that was like in the fifties. Grampa Joe had gone straight at that time, so Ebenezer didn't hang around long. He took off for Mexico and disappeared. My dad was just a kid then, but he liked to tell the story. I always thought it was one of those family legends. Part of it was that he stole something from some famous writer. Dad never got the details right, and my grandfather was dead before I was born. I figured it was all bullshit."

"Until Thandy showed up with the manuscript pages, asking questions," I said.

"Wait," Grady said, lighting another cigarette. "Why the hell would your uncle steal the goddamn suitcase in the first place?"

"Ransom?" I said with a shrug. "No, Hemingway didn't have any money. Never mind."

"He wasn't poor then," Milch said. "He just liked people to think he was. Added to his street cred. And anyway, his woman had plenty of dough," Milch said, his grin turning from friendly to smarmy. "Pauline Pfeiffer, the mistress. She had dough to spare and she loved him, but that's not why Uncle Ebbie stole it."

"Then why?" Grady asked, and I could tell Milch's story had hooked him.

"He stole the suitcase, my friends, because Mr. Ernest Hemingway asked him to."

"What?" Grady and I said together. Digby remained quiet on the issue.

"It's all right in there," Milch said, stabbing the leather portfolio with his finger. "He says the thief is Ebenezer Milch, doesn't he? They have a conversation about Hemingway needing to suffer, to lose something, in order to get published right?"

"You're saying Hemingway told him where the suitcase would be? He set the whole thing up?"

"Precisely. Why else would he put everything into that one suitcase? It's all right there if you look."

"He says he knew Ebenezer Milch and, yeah, there's that conversation, but it doesn't say he took the suitcase," I said. I laid a hand on the portfolio and pulled it toward me. I did it without thinking, a reaction to Milch touching it.

"He did take the suitcase," Milch said in a low whisper that made me lean in to hear him. "I told you that's the family legend, right? The manuscript proves that he knew Hemingway, right? So if that's true, why not the rest of it?"

"It's a stretch is all I'm saying," I said.

"Look, Dad kept that postcard in his wallet. Like a good luck charm or something. Had it on him when the cops blew him away. That's his blood there." He pointed to the rust-colored stain. "Last known whereabouts of Ebenezer Milch the First is what that is. He was down here in Mexico, and I'll bet dollars to doughnuts the suitcase was with him. So here's what I'm thinking: you guys know how to handle yourselves, and after what happened on the road I feel like I owe you."

"No shit," Grady said. "You sent us up there to die."

"No, I didn't," Milch said, affecting a frown. "I was hoping you'd make the deal. I needed the money."

"You tried to make a break for it," Grady said. He downed his cup of coffee in one gulp. He gagged on it, tossed the mug aside, and picked up a bottle of something unidentifiable from under the bar.

"I only left when I didn't hear from you," Milch said.

"No, you tried to bolt the moment we left," Grady said. He shook his head and waved his hands in front of his face. "But forget that. You could've at least told us who Thandy really is." Digby took the bottle from Grady and replaced it with another mug of coffee.

"Oh, come on. If I told you the truth, you wouldn't have gone," Milch said, as if this was a perfectly valid reason. "Shit, we're in this together now, right? How about I cut you in for thirty percent and we all go to Tequilero?"

Before we could say another word, a loud, shrieking beep pierced the room. I winced from the noise and looked around for the source. Digby pressed a button on his watch and the beeping stopped.

"Sorry to interrupt," he said, "but that's three hours since you got back, Boss. Four since the incident up on the road."

"So what," Milch said. For the first time since we moved to the cantina, he sounded irritated. He had been working us, trying to get us on his team. He'd been close, and the shrieking alarm bell had interrupted his rhythm. It pissed him off.

"So, it's about an hour from that roadblock to the nearest town," Digby said. "If Thandy is alive, that's where he'll go."

"He's tied up on the side of the road somewhere," Milch said. "Probably dead."

"He was alive when they left," Digby replied. "Can't assume he ain't alive now. Let's say he gets loose, goes back to the roadblock, or maybe the nearest town. At the very least, that's an hour down. The colonel won't want anything to do with him, I'm guessing, but we can't be sure. Let's say he's on his own. He'll have to find himself some new help. I'm guessing he used some sort of liaison to hire the colonel. He'll make a call to the liaison. He'll have to explain what happened. He'll offer more money for more men, but I doubt he'll get it. He'll have to go with someone new. If he's lucky, and let's assume he is, it'll take him a couple of hours at most to rustle up a new posse."

"I left him tied up in the desert, rolling down the side of a mountain," Grady said. "He's most likely dead."

"Did you see a body?"

"No."

"A rule I live by," Digby said. "No body, no death."

"That's a rule you live by?" I said. "This situation comes up often enough that you have to have a rule for it?"

"It's wise to assume he's alive," Digby said. "It's wise to assume Thandy's got a truck full of men hauling ass down here. It's wise to assume they will be well-armed and there will be no fooling around. It's wise to assume I won't be able to handle them when they get here."

"Who are you, Digby?" I said, not for the first nor for the last time.

"The handyman," Digby said, without a touch of irony. "If they're leaving from Ensenada, it will take them three hours to get here. We need to be gone by then. We head south. When we get to La Paz, I can arrange transport up the coast to Cali. Or," he gave a long, hard look at Milch, "Tequilero is a hop, skip, and a jump from La Paz. I can get you out or I can get you in deeper, Boss. What I will not do is wait here to reenact the last stand of Davy Crockett." He struck a match against the wall and held the flame to the tip of a cigarette. He took a deep drag and exhaled, examining our faces through the scrim of smoke.

"Point is, Boss," he said. "You don't have to go home, but you can't stay here."

PART 2

The Killers

Chapter Thirteen

The decision was made with a certain tacit ambiguity. No one actually said the words—and in this way no one took the responsibility—but twenty minutes after Digby had told us to shit or get off the pot, we were gathered in the parking lot. I had my backpack full of the few things I'd brought with me plus the leather portfolio. I was kitted out in my corduroy sports jacket and jeans. Grady was dressed the same as always, plus a duffle bag stuffed under his arm. Milch held his tiny suitcase. Digby carried nothing, but he didn't have to. We were taking his home with us.

Digby lived in a mobile home, emphasis on *mobile*, de-emphasis on *home*. The outer shell was made of pale beige fiberglass, huge chunks of which were missing. Dingy pink fluffs of insulation sprouted from these holes like hair on a mange-riddled dog. A twisted wire coat hanger secured the door to the living area, which was unnecessary, as there was nothing inside that could be stolen. There was a sink, which didn't operate, and a stove, which couldn't operate safely. The shower unit had been turned into an amateur marijuana hydroponics laboratory, but it had not been in use for some time. There was a stack of apple crates for a table, and a mattress, which was surprisingly clean, in the back corner. Every window save the windshield was broken or missing.

This was our getaway car.

There was a part of my brain that housed my mother's voice. It told me to take Digby's exit plan when we reached La Paz and hitch a ride on a boat heading back to the States. I wanted to float the idea to the others, but a sort of camaraderie had overtaken us since the decision to leave, an adventurous esprit de corps, like a band of brothers setting out together for parts unknown. We'd been called to action, crossed the threshold, sat in the belly of the whale, and I didn't want to spoil that by voicing my concerns. Besides, there was a louder, more obnoxious voice egging me on in another part of my brain. When it spoke I could smell the faint odor of whiskey and newsprint in my nostrils.

We drove through the night, heading south. Along with some sleeping bags, Digby had procured a cooler full of sandwiches and beer for the drive. He drove and Milch kept him company. Grady and I sat on our bags, watching the stars go by through the hole in the roof. We stopped once for gas and once to take a leak. No one said much, little more than a grunt here or there. I think we were all afraid to speak, afraid that if we talked about what we were doing or, more to the point, *why* we were doing it, then it would fall apart. Money, glory, professional redemption—these vainglorious incitements may have paled to the relative danger we were facing. Thandy, most likely alive and monumentally pissed, would not give up his own search for the suitcase. Even if he did, we were heading into one of the most dangerous places in the world. I knew about the cartel wars and the specific perils involved with them, but what about, as our former secretary of defense called them, the "unknown unknowns"? And so, we kept our mouths shut, hoping like the inverse of a birthday wish that if we said nothing then nothing would happen.

Sometime around what my mother used to refer to as the witching hour, I fell into a half sleep in which my hypnagogic dreams seemed more real than reality. A face appeared above me in the hole in the roof. It was not formed of clouds and stars like Mufasa, or a blue haze like Obi Wan Kenobi. That would have been nice. No, this face, haggard and broken like sunbaked leather, was formed out of the distilled ether of disappointment. He said nothing, just looked at me with that look, the condescending look of paternal pity, disappointment, and snark. It was a difficult combination to pull off, but my father had perfected it over the years. I had first seen it when I tried out for Pop Warner football. He told me I wasn't big enough. I eventually became the starting-place kicker for the high school team, but Dad felt this only proved his point. I saw it when I came home from middle school, beaten bloody by a couple of older kids. The last time I saw it was the day he left us. I told him, in what I had imagined to be bravery, that we didn't need him anyway. My father got down on one knee, put a hand on my shoulder, and with that look on his face he just shook his head. Then he left.

We reached La Paz by two in the morning, and revelers were still roaming the streets looking for a good time. The majority of them were dressed for the nightlife: a few women in cocktail dresses, and the odd man in an open-collared shirt. The last dregs of a Saturday night in a town that catered to rich tourists. As we drove past, I looked out the window at the nightclubs and after-hours bars the way a homeless man might covet the food at an open-air café. These people were my people, drowning themselves in pleasure and narcissism. I was desperate to join them, but Digby didn't stop for margaritas. He kept the RV rolling toward the seedy fringe these people would never condescend to visit.

The public ferry east across the Gulf of California wasn't due to leave until the following evening, and Digby felt we shouldn't wait for it. The idea of waiting around all day with a likely posse coming down on us was, at best, unappealing. There were one or two commercial vessels that could take us across, but Digby nixed that as well, saying it would be a good idea to keep our departure "low-key" and "off the radar." He knew a guy who could get us across, and we all went along with it. He also knew someone in Tequilero who, he believed, could help us, and we went along with that too. Part of it was that it was the closest thing we had to a lead on the suitcase, but it was mostly that going along with Digby was the natural inclination of anyone who met him.

The nightlife and, for that matter, the streetlights ended abruptly at La Paz Street, as if there were a city ordinance mandating wretchedness in the docks area. Digby pulled down an unmarked alley, and we parked next to a Dumpster in front of a rusted metal door. Digby got out without a word and started for the door. Grady started to follow, but Digby held up his hand, freezing Grady with one foot hanging out of the RV. He pulled it back in, closed the door, and twisted the wire-hanger lock.

"You notice he calls me 'Boss,'" Grady said out the side of his mouth.

"I feel like that's more of a ceremonial title," I said. Digby knocked on the door several times and waited with his hands held out to his sides as if he were carrying invisible pails of water. A Judas window in the door slid back, and a shaft of gold light flowed out onto Digby's face. He nodded at something and turned slowly around, lifting his jacket up and out. When he finished, the door opened just far enough for Digby to slide inside. It closed again and the slice of light went with it.

"So we just wait then?" Milch asked. "It'd be nice if he told us what was going on."

"Who says I don't know what's going on," Grady said, and winked at me. "You just sit tight, Milch." We waited five minutes exactly. I know because I occupied myself by following the second hand in the lumines-cent clock on the dash. The door opened again and Digby edged out. He walked slowly to the cab and climbed inside.

"We got a ride across the Gulf," he said. "But it's gonna cost us. Anybody got five hundred dollars?"

"Not on me," I said. "Is there an ATM around here?"

Digby snickered and shook his head. He glanced up to make sure Milch wasn't watching and picked at a piece of duct tape on the driver's seat. It tore away and he slid his hand inside it. When he pulled out a wad of cash, I cocked my head and gave him a quizzical look.

"Better than Bank of America," he said with a smirk. He eased the bills into his jacket pocket and started up the RV. Another few minutes, a couple of twists and turns, and we pulled onto a grim pier made of weathered wood. There was a ferry at the end of it large enough to handle the RV, but old enough to make the venture questionable. We all held our breath as we drove onto it.

The ferryman was a young Mexican dressed in khaki pants and a worn-out Styx T-shirt. He shook Digby's hand vigorously and they talked while we sat in the RV. When their chat was finished Digby clapped him on the shoulder and jogged back to us. I felt a jolt as the ferry pulled away from the dock. My stomach lurched along with the rhythm of the water. I closed my eyes, but it didn't help.

"Ride's gonna take at least three hours," Digby said, after climbing into the back of the RV and closing the door. "That's if this rust-bucket doesn't sink on the way over."

"Can we get out?" Grady asked. "Walk around a little."

"Sure, but stay by the RV," Digby said. The ferry's rails barely left room to open the RV's doors. The captain's cabin, housing the wheel, was about two feet from the front bumper, and the RV's rear scraped against the aft rail with a distressing grate each time we hit a swell.

I climbed up the RV's rear ladder and stretched out on the roof, careful to stay clear of the hole and the jagged fiberglass that surrounded it. Grady joined me, dragging the cooler with him. He tossed me a beer and a ham sandwich. Beside us the Gulf of California chugged by. It looked rough and uninviting. I stretched my legs and watched the stars peek out from the wisps of a few early-morning clouds. Grady was silent, sipping his beer and taking the occasional peek at the ferryman standing at the wheel. Our captain was steering through a grotesque blackness with just a penlight to check his instruments.

"You know we're smuggling something, don't you?" Grady said, crushing his can and tossing it through the hole in the roof. It rolled back and forth on the floor below us as the boat rocked, adding an annoying accompaniment to our conversation. I handed him another beer without being prompted.

"What makes you say that?" I asked.

"For one thing, we don't have any lights on. A little dangerous for heavily trafficked waters," Grady said, cracking his beer and looking back at the cabin. The ferryman looked back at us and Grady gave him a friendly wave. The ferryman nodded back and checked something with his penlight. "Secondly, that radio ain't tuned into the harbor. He's listening to the *judiciales* radio ban. Shit, we paid this fucking guy five hundred dollars and we're his damn cover."

"What are we smuggling?" I asked. Grady shook his head.

"Maybe just us. I don't know."

"One of Hemingway's last books was about a smuggler in Cuba."

"How'd it end?"

"Badly," I said. "Must make you uncomfortable, you know, former agent and all."

"I can handle it."

"Was it tough being an agent?"

"Just the paperwork."

"Why'd you leave?"

"Why don't you ask the question you really want the answer to, Coop?"

"What question is that?" I asked.

"Was I dirty?" Grady said. He was looking past me, over the edge of the ferry, at the gently rocking waves.

"Were you?" I said. He knew what was on my mind, and there was no reason to pretend otherwise.

"You wondering if you can trust me?" Grady asked.

"No," I said, then after a moment, "Yes."

"Then I guess it depends on what you mean by 'dirty,'" he said. I listened to the radio static mix with the waves against the boat. It was clear that was all he was going to say on the subject.

"Fair enough," I said.

"There's gonna be a moment," Grady said, motioning for another beer. I obliged. "I'm gonna tell you we gotta ditch Milch. When I do, don't question it. Just do what I say."

"You think he's that bad?"

"I'm just saying I don't trust him," Grady said.

I ate my sandwich and Grady drank his next beer. I tried to listen to the scratchy tones coming from the ferryman's radio, but the Spanish sounded even more foreign than usual. I closed my eyes and was just about to fall into sweet sleep when Grady spoke again.

"Why'd he do it?" Grady asked. "Hemingway, I mean."

"Why'd he get Ebenezer to steal the suitcase?" I said. I had been thinking about the same question for most of the drive. I tried to conjure a portrait of Hemingway as he was in Paris. Up to that time the most interesting thing he had been a part of had been World War I. His poor eyesight had kept him out of the army and so he had joined the Red Cross as an ambulance driver. Everyone knows the story of his injury and his ensuing infatuation with Agnes von Kurowsky, the nurse who tended to him. An infatuation that ended bitterly for Hemingway when Agnes spurned his love, not for another man, but for the idea of future men who would be better than poor Ernest. Her reasoning was that he was just a kid, but more to the point, he was not a man.

Kept out of the military due to a physical defect, and kept from love because of a character defect, the Parisian-era Hemingway was obsessed with the idea of manliness. It didn't help that the people with whom he surrounded himself were all successful either critically or financially. Hemingway, on the other hand, was struggling to get just one of his stories published. He'd already lost at love, despite the presence of both Hadley and Pauline. A failure in his chosen profession would certainly complete the emasculation double whammy.

Lying about the suitcase made perfect sense, at least to me it did. Hemingway wrote down his entire life as idealized fantasy in most of his novels. He reinvented every pathetic trial he'd endured. His failure to become a soldier was turned into the story of a brave ambulance driver. He inflated the story of his injury with each telling. He down-played his involvement in the Red Cross, going so far as cutting his uniform so it would look like a real soldier's. His inability to satisfy a woman was rewritten as the manliest love story ever told, *A Farewell to Arms*. The line between his fictional life and his real one became increasingly obfuscated until it was completely obliterated in *A Moveable Feast*. If Hemingway's career had been built from lies, then why *wouldn't* it have started with one that would be the cornerstone for all the others to come? A lie that could earn him sympathy with influential friends, while at the same time pinning his failures on a woman, sounded like a pretty good gambit for the young writer. Why the hell not? Fiction writers are really nothing more than excellent liars anyway. Why should he have consigned those lies solely to the written word?

I explained all of this to Grady, ending with the coda, "He would have been desperate."

"You said he was working for a newspaper. He had a job. He had a wife, a girlfriend too. He was doing pretty good."

"I'm not sure Milch has the timeline right about Pauline," I said.

"Still though."

I opened my eyes and the night's sky looked like sugar spilled over dark linoleum. I tried to find some constellations I could recognize. I couldn't.

Hemingway did have a decent job, a loving wife, and an interesting life in a major European city. If he had been an ordinary man, it would have been more than satisfying, but Hemingway was not an ordinary man. He was a writer. Few professions draw such insecure, narcissistic, paranoid, depressive, and needy applicants as the writing life. The need to be published, to be validated, churns in the writer's breast like a nonstop, manic engine. The writer's waking life is filled with dreams of success, and his sleep is plagued by nightmares of failure.

I thought back to the first time I tried to get a novel published, the one that eventually failed. My work was my raison d'être, a mooring line to my worth as a person. Each submission felt like I was sending my firstborn out into the world, and each rejection felt like a serrated blade slashing into my soul. I remembered the clenched fists and bitter tears. The process took two years to complete, but it took decades off my life. And I wasn't surrounded by F. Scott Fitzgerald and Gertrude Stein rubbing it in with their easy genius.

"He would have been desperate," I repeated. It wasn't worth explaining to a man like Grady. Like war, it couldn't be truly understood by anyone who hadn't been through it. Except going to war was at least brave, noble even. There was nothing noble about writing, at least not the way I did it.

"You're looking at it like he was a character in a book," Grady said, crushing his beer can and tossing it playfully at my head. "He was real. Flesh and blood, not words on a page. No one really thinks that way in real life."

"Writers think that way," I said. "Hemingway thought that way."

"Bullshit" he said with a sniff.

"Fine, then," I said, and laid my arm across my eyes. "How about this. A lot of historians think he had hemochromatosis. His body couldn't process iron, and it affected his brain. It's why he put a shotgun in his mouth in Idaho. Maybe he was crazy in Paris, too."

"I can buy that," Grady said. "Then again, just being in Idaho was probably enough to make him blow his brains out." I felt him waiting for a reply. I didn't give him one. Instead I let the wariness of the day wash over me and I drifted away. I dreamed of a mountain made of books smoldering under pink flames, and in the shadows, I heard my father laughing.

Chapter Fourteen

We arrived in Tequilero just as the sun skulked over the Madres and illuminated the tiny town coiled up in the foothills. Grady drove our vehicular dinosaur as Digby guided him through the small city like a U-boat through enemy waters. The buildings fluctuated in shape and size from small and deflated to large and ornate and back again. We turned down a dusty street strewn with debris and infested with stray dogs, and parked in front of a two-story wooden building with batwing doors and a host of faded beer signs on the front. He cut the engine and we sat in silence, listening to the town wake up.

"Who's this guy now, Digby?" Grady said, looking through the grime of the cracked windshield.

"A guy I used to know," Digby said. He pulled his pistol out of his gun belt and checked the cylinder. Satisfied, he slapped it home with a flick of his wrist, and slipped the gun into the waistband at the small of his back. He slid the gun belt off and tossed it on the floor between the front seats. "He's been around Tequilero forever. If Milch's uncle came through here, he would've known him or his father would have. He'd also know if Thandy hired any talent to come looking for us, too. If he's alive." He leaned back so he could look at me. "You come in with me, Coop. Mr. Doyle and Milch can hang out here and keep a lookout just in case."

"Why can't I come in?" Milch asked, rousing himself from his slumber. He had slept for nearly the entire ride from the ferry.

"Because Coop is a writer. That'll be our in," Digby said.

"A writer?" Milch said. "Look, man, if you need a writer I can play a writer."

"Not in there you can't," Digby said. "Do you know where we are now? Tequilero is at the edge of the Monte."

"The Monte?" Grady and I said together.

"The Wild," Digby said. "The Monte is the Madres proper, where civilization ends. You'll find no god in the Monte, but you'll find shrines to Jesus Malverde, the patron saint of hit men, bandits, *narcotraficantes*, and other bits of human filth. These are the people you will have to deal with. People Thandy will have to deal with. These people keep their own council and they have no trust reserved for outsiders. In the Monte, blood is currency and death is the language."

"And you speak the language?" Milch asked with a scoffing sniff. Digby tossed his cigarette out of the window.

"Fluently," he said, and stabbed his finger at the dilapidated hovel across the street. "And so do the people in there. They know your kind. They'll smell the grift on you. You won't get more than four words out before they slice open your throat and pull your tongue out through the hole."

Milch looked unimpressed. I did not share his skepticism.

"Maybe Grady should go," I said. Digby slapped me on the shoulder.

"You'll be fine," he said, and got out. He started across the street without waiting for me. Grady nodded some encouragement and I crawled out of the RV. I could hear the tendons in my legs creak as I half-jogged to catch up with Digby. I had slept intermittently while on the ferry, but when we had reached the dock, a rickety structure that tilted back and forth with each incoming wave, Grady had shaken me awake and shoved me into the front seat so I could keep him awake while he drove. I was on about two hours of sleep and no coffee, about to walk into a building filled with people who are adept at a Colombian necktie.

A filthy Rottweiler stood at attention at the door. It growled at us, a low guttural noise, but Digby passed by and pushed through the batwings without breaking stride. The Rottie's head followed him and then snapped back to me. The growl grew louder and he raised his hackles as if to pounce.

"Leave him be, *cabrón*," Digby said. He had reappeared at the door, arms hanging lazily over the batwings. His tone was bucolic, his manner disinterested. The beast sat down on its haunches, stopped growling, and panted contentedly. I inched by it and slipped through the batwing Digby held open for me.

"I remember when that dog was just a puppy," he said. "Try not to fall behind."

We stood in a large open room with a bar at one end and a few sporadic tables filling out the rest of the floor. The paint on the wooden walls had faded into an indiscernible color—I don't know, maybe it was green—and the splintered floorboards were caked with so much dirt I originally thought there wasn't any floor at all. The bar was a sturdy burled walnut, and the lacquer had been filled with chips and divots, giving it a veteran appearance. Glass shelves lined the wall behind it, but there were only a few bottles, and thick layers of dust obscured the labels of each one. At the end of the bar, a staircase built from unfinished wood climbed to a balcony that circled the room. There were four doors above the bar on the second floor.

A crew of four Mexicans sat at a table in the corner. It was not yet seven o'clock and they did not look like early risers. It must have been the end of a long night or series of nights. They were going through the motions of playing cards, but if it was poker then it was a version with which I wasn't familiar. One of them sat with his head back, staring at the ceiling, and half of the cards in his hand were facing the wrong way. The other three noticed our entrance with casual interest.

The bartender sat on the bottom step of the staircase, reading a newspaper, when we approached. He was a thin man with a sparse beard and an apron that looked like a work from Pollack's late period.

"I'm looking for Virgil Scripes," Digby said. The bartender looked up at him and gave an indifferent sniff. He shoved his hand in his apron pocket, pulled out a pack of smokes, and tapped it against the wooden step. He pulled out a cigarette with his teeth and searched his pockets for a light. I offered him my silver Zippo, the one with the shamrock on it. He took it without looking at me, lit his cigarette, and tossed it back without thanks.

"I don't know him," the bartender said.

"Then find someone who does," Digby said. "Make your calls." The bartender took a drag on his cigarette and his eyes moved to the men in the corner. He sucked his teeth and stood up, moving behind the bar. He was almost to the door at the other end when Digby called out to him.

"I'll need a room, too," Digby said, and fished out a wad of cash from his pocket. He peeled off two twenties and laid them on the bar. The bartender nodded toward me.

"He want anything?"

"Coffee, please," I said. The bartender tilted his head as if he had trouble hearing me.

"Put on a pot of coffee for my man here," Digby said. The bartender breathed loudly through his nose and pushed through the swinging door and out of our sight. The money was presumably safe on the bar.

"Is this a whorehouse?" I asked Digby. He laughed and shook his head.

"No," he said. "It's a bar. There are some rooms upstairs for people to flop if they need it. Forty bucks buys a shitty mattress and the bartender's silence should the *judiciales* show up. The guy we're waiting for won't show up for at least half an hour. I'm gonna go take a nap. You stay here and have a cup of coffee."

"By myself," I said.

"The dog doesn't come inside," Digby said with a smirk.

"I'm not worried about the dog," I said, although I was. "It's the three *hombres* in the corner who haven't stopped staring at us since we came in that scare me." Digby looked over his shoulder at the men, who had given up any pretense of playing cards. They were now actively gawking at us. The fourth man was still staring at the ceiling, and I realized he must sleep with his eyes open.

"Don't be racist," Digby said. "Just wait down here and keep an eye out. You'll know the guy when you see him."

"Virgil Scripes?" I asked.

"No, I'm Scripes," Digby said, and then added, "Sometimes at least."

"But you said you're looking for him."

"That name hasn't been used around here for a while," he said. "It'll attract some attention, get spread through the channels. Levi'll hear it and come by to see who's asking for me."

"Why not just ask for Levi then?" I asked. Digby shook his head and looked longingly at the stairs leading to a bed and rest. I couldn't blame him.

"Because nothing gets said around here that doesn't hit at least three sets of ears. I don't want to advertise that I'm back in town. You'll have to trust me on how these things work," he said. "Scripes is an alias for an alias. Only Levi would know it, and only Levi would be interested in someone asking about that name. It pays to be careful." He patted me on the shoulder and offered a smile before starting up the creaking stairs. I called to him in a loud whisper.

"Digby," I said. He half turned, offering only his ear. "Who are you?"

"I'm just a guy does odd jobs at a small hotel in Baja," Digby said, weariness creeping into his voice.

The bartender had left his newspaper on the bar, and I spent the next half hour trying to decipher the front page. The man pictured was a fat, wrinkled white man in a panama hat and aloha shirt. There was a second picture involving a large white sheet covering something about the size of a body inside what looked like a medieval prison cell. I translated the words using my mental film library. For instance, *Goonies* and Corey Feldman taught me that *muerte* means "dead," but most of the words like "*Americano*" were easy to figure out, and, along with a few others such as *Ensenada* and *librero*, I eventually got the gist of the story. A Mr. Philip Norwood of San Diego, who may have been a book dealer, was murdered the night before while in the custody of the *judiciales*. He had been arrested, as far as I could tell, for smuggling, but I couldn't understand the details of it. The murder had taken place after we had already escaped. That meant Thandy could have ordered the murder before Grady kicked him over the side of a mountain, or the *judiciales* decided to kill Norwood when they didn't hear back from him. The third option was that Thandy had made it back to civilization in time to order the hit on Norwood before coming after us. And then there was the fourth option: I got the translation completely wrong.

"You lookin' for Virgil Scripes?" a voice said from the doorway. It sounded like pure maple syrup and had a rhythm to it that made the simple phrase sound like a soul song. The voice belonged to a tall black man wearing a faded Jimmy Cliff T-shirt, the last pair of bell-bottom jeans in North America, and leather thongs on his feet. His Afro was shot through with waves of white, but his beard was the color of strong coffee. Though his smile was sleepy, his eyes were alive, sizing me up like a gunslinger before the draw.

"This the one?" he said to the bartender, who had materialized at his spot on the bottom step.

"Him and another guy upstairs, Levi," the bartender said. Without prompting, he reached under the bar and brought up a bottle of Jack Daniels.

"Let's go meet your friend," Levi said, and grabbed the bottle. He took a pair of aviators from his belt loop, slipped them on, and made for the stairs. The bartender leaned over to let him pass. I followed.

Levi stopped at the top step and leaned over the banister. The bartender was looking at us, and he held up two fingers. Levi nodded and moved to the second door, the one Digby had entered. He stepped to the other side of the door, pointed at me, and mimed knocking. I reached up, but just before my knuckles touched wood, the door opened. It looked like the room was empty until I spotted Digby through the crack between the door and the jamb. He was smiling. Levi put one hand behind his back and cautiously poked his head inside.

"That you, Virgil?" he said.

"Thought you were a Bacardi man," Digby said from behind the door. Levi slowly turned his head to the door.

"Rum don't get the job done like it used to," Levi said, and scanned the rest of the tiny room. He stretched a long leg across the threshold, and the rest of his body slid inside in one fluid movement. All the while he kept his hand behind his back. I followed.

When I was clear of the door, Digby pushed it closed with his foot, revealing the gun he held on Levi. Digby eased the hammer down with a click, and I heard the same sound echo behind Levi's back. Digby lowered his revolver, and Levi held up both of his now-empty hands with a wide wave.

"You expecting trouble?" Levi asked, and nodded at Digby's .45.

"Always," Digby replied. "Was that your Colt I heard behind your back?"

"You know me," Levi said. "Always prepared. Could've been a Boy Scout if I liked shittin' in the woods." Digby chuckled and waved his hand at a small Formica table. Levi took a seat on one of the two chairs and Digby took the other. Seeing as my only option was to sit on the soiled mattress in the corner, I chose to lean against the wall.

"Bad idea, you coming here, man," Levi said. "La Dónde's still looking for you."

"Who's that?" I asked.

"You don't know?" Levi said. "Baddest hitter in North America."

"Is that all?" I said, glaring at Digby. "The baddest in North America, not the world?"

"A guy operates out of Ireland's pretty good," Levi said matter-of-factly. "I ain't into hyperbole."

"Thank God for that," I said. I bit my lower lip trying to remain calm. "And this guy's looking for you? That's fucking fantastic. You couldn't have told us about this?"

"La Dónde is a woman," Digby said. "*La* is feminine. You really should learn the language, Coop. And I didn't think she'd still be looking for me."

"You didn't?" Levi said with a dubious look.

"I didn't think she'd be *actively* looking for me."

"It's a standing order, Virgil," Levi said. "Anyone sees you and don't call her gets a shitload of trouble." He wasn't smiling anymore. His expression was quite pained.

"Getting on her bad side could cause a lot of problems for a man in your line of work," Digby said, and set his revolver down on the table next to the bottle of Jack. He sounded almost sad.

"A lot of problems," Levi conceded. The feeling in the room had changed. Something was going down that was beyond my understanding.

"How long until her people show up?" Digby asked.

"About ten minutes," Levi said, and held up his hands apologetically. We'd been sold out. I could figure out that much. The only question was what Digby was going to do about it.

"Ten minutes, huh," Digby said, rubbing the bristles on his chin. Levi nodded slowly. Digby reached for the bottle of whiskey. "Just enough time for a drink."

Chapter Fifteen

Levi Monroe had been just a boy when his father, Lincoln, was swept up in an early sixties' version of the Back-to-Africa movement. Lincoln changed his name, renounced his American citizenship, and took his whole family to Liberia. Their stay lasted exactly three months. Three months of malaria, sweltering heat, and no employment. Lincoln changed his name back, but in the wake of the Kennedy assassination, the Cambridge Five, and the Profumo affair, the authorities were leery of someone who had voluntarily given up their right to be an American. They told him, sorry, but no take-backs. Lincoln had a choice between Canada and Mexico. He chose Mexico because, in his words, he didn't go back to Africa only to end up in the whitest place on Earth.

Lincoln traveled to the Monte because he'd heard it was a place where a man could be free. Of course, this had meant men without families, and Lincoln soon discovered that traveling through the Wild was infinitely more difficult with a wife and child. They settled in Tequilero, where Lincoln opened a tavern.

The drug-running business was picking up steam, and the Madres, with its lack of law enforcement and vast amounts of land, was at the heart of it. The people who frequented Lincoln's tavern were smugglers, thieves, pot farmers, and occasionally sheep ranchers. Lincoln's place gained a reputation as a joint where people could conduct business without fear of the *judiciales*. Lincoln studied his clientele, and he knew who was doing what, where, why, and with whom. That kind of information made him a powerful resource to the dangerous men who spent most of their time out in the Wild incommunicado. Lincoln became a *casamentero*, a broker, a man who could point you in the right direction for whatever you may have needed, legal or illegal. All he asked was a reasonable fee. When he died, he passed the job onto his son, Levi.

"So you're going by Scripes again, huh?" Levi said. He took the bottle, spun the cap off with his thumb, and took a pull.

"Figured it was a name only you knew," Digby said with a smile. He leaned back in his chair and slid his hands in his pockets. "I was trying to fly under the radar."

"Is that how you know him?" Levi said to me. "As Virgil Scripes?" I looked to Digby for help, but Levi laughed and held up a hand. "Fuck it. I don't even want to know. Virgil's got so many names I bet *he* don't remember what you call him. The real question is, what's he call you?"

"Shouldn't we be leaving?" I said, feeling a nervous heat creep up the back of my neck.

"This is Coop." Digby answered Levi's question, ignoring mine. "He's a writer from Chicago."

"What's he write?" Levi said. It was clear I wouldn't be speaking for myself in this conversation. It dawned on me that this was probably Digby's reason for bringing me rather than Milch. I doubted our con-man friend would have liked holding his tongue.

"Right now he's doing a book on Ernest Hemingway," Digby said. In my head I let out a sigh of relief. I didn't want to have to explain Toulouse and his vampire detective to this man. I'd only known Levi for a few minutes, but his opinion, for some reason, had come to mean a lot to me. "There's a guy down here he wants to interview."

"Why bring him to me?" Levi said. He slunk down in his chair, knees spread, and his hands on his thighs. He pulled a cigarette from behind his ear and lit it while Digby told him about a thief named Ebenezer Milch who'd come through Tequilero in the late fifties. It was all so relaxed, as if armed killers were not on their way. As if we had all the time in the world to chitchat. I couldn't even remember how much time had passed since Levi had told us we only had ten minutes. It seemed like hours.

"Shit, that was before my daddy's time," Levi said, and rubbed his chin dramatically.

I started to do a little nervous dance like I had to take a major piss, and I realized I did.

"He was here for a while. People would have known him. Your daddy might have when he first started."

"Come on, Digby," I said, and my voice almost cracked. "People are coming to kill us."

"Relax. They're not coming for you," Levi said. "They comin' for him." Then a cocky smile spread over his face. "La Dónde gonna wanna kill Digby, here, her ownself."

"What about me?" I said.

"Yeah, they probably gonna kill you too, if I'm being honest," Levi said, scratching his ear.

I sank to the floor and put my head between my knees.

"This man Ebenezer may have been going by a pseudonym," Digby said.

When Levi didn't answer right away, I thought I'd clarify. "An alias." I said, lifting my head up and whacking it against the wall. I hardly noticed the dull throb at the back of my skull.

"I know what a pseudonym is, motherfucker," Levi said, shooting me a hard look. "You racist or something?"

"He didn't mean anything, Levi," Digby said, and shot me a warning look.

"I'm just fucking with him," Levi said, chuckling and scratching his chest. "Shit, I just ain't never heard of this guy. I feel bad, ya know. I wanna help you out, man."

"See, he doesn't know the guy. Let's just go," I said. I had been concentrating on the closed door, imagining a troop of desperadoes breaking it down in a fury of broken wood and bullets.

"You know, you should lay it on Elmo," Levi said. "He knows every cat since way back."

"I wouldn't go there unless I absolutely had to," Digby said, and raised his glass. "Thanks anyway."

"It's cool," Levi said. "If this writer wants to interview someone about Hemingway he should go up to Chavez's place anyway, you know, up in Los Ojos," Levi said.

"Why's that?" I said.

"He met Hemingway." Levi said. "Back in like '58. Used to tell me about it all the time. Says he came to watch the fights. It's a good story for a book, man."

"Los Ojos?" Digby said, picking at his front tooth with his thumbnail. "I don't know anybody up there."

"Never met Chavez?"

"Not formally."

"He alright. Gotta flatter the motherfucker. Make him feel important. I'd make a call, but if it ever got back to *her* I helped you . . ."

"I get it," Digby said.

"Los Ojos," I said. "Great, let's go." I started for the door. I had a loosely structured plan to run as fast as I could to the RV. After that I would improvise. My hand was raised, poised to pull open the door and make a break for it, but the dog out front began barking with spastic intensity and I froze. Levi cocked his ear to the door as if the thunderous bark were hard to hear.

"Oh, Virgil," Levi said with a mischievous grin. "I do believe the rest of your party has arrived." Digby scratched his chin and rubbed his eyes.

"Yeah," he said. "I guess we'll take our leave." He took his gun from the table. Someone downstairs pounded against the ceiling, three quick dull thumps, then nothing.

"Miguel says there are three of them," Levi said, looking down at the spot from which the sound had emanated. "Inside at least."

"Just three?" Digby said, took the last swig of his whiskey, and cocked his revolver. "Good. For a second there I thought we were in trouble."

Chapter Sixteen

Digby moved across the room in two long strides, took a fistful of my collar, and redirected me toward the window. I went without protest. The window opened onto a narrow alley. The building across the way was a dilapidated, rotting mess. It was close enough for a jump onto the ledge, but I doubted the deteriorating plaster and wood could hold our weight, and the alley floor below was a thick jungle of discarded appliances and car parts so rusted and muddled that it was difficult to tell where one sharp tetanus-inducing piece of scrap ended and another began. Though the drop would not have been far, I imagined dying slowly and painfully with several nasty objects impaled in some of my favorite body parts.

Digby put a hand on the back of my head and shoved it through the open window. There was a ledge just wide enough to accommodate my boots. Digby stuck his head out next to mine, pointed to the ledge, and waved down toward the corner of the building; indicating that I should get out there and then make room for him.

I stepped onto the ledge and immediately regretted wearing cowboy boots for this adventure. I placed the treadless soles on the weather-worn wood, slick with mold and morning dew, and said a silent prayer that I wouldn't die as a result of my flare for costuming. I turned to move back through the window, but Digby was already halfway out and my only choice was to keep moving. As I sidled down, the ledge creaked in protest or maybe warning, but I was able to get to the corner and grab the rusted tin drainpipe for balance.

The broken window in the building across the alley reflected the room we'd just left, and we could see a Mexican dressed in a fine suit and Ray-Bans enter the room alone, just as Digby brought his second foot through. Digby put a finger to his lips and I shot him the bird. I didn't need to be told to be quiet.

"Dónde?" the Mexican said to Levi, who was still sitting in his chair with the whiskey bottle in his hand.

"I know who sent you, asshole," Levi said. The cool amiability he had showed us was gone, replaced by a baleful serenity. Even though the Mexican was holding a gratuitously large handgun, Levi was the one in control.

"*No, dónde está el hombre,*" the Mexican repeated, but this time it was less demanding.

"Where you think, motherfucker?" Levi said. "They went out the window." I would have toppled off the ledge onto the rusty shards below if Digby hadn't reached out and righted me again. In the window's reflection, the Mexican cocked his head and shrugged. Levi sighed and translated. "*La ventana.*"

The Mexican nodded, racked the slide on his gun, and marched to the window. He shot his head out, looking first down at the scrapyard and then at the window across the way. He noticed us in the reflection and, in the moment it took him to realize we were right next to him, Digby brought his leg up and his heel down on the Mexican's jaw. There was a sickening crack, like breaking crockery, and the Mexican, who had been leaning precariously out the window, tumbled out. He did a half-gainer and landed on top of a pair of discarded lawn-mower blades.

The brittle ledge under Digby gave out, and he nearly followed the Mexican down to his ignominious end. He grabbed the windowsill and hung there, one arm waving behind him, still holding his gun, dangling over broken metal and a dead Mexican.

"A little help," Digby said with a calm tone. I stepped over the piece of broken ledge and dove headfirst back into the room. I reached back through the window and helped Digby inside. Levi watched the whole thing with an amused grin.

"I forgot to tell you," he said. "I've been letting Miguel use the alley to store some junk. It's a little dicey down there."

"No shit," Digby said. He moved to the open door and peeked out. "The other two are still downstairs. I guess we'll just have to shoot our way out."

"Fuck that," I said, walking over to the soiled mattress. "There may be two down there and fifty outside. We go out the window."

"Fifty sounds excessive," Levi said. I grabbed the mattress, ignoring the fouler stains, and dragged it over to the window.

"I would describe everything you two do as excessive," I said. The mattress was a twin and old enough that it bent in the middle considerably. I folded it onto itself and got the end through the open window. Digby, catching on to my plan, helped me shove it through. It landed on top of the Mexican, adding another gruesome layer of cushioning.

"After you," I said, and Digby shook his head.

"What if they come up here after I jump?" he said.

"You're just chickenshit," Levi kidded him.

"You may be right," Digby replied. I climbed outside without further comment. I hung down from the sill as far as my arms would allow and kicked out my legs, turning in the air. My ass landed on the mattress with the sound of creaking metal and the squelch of the dead man underneath. I kicked a few auto parts aside and gingerly slid off the mattress. I was barely on solid ground when I heard Digby hit the mattress behind me. I didn't wait for him. Winding through the debris and picking my way through the junk, I was very glad now to have my boots.

I nosed around the corner to survey the situation out front. The street was deserted. Apparently, the people on this end of Tequilero— the playing-card enthusiasts in the bar notwithstanding—slept late. Digby crept up behind me and put his hand on my shoulder.

"You cool if we just run for it?" he said. I looked over my shoulder. He was grinning and his eyebrows were raised sardonically.

"Are you enjoying this?" I asked.

"I'm enjoying you enjoying it," he said, and pointed across the street. The RV was still tucked between two buildings. The windshield was obscured by shadow, and it was impossible to tell if Grady and

Milch were waiting for us inside. "You run like hell and I'll keep you covered. I'll be right behind you."

"You'll be right behind me or you'll keep me covered," I said.

"I can do both."

"I guess we'll find out."

Digby snorted a laugh and prodded me in the back. I took a tentative step away from the building's relative cover. My left foot joined my right and I moved forward in a stuttered shuffle, keeping my eye on the front door of the bar. The Rottweiler stared at me until something inside the tavern caught his attention. He spun around on his haunches, growling at the batwing doors, one of which was swinging more swiftly than just the wind would allow.

"Faster than that, Toulouse," Digby said. He stepped out behind me, turned on his heel with the same animal precision as the dog, and raised his gun. Several things happened in unison, or close enough that they have melted into one event in my memory. Digby fired into the darkened doorway. A tall Mexican, dressed in the same dark suit as the one upstairs, pushed through the batwings and raised a sawed-off shotgun. Digby's bullet caught him in the throat before the shotgun could clear the door. He fired back through reflex and the door exploded. A chair burst through the large plate-glass window. Another suited gunman, standing in the now-empty frame, raised his own sawed-off. The cacophony of gunshots, exploding doors, and shattered glass shocked my senses, and my muscles turned to pure instinct. My legs pumped without my permission, and my arms flailed with unconscious abandon. I heard the shotgun fire, I heard Digby fire twice. I could not say in what order these things occurred, but the chronology must have been in Digby's favor because when I slammed into the RV's grille and turned around, he was striding, maybe even strutting, across the street without pursuit.

I scrambled around to the driver's side and pulled open the door. Milch was sitting in the passenger seat. He had one of my books in his hands, but his focus was on the street in front of him. His mouth hung open and his eyes were glazed like a stoner watching SpongeBob. I climbed in behind the wheel and smacked him hard on the shoulder.

"Jesus," he said, and I couldn't tell if the blasphemy was directed at the slap or what had just happened across the street.

"Where's Grady?" I asked. Milch jerked a thumb over his shoulder.

"Taking a leak," he said, and tossed the book onto the dashboard. Digby climbed into the backseat and leaned in between us.

"Let's go," he said, as if he had just finished picking up his dry cleaning.

"Grady," I said. "We're waiting for Grady."

"Like hell we are," Milch sputtered. "People are shooting at us, he's taking a leak. That's his tough luck."

I looked at Digby, hoping for a cue to take, but his eyes were on the street. When he did glance at me, there was only a vague curiosity. The decision, it appeared, was mine, if only by virtue of the fact that I was sitting in the driver's seat.

"We're waiting," I said, dismayed at how weak it sounded on the way out. Milch reached for the keys, and I pulled them out of the ignition, holding them over my head while I pushed at Milch with my other hand. We were locked in this struggle when Grady opened the back door and plopped inside.

"Goddamn it," he said, looking down at his crotch. He was furiously rubbing the fabric of his pants. "I caught my balls in my zipper and pissed all over myself. Was that gunfire?"

I put the key in the ignition, turned it, and the engine came on with a mechanical belch. I pulled out onto the street and pressed the accelerator as far as the old beast would allow. The bar receded in the rearview mirror. No one was coming out, and I heard no sirens. Apparently the cops in Tequilero didn't get up that early either.

"I take it the meeting didn't go well?" Milch said.

"As well as I expected," Digby said. He climbed halfway into the front seat and grabbed my novel off the dashboard. He settled back onto the floor, licked his finger, and flipped through to find his place. "Take the next left and then keep going until the road starts to rise. Then I'll take over."

"We heading further into the Monte?" Grady asked.

Digby nodded and hunkered down to catch the sun on the page.

Chapter Seventeen

We ate the last of Digby's sandwiches a half mile off the road, under a copse of juniper trees. The ice in the cooler had melted and the beer was warm, but the plastic wrap had held firm and the sandwiches were not soggy. I was grateful for that small miracle. I went with the ham on rye. Digby had cut the crusts off.

"I want to get it on the record that I am not comfortable with the number of dead bodies I've come in contact with recently," I said over the wad of pork and dairy in my mouth. "For that matter, I'm not entirely on board with the method in which the bodies are being produced."

"The fuck you talking about?" Milch said. He was finishing his second can of warm beer. I hadn't seen him eat a sandwich.

"It's new to him," Grady translated. "What did you expect, Coop?"

"I wasn't expecting this," I said. I wadded up my plastic wrap and threw it into the empty cooler, where it joined the rest of the garbage.

"Yeah, no shit," Milch said. He had finished his beer and tossed it in the dirt next to the junipers. His back was against the RV, pressed into the slim sliver of shade it provided. He leaned against it with his hands in his pockets, like a punk staring down a patrol car as it cruised by. "Why didn't you tell us you had a contract out on you, Digby?"

"I didn't think it would come up," Digby said. He was sitting on the bottom step of the RV, his arms resting on his knees. He had a strange, nervous look that seemed wrong on him, like formal wear on a hobo. "It's been a long time."

"Yeah, you know the cartels," Milch said. "They usually let things slide over time."

"Not the cartels," Digby said. "Just a woman."

"Apparently, though," I said, "she's some kind of super-assassin. Best in the world."

"Come again?" Grady said.

"Second-best, sorry," I said. "There's talk of a guy in Ireland who may or may not be better. This is all from Levi, mind you." I shook my finger at the humped-over shape of Digby. "Your friend, whom I only just met, but he seemed to know what he was talking about. Of course, he also completely fucked us over."

"I already explained that," Digby said. He had. Over the several-hour drive from Tequilero, Digby had tried to explain the various coteries, confederacies, and connections to which Levi was beholden and that motivated his apparent betrayal. The Sierra Madres' underworld network was a byzantine system of alliances and blood oaths that reminded me of Europe circa 1914, and just like the Industrial Age empires it could erupt in war at any given moment.

A hitter, such as La Dónde, needs clients. Levi's job was to arrange the meeting with the client for a percentage of the hitter's fee. La Dónde was one of his clients, and a profitable one at that. Once the meeting was made and the percentage taken, however, the *casamentero* was under no obligation to see the job done. Levi was free to pursue his best interests or succumb to fealty for an old friend. By screwing over both La Dónde and Digby he had not, in the twisted logic of the Monte, done either of them a disservice.

"What the hell kind of name is La Dónde?" Grady said. He had been quiet since Tequilero, which I hoped was due to the embarrassment of catching his balls in his zipper during a gunfight, but I feared something else was seething inside him.

"It means 'the where,'" Digby said. "I called her that because you never knew where she was until it was too late."

"*You* called her that?" I said.

"Back when we were partners."

"Partners?" Grady said. He fished a piece of his sandwich from his cheek with his tongue. Somehow he made this disgusting move look menacing. "What kind of partners?"

Digby pulled his pack of cigarettes out of his shirt pocket and dragged one out with dry lips. He slipped his lighter from his jeans and leaned forward into his hands to shield the flame from the wind.

"We were lovers," he said.

"What does that mean?" Grady asked.

"It means they fucked in the nineteenth century," I said.

"It ended badly," Digby said, his eyes squinting from the cigarette smoke.

"You cheat on her?" Grady asked.

"Something like that," he said.

"I'm no expert by any stretch," Milch said, "but it seems to me that you don't cheat on the deadliest killer in the world."

"Second-deadliest," Digby corrected him, "but no, you don't do that."

"You want to just tell us what happened instead of mumbling like a mopey fucking character in a Nicholas Sparks book?" I said. I had lost patience with the demureness of my fellow travelers. Their secrets, as well as their unsatisfying explanations, had begun to weigh on me. I wanted answers instead of the mandala of half-truths, heavy silences, and knowing looks I had been getting.

"Were you a hitter, too?" Grady said.

"Not for a long time," Digby said. He dropped his cigarette in the dirt and crushed it out with the heel of his boot. "It's irrelevant. I made a mistake, but it doesn't matter. She doesn't know where we're going."

"How do you know that?" Milch asked. "How do you know Levi didn't tell her where we're going?"

"Where *are* we going?" Grady said.

"Some place called Los Ojos," I said.

Grady shook his head like a wet dog. "Never heard of it."

"Wherever we're going," Milch said, "how do we know Levi didn't tell this bitch all about it?"

"I don't, but we're not going there," Digby said. "I'm taking you guys south to the closest airport."

"Well, isn't that just fucking special," Milch cried, throwing up his hands. The RV rocked and swayed as he pushed himself off of it. He stood over Digby with his hands on his hips like a parent discovering his son doing something he shouldn't in the bathroom.

Digby looked back at Milch, squinting in the sun. "Are you, of all people, upset I didn't tell you who I used to be?"

"I get it," Milch spat. "That's supposed to be you being clever, right? You know what, though? At least when I misrepresent myself, it's in the interest of my profession." He turned and kicked the dirt. A rooster tail of dust sputtered into the air and a gust of wind blew it back into the grifter's face. He sputtered and swiped at the air in comical frustration. He took a deep breath and waved his hand at Digby and Grady. "And here I was thinking I was rolling with Josey Wales and Denzel Fucking Washington."

"Who's Denzel Washington?" I said.

"The actor," Grady answered. He was wiping his hands on his jeans.

"No, I mean which one of you is supposed to be Denzel?"

"Grady," Milch said. "Told me he was like Denzel Washington in that movie."

"*Crimson Tide*?" I said.

"Time to go," Grady said as he stood up and backhanded Milch all in one motion. Milch spun from the blow and fell into the RV. He put his arm out to stop himself, but it went through the weak and cracked fiberglass, and he slid through until his face struck the wall. The impact snapped his head back and he fell onto his ass in the dirt.

"What the fuck was that for?" Milch said, rubbing his wrist. A small, red welt was forming under his eye, and a thin rivulet of blood trickled from his nostril. He looked up at Grady with more bewilderment than anger.

"You were out of control," Grady said. His back was to me as he stood over Milch. His hands were unclenched at his sides and he spoke calmly. Milch's eyes flicked to me and then back to Grady's face. He saw something there that made him raise his eyebrows and laugh.

"Maybe I was," he said.

"Yeah," Grady said. "The question is, what do we do now?"

Milch licked the blood from his lip and shrugged. "There's no fucking question," he said, and spat a bloody hunk on the ground. "We go to this Chavez's place."

"Digby," Grady said, keeping his eyes on Milch. "Those guys at the bar. They work for La Dónde, or were they contracted?"

"I don't know. I haven't seen her in years. I don't know what kind of organization she has now."

"But they were after you, right?"

"Yes."

"Would Levi tell her where we're going?"

"I doubt it, but I can't be certain."

"So Digby stays in the RV while we talk with this Chavez guy," Grady said, offering his hand to Milch. Milch took it and Grady helped him to his feet.

"Exactly," Milch said. "We've got nothing to worry about."

"You want to weigh in here, Digby?" Grady said.

"They're after me, not you," Digby said. "I think we can assume we're safe."

"'Assume'?" Grady said. "But I thought you were the guy who says the wise man never assumes anything."

"We're already out here," Digby replied. "None of this fits under the category of *wise*."

"Good enough for me," Grady said. He picked up his garbage, dropped it in the cooler, closed it up, and slid it back into the rear of the RV. "We got a fortune in a suitcase out there, boys." He climbed inside. After a moment, the engine came to life and a small, steady stream of grey smoke puffed from the muffler. Milch climbed into the front seat, patting me on the back as he passed. Digby entered through the back door and held it open for me.

I didn't move. I stood with the last bite of sandwich stuck in my cheek like a wad of chewing tobacco. It was insane to keep going at this point, especially for nothing but a story. I'd already had plenty of adventure to draw on, and I could write a pretty good book on just what happened in Tequilero. All I would have to do is come up with an ending, and therein lay the problem. I am not just a writer, but also a reader. I have a voracious appetite for the written word that borders on addiction. Surely, just as the dipsomaniac is unable to stop until the very last pour from the bottle, I cannot stop a story until it is done. I must know how it ends. I have read some terrible, pathetic, and appalling works simply because I could not stop. Whether it is Tullamore Dew or rotgut, I must finish the bottle.

And then there was the voice in my head. Stinking of literal alcohol and garnished with derision. *He* was telling me what I could not do. *He* was telling me I would die out there screaming like a child. *He* was telling me how small I was. *He* was telling me to quit, to give up, to be the impuissant scribbler of fiction I knew that I was deep down .

He could go fuck himself.

And then Grady emerged. He dropped heavily to the ground and stomped up to me. His great, shaggy head blocked the sun. He looked over his shoulder to make sure we didn't have an audience.

"Problem?"

"There's an argument going on in my head between my parents," I said.

"Yeah, that's a problem. What does your mom say?"

"She says this is the stupidest thing I have ever done in a long and rich history of stupid things."

"Is that all?"

"She says I don't really know you," I said. "That I shouldn't put my life in the hands of a man I've known less than a month.

"What does your dad say?"

"We don't have time for those kinds of issues," I said.

"So you're not going?"

"I'm what you might call conflicted."

Grady sighed and threw up his hands. "Alright," he growled, and looked over his shoulder like a man about to tell a dirty joke. "Here it is. They were two kids. College kids, but smart, you know? They had a decent smuggling op going, grass mostly, but sometimes the hard stuff. That's where I came in. Anytime they brought in coke or heroin, anything like that. They called me. They told me where and when, and I'd set up the raid. They would always be gone before I got there, but we'd get their buyer. Do you understand?"

"I think so," I said. Why was he telling me this now?

"We offer rewards for that kind of information. Bigger the bust, bigger the reward. Deal was I got half and they could count on me to tip them off if the heat was onto their grass shipments."

"So you were on the take," I said. Grady shook his head and clenched his fists.

"No," he said. "I never took a bribe. I just kept my part of the informant reward. Happens more often than you'd think."

"So that's it?" I said. "That's where your money came from."

"No."

"Then where?"

"Shut the fuck up and I'll tell you," Grady said. He closed his eyes and took a deep breath. "This was New Orleans, right? Lots of smugglers. Lots of competition. One day, this fat Frenchman knocks on my door. Shoves a briefcase full of cash in my arms. Tells me I don't work with those kids anymore. Tells me next time they call me about a raid I should call him."

"You did?"

Grady nodded.

"What happened?"

"I don't know," he said. "I left the next day. Haven't been back since. Haven't called anybody. I imagine they didn't fare well."

"That's it?"

"That's it. That's who I am."

"I have to be honest, Grady, that doesn't make me feel better," I said.

"It should. That's the darkest thing about me and I told you all of it," Grady said. "Only thing I can give you is my trust. I just gave it to you. If that ain't good enough for your mom, then she can go fuck herself." He turned and made for the RV. He was inside before I could say anything.

I looked behind me. Shrubs and desert. I looked to my left. Desert, but no shrubs. I looked to my right. Mountains obscured by the hazy heat and the one cloud in the bright-blue sky. In front of me was a dirty, poorly maintained RV, a former hit man, a grifter, and a friend of less than thirty days whom I realized I didn't know at all.

I climbed aboard.

Chapter Eighteen

We drove west into the hazy blue-grey horizon. Mountains rose and fell beside and under us. The road had become little more than a subtle path about fifteen feet wide and was discernible only in that there were slightly fewer shrubs and the rocks in it were only the size of small dogs. We passed through sparse cottonwood forests, scabrous ridges, and utterly depressing former *ejidos*, the communal subsistence farms that gang-reaped the once-fertile land, leaving it naked, broken, and damaged.

The days in the Mexican desert were long and even longer when traveling in silence amongst men you couldn't trust. Funny thing, doubt—it marches into your brain and sets up camp without any invitation. It's nothing much at first, just a fire and a pup-tent. But that tent can become a settlement, and, if left unattended, it can grow into a thriving metropolis, overgrown and overpopulated. The town of doubt about my compatriots had become large enough to warrant its own McDonald's.

And then we were on foot, Milch and I, dusk coming on fast and the falling sun at our backs. We only had to hoof it for half a mile, but my feet began to hurt after less than fifty feet of the hard-packed dirt that served as a road. Walking into town had been, of course, Digby's idea. There was one road into Los Ojos, and one road out. The RV would be as inconspicuous as a streaker blowing across the stage at the Oscars. After the incident at Tequilero, it wasn't a good idea to be seen with it.

That went for Digby, too. He was our guide in the strange wasteland of the Sierra Madres, but he had become a liability. We couldn't be seen with him, and any connections he might have had were forfeit. He could point us in the right direction, but he couldn't go with us. He was like Moses except he used to kill people for a living, and where we were headed was as far from the land of milk and honey as one could possibly get.

Los Ojos.

There had been a farm there once. By all accounts it had been an alfalfa farm. In the 1970s there had been an American program to deploy the herbicide paraquat over the many marijuana fields in Mexico. Not all of the fields the US hit had belonged to reefer farms.

Cracked and sun-bleached wood pillars stood every few feet along the road like old vets watching a Memorial Day parade. They had been part of a stockade fence in another life, and beyond them was the collapsing husk of the barn. It wasn't much more than a leaning frame with a few recalcitrant, weathered boards hanging on like old and unloved relatives. The corpse of a John Deere tractor sat beneath the remnants of the roof, rusted and useless. The land around it was barren, burnt, desolate. That side of the road was failure. On the other side, however, was death.

When Digby said we were heading for a ghost town, I imagined the comical western burg from that episode of *The Brady Bunch*, the one where the old prospector locks them in jail and steals the family station wagon. What Milch and I found was not a series of old-timey western facades, but a spattered grouping of ashen, dead buildings huddled around a dry and blackened stone well. There were a few burnt-out buildings that looked like a herd of felled mastodons. One might have been the general store, maybe the town hall, or maybe it had never been anything. The rest of the buildings were too rotted, some to the point of near disintegration, for my imagination to assign any past to them. It was a putrefying graveyard of dead architecture. Gleaming chrome and sheet metal pocked the spaces between the carrion buildings. Motorcycles mostly, with the occasional muscle car or Escalade nestled in amongst the choppers and hogs. They were vehicles for tough men; not a Camry in the bunch.

There was a small shack on the far edge of town. The sun glimmered off the slanted corrugated-tin roof, and I had to shade my eyes as Milch and I walked to it. The walls were made of white stucco, and the door was solid steel painted the color of dried blood. It was the size of a toll booth. Though no sign announced it, I knew this was Chavez's place. I knocked three times on the claret door and waited.

The plan was simple, which did not preclude it from going to hell and ending with my bloody corpse in a shallow grave out in the desert. Digby would drop us off so we could come in on foot. Grady would go with Digby so they could discuss what Digby had dubbed "Plan B." They would take the RV and blow past Los Ojos and on to the next town for better and less conspicuous transportation. What this would be or how they would obtain it was not information he was willing to share. Maybe they were going to trade the RV, or maybe Digby had a few thousand more dollars stashed in the upholstery. It wasn't my problem. Part two of the plan was my problem, and it was infinitely more difficult.

The door opened and a large Mexican man in a tuxedo stepped out of the darkness. It was impossible to imagine this hulking man in formal wear occupying the small hut from which he had emerged.

"*Si?*" he said.

"I don't speak Spanish," I said with a sheepish look at his magenta cummerbund.

"Sir, this isn't a place for tourists," he said in unaccented English. He offered an uncomfortable smile and held his hands out in a gesture that was both conciliatory and admonishing.

"I'm not a tourist," I said, pretending not to be shocked by the Mexican's command of my native tongue. "I'm an author."

"This isn't a place for authors, sir," the Mexican said. He sounded bored, as if I had woken him from his evening nap.

"That's not what I hear," I said. "I understand that this place was visited by Ernest Hemingway shortly before his death."

"Maybe," the Mexican said, unimpressed. Milch tugged at my elbow and stepped in front of me.

"My name is Joe," he said, flashing that shark-tooth smile of his. "And yours?"

"Luis."

"Luis. I have never met a Luis before," Milch said, rubbing at his lower lip as if he were cycling through his life, looking for any other men named Luis. "That means that from now on whenever I hear the name Luis I will be forced to think of you. You will be the yard stick by which every other Luis will be measured. Do you think you can handle that responsibility?"

"I can handle it," Luis said, and there was the slightest infinitesimal hint of a smile at the corners of the doorman's mouth.

"I knew you could," Milch said, and put a hand on the man's ham hock of a shoulder. Luis didn't flinch, look at the hand, or back away from it. He showed no offense at the gesture, and instead leaned closer to Milch, eyebrows raised, waiting for his pitch. "Now, my man here is telling the truth. He is an author. It's not important that you know his name. The important thing is the name by which the world knows him: Toulouse Velour."

There is a scene from *Romancing the Stone* that flooded back to me. Michael Douglas's wayward adventurer and Kathleen Turner's romance novelist show up at the door of a South American drug lord, looking for help. Of course the drug lord, played by El Guapo from *¡Three Amigos!*, was a big fan of Turner's novels and invites them in for cocktails. As Luis squinted at my face going through his mental Rolodex, I had a fantasy that this would go the same way. Luis would declare his undying love and affection for Alasdair MacMerkin and beg me for details on the next installment. He would become a loyal major-domo during our brief sojourn at Chavez's place, getting us whatever we needed with a dopey hound-dog smile. This fantasy lasted about three seconds before Luis clicked his tongue and shook his head.

"Never heard of him," he said.

"I'm not surprised," Milch said, undeterred. "But regardless of that, you have to understand that this man here," he pointed at me with the flourish of a car model showing off the latest concept car, "is an industry unto himself. Are you familiar with the term *ten percenter*? Well, that is my man here. He shits out bestsellers before breakfast. You understand what I'm telling you? And now he's writing a story on Ernest Hemingway, and all he wants to do is talk to your boss."

"No one talks to Mr. Chavez," Luis said.

"That's not completely true, though, is it, Luis?" Milch said. "I mean someone must talk to him. He's a businessman. Businessmen don't do business without talking, am I right?"

"People talk to him, I guess," Luis said.

"OK, yes, see, there we go," Milch said. "So there must be a process, right? Standard operating procedure for talking to the big man?"

"You have to know somebody."

"I do know somebody," Milch said, and gave the doorman a light pat on the cheek. "I know you, Luis." Milch placed himself between the doorman and myself. He reached into his jacket pocket and pulled something out in his fist. Luis looked at Milch's hand and then his face. He took the thing in Milch's hand, stepped back, and waved to the open door. When he spoke, it was in the bored, robotic monotone often heard from carnival-ride operators.

"Step inside. Keep your arms to your side and limit your movement after the door closes. There will be thirty seconds of complete darkness before the descent. There will be a small jolt at the beginning. Do not be alarmed. The descent will last two full minutes. Do not open the door. The door will be opened for you."

We stepped into the shed. In the brief moment before Luis slammed the door behind us, I took in the measure of the room. There was nothing. Rough stucco walls and a tear-drop steel plate for a floor. The door closed and then there wasn't even that to look at. The darkness was complete.

"What did you give him?" I said. I had expected there to be an echo, but there wasn't enough room in the empty space to create one.

"A grand," Milch said. I couldn't see him even though he was close enough that I could feel and smell his breath on my face. I became keenly aware that neither of us had showered in three days.

"In cash? Where'd you get that kind of money?" It was warm inside the shack. It had been baking in the desert sun like a Bundt cake all day.

"From the First American Bank of Digby's front seat," he said. Even in the dark I knew he was grinning.

"He gave it to you?"

"It was a one-sided two-party loan."

"You stole it."

"More or less. I figured I'd need it to get us in."

"So that makes it all right?" I said.

"Yes," Milch said without any humor. "Look, I took the grand and I used it. That's all."

"How do I know you didn't take more?"

"Because I would imagine Digby knows how much is supposed to be in there. When we're done here, you tell him what I took. If he can subtract, he'll know if I'm lying."

I had no reply for that.

The floor dropped out from under us.

Chapter Nineteen

It was a two-inch drop. It lasted less than half of a second, but when we stopped my teeth smacked together with an audible clack and my mouth filled with the warm, coppery taste of my own blood. There was a metallic screeching of gears, and the floor continued to descend with a lurch that eventually smoothed out into a consistent drop at a slight angle. I leaned against the wall but found that it was moving upward, or rather it was staying where it was and the floor was lowering.

The dark abated and a series of incandescent lights dug into the rock walls passed by. I pulled my handkerchief and inspected my mouth. My tongue was fine and not, as I imagined, cleft in two. I spat a small hunk of my cheek into the hanky and stuffed it back in my pocket.

"He told us there would be a slight jolt," Milch said, the amber lights reflecting off the walls gave both his smile and laughter a ghoulish quality.

The ride took forever, or two minutes, depending on whom you asked. The floor settled into an open bay with more rock walls and lights set into them. A tall door stood opposite the elevator about three feet away. It was steel, with the same tear-drop pattern as the elevator, but with rivets the size of a man's fist embedding it to the rock. The doorknob was a large hoop of brass about the size of a basketball. We were, I imagined, in some sort of antechamber. It looked like the staging area for a mining operation, and I realized that's where we were. Los Ojos had been a mining town once. When the lode ran dry, the town died. Chavez had hollowed out the carcass and made a home there. The brass ring turned from the other side and the door opened with a soft whisper, as if it weighed nothing at all.

There were fewer lights in the main room than there had been in the antechamber. I got the sensation that the room was cavernous and went on as far as my imagination would let it. A cluster of spotlights hung from the ceiling, illuminating a raised platform. Canvas stretched across the floor of the platform, and it was surrounded on all sides by four padded ropes painted red, white, and green, tied to a pole in each corner. It was a fine boxing ring, although I'd never seen one in person before, so I could be wrong.

The white light ended at the edge of the ring as if the line between light and dark had been drawn with a thin black Sharpie. There were sounds in the darkness, rumblings and murmurs. Things moving, settling into seats, exchanging opinions and cash. Now and then a part of them would emerge, a white cowboy hat with a silver buckle, jewels sparkling over tanned décolletage. There was power and money out there in the shadows, and it sent an icy shiver through my spine.

There was a bar to my left. A green neon sign promised cold beer. A red one made sure I knew top-shelf liquor was also available. A grinning little man in a tuxedo stood with a brass phone receiver to his ear and his other hand resting on a crystal tap. I wondered how he could see enough to know what the hell he was pouring.

He nodded as he spoke into the phone, but he kept his eyes on Milch and me. He hung up the phone onto an antique cradle and signaled us by crooking his finger. I followed without looking at Milch for consent. When I reached the bar, my con-man compatriot sidled up next to me.

"Gentlemen," the bartender said as he placed a beer in front of each of us.

"This for us?" I said.

"I put it in front of you, didn't I?" the bartender replied. "Don't worry. It's on the house. Now, if you could wait here, Miss Samantha will be with you in a moment. She will take you to Mr. Chavez."

"Excuse me?" I said. I had planned on some finagling to get in to see the head man. I was prepared to lie, or let Milch lie, or offer a few more bribes. I did not expect to be given an escort and a beer with minimal effort. The Catholic in me mistrusted this unearned good fortune. The writer in me just thought it was poor plotting.

"Miss Samantha will explain, sir. Ah, here she is now," the bartender said, and pointed behind us. She emerged from the dark as if she had been created by it. She was blond, the hair pulled back in a cascading bun over her head. Wisps of golden curls dripped over her cheeks. She wore head-to-toe khaki in the British military fashion, but I don't think Montgomery ever had a body like hers. She had the type of beauty that a man could not take in all at once, and so I had to look at her slightly askew, as if I were trying to get a glimpse of the sun during an eclipse.

"Mr. Velour?" she said. Her voice was like silk and it wafted over me like a sonata. She arrested me completely.

"Coop," I said. "Velour is my professional name." Samantha looked confused, but I couldn't think of anything to follow up with. Milch grabbed his beer off the metal bar and took a long swig before he took her hand.

"What's the deal here?" he said, waving his hand around the arena. Samantha put her hands in her jacket pockets and pushed her bottom lip out in a look of contemplation.

"It is an underground boxing ring," she said, and turned to me. "You're a writer, yes? You're here for the Hemingway story, right?"

"Yeah, how did you . . ."

"Twenty cents on every dollar made in this joint goes to Mr. Chavez," she said. She turned and continued talking, not looking back to see if we followed. I strode after her immediately, but Milch paused to finish his beer and then chug the one I had left behind. He caught up to us as she was finishing her explanation. "You gave Luis upstairs a thousand dollars. Two hundred dollars of that is Mr. Chavez's. Luis did the right thing and called Mr. Chavez while you were in the lift."

We moved past the empty ring on the opposite side of the ghostly murmurings in the dark. My feet crossed from rock to steel grating, and Samantha started to rise in front of me. I expected stairs but found that we were ascending gradually on a low-grade ramp. Milch stumbled behind me and caught himself on the wall. I hoped he was just surprised by the rise in the floor and that the beers had not gone to his head. I'm not sure I wanted to be partners with a drunk Milch. Shit, I wasn't sure I wanted to be partners with a sober one.

"The SOP in this situation is for Luis to take your money, let me know about it, then send you down here. We let you hang around until you get bored and leave. If you get bitchy and demand to see Chavez, then we'll escort you out. Today, though, is different."

"Why is today different?" I asked. We had reached a narrow hallway with cages stacked along the sides. Inside the cages, roosters cocked and crowed and scratched. Brown, red, green, yellow, and as big as bulldogs. One of them eyed me like I was a juicy piece of steak, which confused me because I thought chickens were herbivores. Samantha was difficult to hear over the ruckus they made. And then there was the sound of the fans. Huge industrial blades set into the rock ceiling.

"Today Chavez finds you interesting. He likes writers." We passed one final large cage set into the stone wall. A large ball of thick black fur snored in the far corner on a bed of hay. As we passed it, the ball shifted and I could see a snubbed brown snout and coal black eyes. They had a fucking bear. I hoped the cocks didn't have to fight it.

The hall ended with two double doors made out of dark wood. A scene was carved into the wood—two large men stripped to the waist with raised, bare fists. It was lovingly carved and each stroke of the knife was accented with gold filigree. Samantha pushed open the doors and we followed her inside. As the doors closed behind us I heard the bear moan softly.

The office was brightly lit in contrast with the dark hallway. The decorator had been a fan of the art deco movement but did not have access to the proper materials. The result looked something like the stagecraft of a high school production of *The Broadway Melody of 1940*.

A tall statuary of Jesus stood between two silver clamshell wall sconces. Upon closer inspection, I saw that the statue's face had thick black eyebrows and a Fuller Brush mustache, making Him look more like Burt Reynolds circa *Hooper* than Our Lord and Savior circa the Sermon on the Mount. Two wiry but muscular men knelt before the statue, their taped hands lying against the base of a prayer candle between the icon's feet. One wore blue trunks and the other wore white. Their sweat-slicked backs were bare, and their heads were bowed with solemnity. I focused on this odd sight first, and so I was startled by the deep, rumbling voice from the far side of the room.

"They pray to Jesus Malverde," the voice said, and I turned to find a Mexican rising from a chrome desk. He was a full foot shorter than me, and he had the same mustache as Jesus. He came around the desk at a languid stroll in a blue polo shirt and mom jeans. He stopped by the two praying pugilists, and they crossed themselves in unison before they stood up to face him. He placed a hand on each of their shoulders and whispered in their ears. They genuflected, repeated the sign of the cross, and exited side by side through the door that Samantha held open.

"They fight next," the Mexican said. "It will be a good fight. It is always a good fight when two brothers are on the card. So much history will be spilt on the canvas tonight." He extended his hands to us like a grandfather welcoming his grandchildren. "Gentlemen, I am Sugar Ray Chavez."

"Mr. Chavez, my name is Henry Cooper," I said.

"Sugar Ray, please," Chavez said. "And your friend here is Joe. Luis informed Samantha and Samantha informed me. You want the Hemingway story, yes?"

"That's right, Sugar Ray," I said. "I'm writing a book. Sort of an *In Cold Blood*–type of thing." Chavez nodded slowly.

"I was very young when I met Papa," Chavez said. He guided us to matching rattan deck chairs that sat in front of the gleaming desk. He took a seat on the opposite side. He opened a box of cigars and held them out for us. I declined, but Milch took two. One he stuck in his mouth and the other went into his shirt pocket. Samantha arrived silently next to Milch with a lighter. She bent at the waist to light it for him. I reconsidered the cigar, but Chavez had already taken them off the table. With the cigar lit, she moved to stand next to Chavez, her arm slung over the back of his chair so that the tips of her blood-red fingernails grazed his collar.

"I have heard this story many times," Samantha said with a cool smile. She brushed the back of her hand against Chavez's cheek, and the gesture seemed to surprise him. He looked up at her with raised eyebrows as if he were looking for some sort of cue from her.

"Would you rather watch the fight?" he said.

"I do not want to watch it alone," Samantha said. She looked at Milch and a pang of jealousy shot through me. "Mr. Milch is not a writer. He seems like a man who prefers action to stories."

"You've got me pegged," Milch said, and the look on his face was borderline lascivious. She returned the grin and tilted her head in a way that almost made me fall out of my chair.

"Would you join me?" she asked.

"I have a private booth above the ring," Chavez said, beaming with pride. "Samantha will make sure you have anything you may need."

"Is that right?" Milch said, standing up. "I do believe a boxing match is just the sort of entertainment I need on a night like this."

"Don't you think we shouldn't, um," I tried to think of a word that wouldn't make us sound like we were a couple. I failed. "Get separated?"

Chavez let out a booming belt of laughter. Milch snickered. Samantha smiled.

"What do you think will happen to you?" Chavez asked.

"I'm just saying," I said. "You know, the buddy system."

"Well, Samantha will be my buddy," Milch said. He offered her his arm and she took it. She walked with him to a door behind Chavez's desk. We both watched them go, or rather we watched her go. When the door closed behind them, Chavez turned back to me.

"You've got quite a woman," I said.

"Samantha?" Chavez said, and looked genuinely confused. "Oh no, she is not mine."

"She works for you, though, right?"

"Do you want to hear about Hemingway or the girl?"

"The girl," I said. Chavez took a cigar and lit it. I heard the muffled roar of the crowd and then a thin ding that was the bell. The fight had begun.

"I have a better story than Samantha's," Chavez said. He cocked his ear and, as the din of the crowd crescendoed, he leaned back and stared at the glowing tip of his cigar.

And then he told me a story.

Chapter Twenty

Chavez was eight years old when the American first came. This was back when Los Ojos was still a town. After the mine went bust. After the United States flew her planes and dropped her chemical death. Before the fire. The American arrived on a bicycle, an old piece of rust that shouldn't have been able to support a teddy bear, let alone a man. On the back were two bags, a soft olive-green duffel like one carries in the American army and a small cardboard suitcase that looked very old, but well cared for.

The stranger leaned his bicycle against the farmhouse they had converted into a saloon and hotel. He took his luggage inside and a moment later he reappeared in the doorway. The duffel was gone, but he clutched the suitcase to him like it was a wailing child. The stranger's eyes found Chavez's father, and he strode across the yard with graceful, purposeful steps.

"You Javier?" the American said. "I was told there is work here."

Chavez's father nodded and took the American's hand when he offered it. "For those who can do the work, yes."

Father had never given work to a gringo before. He had never expressed any particular prejudice against them, but he had passed on them many times. They had been broken, low men, desperate for work and escape. While the American also seemed to be escaping, he didn't have the look of the desperado. He was tall and large around the chest, which belied the delicate features of his face. Although he was the same age then as Chavez was now, the lines of age were just beginning to show around his eyes, but they were only seen when he smiled and they were not seen often.

Father hired him on the spot.

Chavez never got around to asking his father what he had seen in the American, but it quickly became evident that hiring him had been a good move. The American was skilled as a fighter, although he only offered himself as a sparring partner. He was useful whenever any construction was attempted. He designed the new saloon and was the first to propose using the mines to house the fights. It was behind the bar, however, that his true talent shone. He was a master of all spirits, but it was his daiquiris that drew the crowds. They weren't the frozen abominations that would become popular in the coastal cities, saccharine horseshit to give the tourists a sugar high. The American's daiquiris were for drinking men. Men who knew their liquor and knew the subtle art of making each part sing so that the whole was a libation of harmony.

The American stayed for one year. He made drinks for the gamblers during the day. At night he would make his one glass of Campari last for hours. Between each sip he would hum Cole Porter.

And then the one they called Papa came.

At ten years old, Chavez had earned a spot in the saloon with the American. He fetched him his ice and washed up. It was a good job. The American was kind and mixed Chavez Shirley Temples whenever he hauled the ice from the machine in the barn to the box under the sink. When Papa came, Chavez had just finished hauling a wheelbarrow full, and he sat at the end of the bar, his feet kicking under the stool, sipping on grenadine and 7 Up. The American was having a cigarette behind the saloon. It was a quiet, dreamy May afternoon.

When the writer entered the room, the air swept out of it. Every object, every person, bent toward him as if he were a black hole sucking up their attention with nothing more than his mass. His thinning hair was combed straight back, and his wild, white beard reminded young Chavez of the Santa Claus on the cover of his mother's magazines. Great rings of perspiration hung under the arms of his guayabera shirt. He waited a moment, panting in the doorway, taking note of the faces, the room, the liquor over the bar. His eyes moved quickly, cataloguing, collecting, understanding. He walked with a somber gait to the bar and slapped a raw, well-lined hand down on the bare wood.

"You run this saloon, son?" the man asked Chavez. There was a smile under his whiskers, but it was weary. Chavez felt the man meant to be cheerful, to let him know he was a kind old man, but he couldn't quite pull it off. There was a sadness in the eyes that repulsed Chavez as much as the man's initial entrance had attracted him.

"My father, *señor*," Chavez said.

"I see," the old man said. "But you can pour a rum, yes?" Chavez did not answer, but slid off his stool and retreated behind the bar. He was not a tall child and, as he poured the rum into the glass, he heard the old man's voice but could not see him.

"I understand there is a man here named Milch," the old man said. "Is that correct?"

"I do not know this man," Chavez said. The old man swore under his breath and slapped the mahogany again.

"An American, then? Is there an American here under any name?" Chavez almost answered at once, but he stopped himself before he could say the American's name. He didn't know why. The American would be returning any second. He could not hide him or warn him about the old man. He didn't even know why he would want to. The old man was not a threat. Not here in his father's place. But there was something terrible about him despite the kind smile and twenty American dollars he offered Chavez in exchange for the rum.

"The rest is for you," the old man said. He drank his rum slowly, and some of it ran down his beard and dripped onto the bar. He let out a long "*Ahhhhh*" when it was finished and placed the glass upside down on the bar.

"Ernie," the American said from the far end of the bar. "How good of you to come." The old man, Ernie, turned on the stool, and Chavez could hear his old bones and tendons creak with the effort. The American stood in the doorway, that serene look on his face.

"You," the old man said. The American moved behind the bar, patted Chavez on the head, and shooed him away. Chavez felt the sheer electricity between the two men, and although he knew he should run for his father, he stayed. He wanted to be there when whatever was going to happen happened. It would be a story, and at ten years old he had precious few of those.

The American took the turned-over glass and righted it again. He reached to the high shelf—the one Chavez could not reach—and brought down the unlabeled bottle. This bottle was meant only for men of status and the *judiciales* when they came for their due. The American poured half a glass for the old man. He cut a fresh lime, twisted it over the spirit, and dropped the peel in. The old man did not touch the drink.

"I don't want a long conversation. Do you understand?" the old man said.

"I do."

"I want it."

"What is that?"

"I don't want a long conversation."

"We've established what you don't want, Ernie. I'm still uncertain about what it is you do want. From my perspective, I would think you would want a bath or at least a shave. By the by, I preferred the mustache. You look like Crusoe, for Man's sake."

"Don't test me. Do you still have the suitcase?"

"I've kept it, yes."

"I want it."

"It's not yours to want," the American said. The old man stepped off his stool and raised one hulking hand, his index finger extended out like a baton.

"You went back on a square deal," he said in a rough growl. His head bobbed as if the weight of these words rested on his brow. "What kind of man are you?"

"I suspect I'm the same sort of man you are, Ernie," the American said. He picked up the untouched glass of rum and drank it down in one gulp. He spit the lime back into the ice and tossed the glass over his shoulder. It landed in the sink, and the sound of the glass breaking made everyone in the joint turn to watch. The old man saw that he had gained an audience, and he turned with one foot toward the room so that he could address both the American and the small crowd as he spoke.

"Like me?" he roared, and gave a thick but hollow laugh. "This man has stolen from me and now he insults me." There were about ten men in the saloon. A mixture of fighters and gamblers, who looked at the old man with the dull expression of cattle.

"They don't know you, Ernie," the American said. "They don't care."

"They know me," the old man said with exquisite certainty. "They may not know my face; they know my name."

"OK," the American said. A cruel look came over his eyes, and he called for the room's attention. "Does anyone here know the name Ernest Hemingway?"

Young Chavez was the only one to raise his hand. The old man pointed at him with a satisfied grin.

"There you see? And who is Ernest Hemingway, boy?"

"A writer."

"There, you see?"

"What did he write?" the American asked Chavez. Chavez shook his head and slumped his head over his Shirley Temple.

"Your legend hasn't made it down here yet," the American said. "These people don't have time for you. They do not read. They live and they don't write it down. No one needs your stories here."

The old man looked as though the American had slapped him in the face. He staggered back, his mouth open. The American smiled a black, cruel grin, the sadistic smile of the executioner before he drops the ax.

"So, Ernie, if you've had your drink, and I see that you have, I suggest you fuck off." The American crossed his arms. The old man opened and closed his mouth a few times, then screwed himself up to his full height. He turned to the crowd and found that their backs were already to him; he had already lost his entertainment value. He turned back to the American and held up one righteous finger. What the finger was meant to convey was lost on Chavez, and the American seemed to take no stock in it either. The old man nodded once as if satisfied, turned with a military air, and stalked out of the saloon.

"Who was he?" Chavez asked, watching the man through the door as he skulked through the hot sun.

"A very famous man," the American said, and turned to clean up the broken glass.

"You stole something from him?"

"I did."

"Why?"

"Because he asked me to, and he paid me. Not much, but he couldn't afford much back then."

"Why didn't you give it back?" Chavez asked. The American flinched as a shard of glass sliced open his finger. He wrapped it in a bar towel, and a small rose of blood bloomed over the white terry cloth.

"Love," he said. He dropped the pieces of glass back in the sink. He clutched the towel in his hand as he climbed the stairs to his room. Chavez heard the door close, and he did not see the American again until he left two days later. He carried with him the duffle and the cardboard suitcase. Chavez's father had given him a horse to replace the bike. He didn't say good-bye.

Chapter Twenty-One

"That's my Hemingway story," Chavez said. He told it well, I thought. Not a lot of embellishments. It was simple and a little sad, but there was no punchline. It was not a story to tell in a bar or on the golf course. It was a story you told late at night, sitting on the back porch with a good friend. I decided to believe him.

"I was expecting them to get in the ring, you know," I said, holding up my hands like an old-time boxer. "That would have been cool."

"But they didn't," Chavez said with regret.

"It would have been cool."

"I thought you would want the truth."

"I know. I know," I said, holding up my hands and offering him an understanding look. "I'm just saying."

"Yes," Chavez said with a commiserating grimace. "That would have been cool. Maybe from now on I will tell it that way."

We spent a moment in silence, and I imagined what it would have been like for an aging Hemingway to take on the aging Ebenezer Milch. From the look on Chavez's face, I could see his mind was moving along the same lines. We sighed together at history's lost opportunities. It was a few more moments before I remembered one of the more important details.

"He said he kept it for love," I said. "Love for whom?"

"I don't know," Chavez said. His cigar had reached the band and he stubbed it out carefully and with reverence in a pewter ashtray. "I had heard of Hemingway, but I didn't really know who he was. His name was like, I don't know, don't you know some names that you don't know why?"

"Yes," I said. "There's this guy Jasper Johns. I've heard of him. I think he's an artist, maybe a nineteenth-century politician. Anyway, I know what you mean."

"Yes, like this Jasper Johns. I knew the name, but not the man. I didn't really realize the significance of what I'd seen until about half a year later. My father was reading the paper, and he commented to one of the fighters that Hemingway had killed himself. He had to explain to the fighter who Hemingway was. My father was an educated man, you see. It was then that I realized I had poured a drink for one of the most famous Americans in the world."

"Did you tell your father your story?" I asked.

Chavez chuckled and shook his head.

"No. How could I tell him that the great Hemingway was here and he missed it? No, I never told him. And I never got a chance to talk to the American about it."

"The American's name was Milch?" I said.

"That's what Hemingway called him."

"Do you know what happened to him?

"A few years ago, I was visiting Tequilero and I told the story. It was at the end of the night. Only a few people left in the cantina, a *casamentero* I knew, a couple of whores, and a man I did not know.

The unknown man told me I was not the only man in the Madres to have met Hemingway. He said he knew another man who would tell stories in their camp, but these stories were from Paris, not Mexico. I asked him about the man and he described him. The man was the American, the one Hemingway called Milch."

"Where was this camp?"

"Not far from here, but you cannot go. It is Elmo Booth's place and he does not take in strangers. Not anymore. You need to know someone from his band, and they are not as easily persuaded as my man at the door."

"Elmo Booth?" the name struck a chord like a church bell in my mind. I had heard it only the day before. Levi had suggested we go to see an Elmo, and Digby had shut the idea down, but Levi wouldn't have suggested it if we couldn't go there. Was Digby a member of Elmo's band? Was this another brushstroke in the mysterious portrait of Digby?

"I might know a guy," I said. The door behind Chavez opened, and Milch and Samantha poured in. She stood tall and poised, but Milch hung off her arm like an oversized purse. There must have been more drinks in the private box.

I felt the urge to take a giant piss, and I realized it had been a while since I'd relieved myself. I asked Chavez about the facilities, and he directed me to a small room by the door. I stepped inside the gold-trimmed latrine and went about my filthy business as I thought about what I had learned.

The American's final word to young Chavez bothered me. *Love.* What did love have to do with a theft? It was as unsatisfying an answer for why he kept the case as any other we had come up with. Perhaps if I knew who it was that the thief loved? Was it Hadley? Perhaps he wanted to punish Hemingway for the way he had set up his poor wife, and for using Ebenezer to do it? Maybe, but then why didn't he just refuse to steal the case to begin with? Was there another woman? One he and Hemingway had vied for, and he thought that by keeping the case he could ruin Hemingway and win the girl? What the hell did love have to do with it?

My head lolled back as I unleashed, and I took an interest in the small glass shelf above the toilet. A couple of bottles of what I assumed was expensive cologne—I would have no way of knowing—a vial of mouthwash and three bottles of pink bismuth, Walgreens brand. One of the bottles was half empty.

I zipped up and backed away until I hit the wall, where I froze, staring at the bottles sitting on the shelf, like three pink shotgun shells. They didn't *necessarily* mean Thandy had been there. And if he had been there, it didn't mean he was still there. Still, I had not seen many Walgreens in my time in Mexico, and three bottles of that particular brand found while on the trail of the suitcase was not likely a coincidence. Levi could not have been the only person to have heard about Chavez's run-in with Hemingway. It was quite possible that Thandy could have gotten here before us. A wise man, as Digby would say, would assume that he had.

The knock on the door was heavy and insistent. I gurgled something about washing my hands and turned the water on. I was certain that if I opened the door I would find Thandy and a half dozen goons on the other side, maybe even the bear on a leash, waiting to eat me. The knock came again along with a muffled and unfamiliar voice. How long did I have until they decided to just kick down the door and drag me out? What were they waiting for?

I threw cold water on my face and then buried it in the plush towel next to the sink. I was still in this soft facial cocoon when the door opened—I had not thought to lock it—and I heard footsteps come up behind me. I kept my face tight against the terry cloth like a child pulling the covers over his head. The monster in the closet laid a hand on my shoulder, and I sagged under the weight of it.

"You fall in or something?" Milch said. I turned around to find that he was the only one in the bathroom. Through the open door I could see Samantha and Chavez at the chrome desk, talking closely. I dropped the towel on the floor and grabbed Milch by the shoulders.

"We have to leave," I said.

"No way," he said, shaking me off. "I think Samantha likes me."

"Thandy is here," I said, covering my mouth with my hand as I spoke. "We have to go."

"Go where?" Samantha said. She was behind Milch. She had walked the length of the room in milliseconds and without a sound. Her hands were folded in front of her and she had a coquettish and inviting look on her face. I did not blame Milch for indulging in the fantasy that she might have the remotest interest in him.

"Our ride will be waiting for us," I said. I pushed past Milch and out of the bathroom. As I pushed by Samantha, I expected to be overcome by some exotic, expensive perfume I couldn't pronounce, but there was nothing. I made for the door, apologizing to Chavez but not looking at him, and hoping to God Milch would just follow.

I was back in the hallway and the cocks were agitated, flapping their wings and making an awful noise. The bear was up with its snout pushed through the bars of its cage. It reminded me, despite the circumstances, of that one Cormac McCarthy book I managed to read. The bear had appeared on one page and I knew it would be dead by the next. It was a sad thing and this was a sad bear.

The gym had emptied, either because it was between fights or the fights had ended for the evening all together. An old man in coveralls wiped furiously at the blood on the canvas. I kept moving as the sound of heavy footfalls came up behind me.

"What's wrong with you?" Milch said, coming up on my right. I hazarded a glance over my shoulder. Samantha followed us. Chavez, it seemed, had elected to stay behind, perhaps to issue orders to his men, or to tell Thandy it was time to strike.

"We got what we needed," I said to Milch. Even if I had time to explain the significance of the pink bismuth bottles, Milch would think I was just being paranoid. I hoped that I was. As I reached the elevator door and pounded on it like a Hun at the gates of Rome, I prayed I was being paranoid.

"It's this button here, Mr. Cooper. I'll take you up," Samantha said as she reached across me to press a faded-red plastic button set into the wall. There was a hiss and the door unlocked. I pushed through it and found the elevator platform waiting for me. I resisted the urge to sprint to it. Samantha followed us into the lift and the platform lurched, starting the slow, maddening ascent to the world above. I was beginning to feel safe. I even took a moment to take in Samantha's ethereal beauty as the lights lit her in a soft amber glow, and I wondered again what kind of woman goes to the trouble of looking like that without putting on at least a dash of some scent?

There was a jolt when we reached the top, and then another one—albeit only in my heart—when Luis pulled open the door. He waved us outside with a flourish and gifted Samantha a wide, puppy-dog smile. We stepped out into the night air, and I surveyed the scene. No Thandy. No goons. Nothing. Not even our ride.

"I thought you said someone would be waiting for you," Samantha said as she tapped Luis on the shoulder. He bowed like a courtesan and shambled back into his shack. The door closed behind us. The only sounds in the air were insects of which I did not know the names. It was an alien landscape among the burnt-out buildings under the moonless sky.

"They're a little late," I said. So many things could have gone wrong. What if they couldn't find a new vehicle? What if the RV had broken down on the way to the next town? What if the new car had broken down on the way back? What if they had run into Thandy or La Dónde? And what could I do about it? Nothing. I waited with my arms crossed, like I had been stood up by a date.

"Who is this man you are waiting for?" Samantha said. She stood close and in the dark of the night it felt like we were the only two people in the world. "Is it the man who knows Elmo?"

"Who?"

"Elmo Booth. I overheard you tell Chavez that you know someone who can get you in to see Elmo. Is that the man who will be picking you up?"

"How did you overhear us?" I asked.

Samantha laughed.

"I meant he told me while you were in the bathroom," she said. I shook my head and looked at Milch. He gave me nothing but a blank expression.

"Why do you care?" I said with more venom than I had intended. Samantha sighed, and her supplicant look faded into something that looked like irritated boredom.

"Just tell me, Cooper," she said. She reached behind her back and pulled a gun, a Glock, the same type I'd used to blow a hole in a man's foot a few days before.

"Ah, fuck," Milch managed.

"Ah, fuck," I repeated. "Are you La Dónde?"

"Why would you think that?" Samantha snapped.

"Well, you know," I stammered. "Woman with a gun . . ."

"Why can't there be more than one woman in this business?" she said. She looked hurt and, despite the gun, I felt an overwhelming urge to apologize, or at least let her know that I was no chauvinist.

"Of course there can be multiple women killers," I said, holding my hands up even higher. "I just thought, you know, the odds, you know, in Mexico and all."

"I know what you thought," she spat. "There are more than one of us here in Mexico, asshole."

"More than two?" I said.

"No, it's just me and La Dónde," Samantha sighed, looking down with a sad grimace. She shook it away and composed herself. "But Thandy hired both of us and I'm not going to lose to her even if she is the best."

"Second-best," Milch said. "There's a guy in Ireland."

"Wait, you work for Thandy?"

"Yeah, and it's up to two hundred grand to anyone who gets that suitcase. So you're going to take me to it. I don't care what kind of deal the old man has with La Dónde," she said, and shoved the gun into my stomach. I could feel the cold steel through my thin T-shirt. "So you're going to take me to Elmo Booth, and we're going to find that suitcase. And if, *if,*" the gun dug deeper into my guts, "you do as I say and you're a good boy, I promise when I bury you out in the desert it will be deep enough so that the coyotes don't drag you from your grave to feast on your bones."

"I'm sorry," I said. "Was that supposed to be a sort of enticement? Because I have to say it's not really sweetening the pot."

Somewhere in the darkness, an engine roared to life. Twin halogen eyes blared out at us, illuminating a large grille like a beastly mouth full of chrome teeth. It took me a moment to realize what I was looking at, but in that same time Samantha lifted her pistol and fired four shots. I heard glass break, and one of the halogen eyes blinked out. The remaining eye was heading toward us by then, growing larger with each turn of the beast's wheels. Samantha took a professional shooter's stance, feet apart, both hands on the weapon, and aimed for the spot where a driver's head would be.

It was at this point that I regained control of myself and I dove to the ground. Milch had done the same, and we both lay in the dirt on opposite sides of the beautiful woman with the Glock as she stood her ground against some hell-bent machine. It was a one-sided game of chicken, but I couldn't figure out which side had the advantage.

Samantha fired. The door to the shack opened, and Luis appeared in his absurd tuxedo. He reached out, took hold of her collar, and yanked her into the shack, closing the door once she was inside. A second later, the beast rammed the shack with the sound of wood popping, metal tearing, and other sounds one only hears in his nightmares.

Our savior was a large black van with a red stripe running down the side. It appeared that we had been saved by the A-Team. I was prepared to accept that a group of mercenaries from an eighties prime-time action series had manifested in the Mexican desert in order to save us. It seemed like the next logical step in the escalating series of bizarre phenomena we had encountered in the Monte. When the van's side door opened, I fully expected Dirk Benedict to hop out with a wry smile and an M16. I was more than a little disappointed when it turned out to be just Grady.

"Let's go," he said. The shack had been destroyed, leaving a gaping cavity under the front wheels of the van. The driver threw the transmission into reverse and pulled out. I took Grady's hand and he pulled me to my feet. I staggered to the door and fell onto the van floor. Grady shoved my feet inside and climbed in after me. Through the front seat I could see that Digby was driving. The passenger side door opened and Milch appeared, wrinkling his nose.

"It smells like cheese in here," he said.

"It'll smell like blood if we don't get moving," Grady said. He slid the door closed, and once Milch was inside, Digby threw the van in gear and peeled out. We were on the road again, leaving Chavez's place behind in slightly worse condition than we had found it.

PART 3

A Clean, Well-Lighted Place

Chapter Twenty-Two

Aday passed in the van as we headed north and further into the mountains. The van had been bought for cash and, yes, the owner had been a big Mr. T fan. We all shared the driving, but it was Digby who took the lion's share, weaving us through the Madres like Hannibal atop his elephant.

"We're all agreed Thandy hired La Dónde, right?" Grady asked. "The bitch with the gun wasn't lying, right?" He had been driving for over an hour in silence, his hands gripping the wheel at ten and two with white knuckles. The rest of us had spent the time catching each other up.

"Yes," Digby said. He was somewhere near the end of my book, and he spoke as he read. "A man like Thandy prides himself on hiring the best. Samantha was not lying. La Dónde is looking for the suitcase."

"I thought she was looking for you?" I said.

"She's a multitasker," Digby said.

"Who gives a shit," Milch mumbled, poking his head out from under his jacket. He had been sleeping for most of the trip. I marveled at his ability to shut off his system like it had a switch. I, on the other hand, was pretty sure I would never sleep again. "I want to know why Samantha didn't off us when we first showed up. Why did she go with the undercover shit?"

"I'll tell you why," I said. I had been working this problem out in my head since our escape, and I was happy to share my results. "Because we're not the only part of the job. Thandy's offering two hundred grand just for the suitcase. Samantha figures she can't beat La Dónde the killer, but maybe she can beat La Dónde the treasure hunter, right? Levi said Chavez told that story all the time, right?"

"That's what he said."

"So Samantha probably heard about it. She decides to question Chavez, and he tells her to find the case you gotta go see Elmo."

"But you gotta know somebody if you want to get in to see the wizard," Grady said.

"Exactly. So she's up shit's creek. So what does she do? She figures she'll wait to see if we show up. She makes Chavez pull a Lando Calrissian and Bob's your uncle."

"Still doesn't explain why she didn't kill us when we showed up," Milch said.

"Because she didn't have to," I said. "She could afford to put on the act long enough to see what our next move was. When she found out we have an in with Elmo, she decided to make *her* move."

"Dumb plan," Milch said. "She couldn't be sure Digby would cooperate. She should've just followed us."

"She's got competition," I said. "La Dónde is after us, and the suitcase too. She couldn't take the chance that La Dónde would say fuck the case and just kill us before we found it."

"So what is our next move?"

"We go to Elmo's," Digby said. He cracked the back window, lit a cigarette, and slapped me on the chest like he'd just told a joke I didn't laugh at hard enough. "You'll be safe there."

"You sure about that?" I said. Digby tipped his hat up with his thumb and squinted out the window.

"Mostly," Digby said. "I have a plan. I'll take you to the camp and then I'll take the van and go."

"You're thinking she'll go after you and not us," Grady said.

"*Hoping* is more like it," Digby said. He held up his hands, moving them like scales. "She's gonna have to make a choice. Go after me or after you; for love or money." He paused and added, "Actually more like for hate or money."

"She hates you that much?" I said.

"She's one of those women who tends to blow things out of proportion."

"A drama queen who knows how to use a high-powered rifle. You know how to pick 'em, Digby," Grady said.

"You'll lay low at Elmo's until it blows over," Digby said.

"That could be never," I said. "Thandy's not going to give up on us or the suitcase. And what if he just sends people after us while she goes after Digby?" I asked. "He's already hired two hitters. Why not more?"

"He's not Lex Luthor," Grady said. "How powerful do you think he is?"

"Thandy is a white rich southerner," I said. "The classic motivations don't apply with people like Thandy. Money, love, revenge, insanity—his pride is all four of them combined. It's all a guy like him cares about. We hit him where he lives. He'll hire an army if he can."

"This isn't a Tennessee Williams play," Grady said, scratching his beard. "But, considering the shit we've been through, I'm beginning to think this suitcase isn't worth it."

"You want out?" Milch said, coming fully awake. "Is that what you're saying?"

"I'm saying Thandy's pushed us out," Grady said. "I got my pride and I got my money troubles, but neither of them are worth my life, you dig?"

"Unless Thandy calls off the hit, it won't be up to you," I said. "Right, Digby?"

Digby lit a new cigarette off the one in his mouth and flicked the old one out into the brush. "That's about the size of it," he said.

"And I'm telling you this Dixie fuck is not going to let this go. He wants to win," I said. The embryo of a plan was gestating in my tired mind.

"So what do we do?" Grady asked.

I smiled and turned on the radio. There was nothing, but static so I turned it off again. "We play to lose," I said.

Chapter Twenty-Three

"Love, while having the power to spur revolution, is itself evolutionary. History has shown that man's natural inclination is toward fear and hate, but it has also shown that Love can conquer both. Love destroys these loathsome ideals not through one glorious death stroke, but rather it filters them out through the charcoal of generations striving to be better than the one before.
The ones who live here do so with distilled souls."

—Elmo Booth

The words had been carved into the rock with an artisan's deft hand. The rock stood to the side of what we had been calling the road. It was a massive stone, its edges rounded smooth and the face polished to a reflective sheen. It was meant to mark the boundary of the camp, but it was more than that. Depending on who came upon it, the stone was a mass rock, threshold to sanctuary, anchor, or, simply, a line in the sand.

"Your friend's a preacher?" Grady asked after reading the words through the windshield. Digby had stopped the van several yards from the rock and cut the engine.

"He is certainly that," Digby said, rubbing the weariness from his eyes. "But think more *Pale Rider* than Pat Robertson. Stay in the car."

He opened the door and held his hands above the headboard for a moment before getting out. He took a step, then another. The wind picked up and dust swirled in small tornadoes around his boots. He opened his coat, showing the holstered gun and belt for a moment, and then let it close again. He reached the stone and stood by it like a man standing on the edge of a deep canyon.

Even the landscape cowed to the rock and its boundary. The last fifteen miles had been a dust-strewn stretch of barren debris, another victim of the *ejidos*. We were facing east, the wind at our backs. The rock marked the beginning of a field of thick green grass spreading well out of our vision to the north and the south. The breeze blew over the lush blades, kneading them into waves that seemed to rise, crest, and crash against twin mesas about half a mile away, ascending from the sea like a couple of raging Poseidons. The sun was setting behind us and it bathed the mesas in a furnace of red. Despite the brilliant light there were still dark pockets of caves and crags, like aphotic blemishes on the mesas' faces. I imagined nefarious men huddled in those hollows, plotting against us down here in the open desert.

Digby was staring at one of these caves in particular. He held his arms up over his head and crossed them, forming an X. After a moment he brought his left hand down, but held his right aloft with four fingers showing. A small cloud of dust puffed up between his feet, and half a second later we heard the corresponding rifle crack. Digby didn't flinch. He didn't even turn around. He waved us on and walked without waiting.

We climbed out of the van, groaning, grabbing our backs, and stretching our legs. As an afterthought I reached back under the front seat and grabbed the leather satchel containing the manuscript. I had to half jog to catch up to Digby, who still had his eyes on the cave up in the mountain.

"What about the van?" I asked.

"We go on foot from here," he said.

"And we just leave it there?" Grady called. He was behind us, walking, refusing to hustle. Milch was strolling next to him.

"It's fine," Digby said. His fingers, which had been floating over the tips of the tall grass, formed a gun and he pointed it at the top of the northern mesa. "Juan is watching it."

We neared the camp and as the sunlight dwindled, bits of light bloomed all over the sides of the mesas. Some were the crimson hues of kindling fires, but there were a great many with the unmistakable amber glow of electricity. Digby sensed what was perplexing me and he pointed to the top of the flat peaks and said, "Solar panels." Then I was suddenly aware of the humming that had grown steadily with each step we took. It must have been the generators.

"The whole place used to be an Apache stronghold," Digby said casually. "You know Elmo's great-great-grandfather was John Wilkes Booth."

"Booth didn't have any kids," I said.

"Not *before* he killed Lincoln," Digby said. I recognized the smile on his face. It was the I-know-something-you-don't-know grin found most frequently on gossip artists, older siblings, and serial novelists. It was a pleasant shock; the Hotel Baja's laconic handyman was in truth a fellow storyteller. "He had a few of them when he got to Mexico."

"John Wilkes Booth died on the porch of a Virginia farmhouse," Grady said, surprising me. He never struck me as a student of American history.

"That's what they told you, huh?" Digby said, eyeing Grady over his shoulder. "They tell you Hemingway asked a guy to steal his own suitcase? They don't always get the story right, do they?"

"To be honest, I never heard of Hemingway's suitcase until someone tried to kill me over it," Grady said. "But I think they do tend to get the big stories right. Don't you think the army would have torn through the South looking for Booth if he'd survived?"

"Ever see *The Outlaw Josey Wales*?" Digby asked. "All those ex-confederates heading down to Mexico rather than surrender? Think they wouldn't have taken the man who shot Lincoln with them? It's not like they had an effective border patrol back then. They don't even have one now."

"I'm not saying he *couldn't* have escaped. I'm saying he didn't," Grady said. "Who did they shoot in that barn?"

"I don't know who they shot," Digby said. "But I imagine it's a good thing they shot someone. Guy like Booth running around could've ignited another rebellion. I imagine the higher-ups thought it better to end it right there and say he was dead. No TV back then. No Internet. Who was gonna say different?"

"Sounds like bullshit," Grady growled. He picked a long blade of grass and stuck it between his teeth.

"There are eighteen sides to every story," I said, trying to be helpful. "And they're all bullshit. You believe it, Digby?"

"I believe Elmo believes it," Digby said. "That's more important than it being true. He tells me Booth and a bunch of former confederates escaped to Mexico and founded this camp. Their plan was to regroup and launch another uprising. They got sidetracked. The Monte can have that effect."

"So this is a camp full of the-South-will-rise-again shit-kickers?" Grady said, throwing up his hands. "I put up with enough of that shit in New Orleans."

"They gave up on that plan after Booth died. Instead, they made a good living wiping out the remaining Apaches in the Monte for the US and Mexican governments. They signed up with Pancho Villa for a while but were really just privateers working on horses instead of ships. Raided various towns, robbed banks, raped the women, that sort of thing."

"They don't sound like my kind of people," I said.

"Mine neither," Digby said. "It ain't like that anymore. Control of the camp has been passed down to each generation of Booths. Elmo took over in the late sixties and changed everything. It started with taking in American draft dodgers, for a fee of course. After a while the racists and shit-kickers died out, sometimes Elmo helped them on their way. Now, it's more like a halfway house for desperadoes tired of the way of the Monte. Trust me, I used to live here."

"You're a little young to be a draft dodger," I said, reaching instinctively for my notebook.

"Like I said, it's a place to go when you're tired of the Monte," he said. "I was tired of the Monte."

We reached the mesas and walked between them until we were enveloped in darkness, the surrounding light somehow unable to reach us. I flipped open the cap on my lighter. Someone's hand folded over it before I could flick the striker, and another one patted me on the shoulder. It was Digby.

"Shit, I thought Juan was screwin' with me," a voice said from the darkness. The sound bounced off the walls, making it unnervingly omnipresent. An orange light appeared to my right as if the rock had caught fire, but then the light became a straight, widening vertical line, and I realized it was a door sliding back. When it was open, I could see the start of a tunnel tall enough for a power forward to comfortably fit through, lit by small torches set into the walls. A set of stairs was carved into the rock just at the end of my vision.

A squat figure stepped into the light. He was backlit and mostly in shadow, but I could see it was a man wearing a scruffy Henley shirt and faded jeans. He tilted his head and absentmindedly scratched his elbow as he considered our crew.

"You gonna come up and see el Jefe, man?" the man said with a California drawl I had missed the first time.

"No, but give him my best," Digby said. He stepped around me and reached out his hand. The other man took it and they shook once. Digby took the man by the elbow and led him away from us. They had a brief, muted huddle and Digby passed the man something, but it was difficult to see in the gloaming. He said loudly enough for us to hear, "For Elmo. I need to be out of here before Pieta shows up."

"Smart," the man said. "Ran into her a couple of months ago out on one of the farms. I mentioned your name and she got . . ." he paused, looking up at the stars starting to appear between the gap in the mesas. He looked back at us, and I could see the edge of his smile in the firelight. ". . . pissed." He said this as if "pissed" had myriad connotations and that Pieta had exhibited every one of them.

"I expect she would," Digby said. I heard his boots scrape in the sand as he turned around, then his steps echoing off the walls like tympani drums. "Good luck, boys," he said. We watched him go, disappearing into the night, and I felt like a mountain climber clinging to my crampons, watching my Sherpa walk away into a blizzard.

The man he left us with turned and walked into the tunnel.

"I'm Dutch," he said over his shoulder. His drawl pushed each word together like elephants walking trunk to tail, and his rhythm made each sentence sound like a punch line. "I'll take you to el Jefe."

Chapter Twenty-Four

Despite the torches, it was cool inside the rock and I welcomed the relief from the heat outside. Dutch moved swiftly up the stairs, and we stumbled in the low light, trying to keep up. The stairs twisted and turned at random, often passing more tunnels with lights and strange sounds, some of them musical and others of the animal variety. My joints ached and my body begged for rest, but I didn't dare stop. It was clear that if we lost Dutch, we would certainly never find our way out of here.

"Hey, Dutch, you know La Dónde?" I asked. Dutch looked over his shoulder and raised his hand with the palm down and shook it in the more-or-less gesture. "She ever miss? I mean, when someone hires her, is there any chance they don't end up dead?"

"Pieta miss? Not that I know of," Dutch said. "Unless the contractor calls off the hit. But that never happens."

"What about Digby?" Grady said.

"Who?"

"The guy we were just with," I said, and remembered Digby's penchant for aliases. "He goes by a lot of names, I guess."

"Around here, he's Sully," Dutch said. "And Pieta didn't miss. She let him go."

"Why?"

"Matter of the heart," Dutch said.

"Do you think she'll go after him instead of us?" Grady asked.

"Maybe," Dutch said. "It's possible. Pieta's hard to read on shit like that."

"What's her beef with Digby, I mean Sully?" Milch asked. Dutch stopped under a torch, and his features danced in a mix of shadow and light.

"It's Pieta, so the answer's both simple and complicated," he said. He fished into his shirt pocket and came up with a fat, tightly wrapped joint. He wet the end with his lips and struck a match against the wall. After taking a long hit, he offered it to us. Only Grady refused. Dutch continued, "I ain't the one to ask, not my place, but Pieta, she's a passionate lady, even if she is a cold-blooded killer."

"And she never misses," Grady said, crossing his arms.

"Look, I ain't the one to ask," Dutch said. "I'm just in charge of the crops."

"What crops?" I asked.

"I already said too much," Dutch said.

"OK," I said. "Just tell us what Digby did to her."

"He was her *casamentero*," Dutch said, the joint bobbing up and down on his lip as he spoke. "You know what that is? Good, so he got her jobs. She was a killer's killer. I mean she didn't give a fuck. Killed women and children. Heard one time she kidnapped and castrated the twelve-year-old son of one of the Cali cartel's higher-ups just because he didn't pay her on time. I mean she didn't give a fuck."

"So what happened?"

"Sully started to give a fuck." The charred paper on the end of the joint touched Dutch's lip, making him spit and jump. "I already said too much. Let's get you boys up to see Elmo and get you a room. Pieta's supposed to be on her way."

The stairs ended and turned into a ramp. At the top we could see a rectangle of light, the outline of a door. There were drums, and as we neared the top the rhythm became familiar. Then there was a piano and finally the vocals. It was the Stones' "I'm Not Signifying" playing on an old turntable.

Dutch pushed the door open and we spilled out onto the top of the mesa. A field of stars exploded over our heads like fireworks. At this height we could still see a small glow to the west that may have been the lights of Tequilero. To the south there was nothing, just darkness.

In the north there was a larger glow, and I told myself it was Chicago. Finally, I turned to the east. I could make out the Sierra Madres as an inky blot where the stars ended.

A man sat at the edge of the mesa, on a wooden deck chair with his back to us and his feet propped up on an overturned straw basket. He wore a rust-colored duster that he gathered around him like royal robes, and his matching Stetson sat on his head like a crown. His fingers were laced behind his head over silver hair long enough to flip over the duster's collar. A gun belt with twin .45s lay next to the basket. The .45s' custom handles were silver, to match the man's hair. I didn't need to be told that this was our host, Elmo, great-great-grandson of John Wilkes Booth.

We had apparently interrupted dinner. At the other end of the mesa, a man in a leather apron was swaying along to *Exile on Main Street* and flipping steaks on a grill made from an oil drum cut in half. I caught the smell in my nostrils and my stomach lurched. I hadn't eaten since the small sandwich the day before. There was a long table where a dozen or so diners were involved in various stages of their meal. Some were dressed in dirty T-shirts, others in chambray work shirts, but they all wore shoulder holsters.

"You boys hungry?" Elmo asked, turning around in his chair. We managed to grunt an affirmative. Elmo nodded to Dutch, who dashed over to the grill master and whispered something at him. Elmo stood up and turned his chair around, pulling it close to the fire pit between us. He waved his hands at a couple of empty chairs and we took them.

"Welcome to the camp. It isn't the Ritz, but we'll try to make your stay comfortable. Elmo," he said, and tapped his chest with his thumb. His accent was old, southern, and aristocratic, but the gentility had been watered out of it, like a good bottle of booze cut just once too often. In the firelight I could see he had one of those faces that was impossible to put an age on.

"Thank you for having us, sir," Grady said after we introduced ourselves. We didn't bother with aliases, but we gave only our first names. We had agreed in the car it would be better to ease into why we were here, and we didn't want Milch's name to give us away. Dutch arrived with our plates. He explained the sizzling steaks were javelina and the stuff that looked like sliced green potatoes was baked agave cactus. We set the plates on our laps and dug in. Conversation ceased and Elmo just smiled, enjoying us enjoying our meals.

"Ebbie," Elmo said, while tugging at the end of his drooping mustache. Milch looked up from his meal but kept stuffing cactus in his mouth. "Not a popular name among people your age."

"No, sir," Milch said through the chunks of meat and cactus.

"I knew another Ebbie," Elmo said. "Good friend of mine, used to live not too far from here. Come to think of it, you look like him. You any relation to Ebenezer Milch?" We stopped eating, and a piece of javelina dropped from my open mouth. So much for easing into it. Elmo took a look at our expressions, bent his head back, and let out a deep, belting laugh.

"He was my grandfather's brother," Milch said.

"I see," Elmo said, wiping a small tear from his eye. "And you're looking for him?"

"We're doing research for a book," Milch said. Digby had felt it would be best not to let too many people know about the suitcase. He trusted Elmo, but he hadn't been in the camp for some time and he couldn't vouch for everyone there. We decided a book would be good cover. At the very least it was consistent with the lie we'd been telling all along.

"You're a writer?" Elmo said. Milch shook his head and pointed at me.

"Him," he said. Elmo had a look like he had sniffed a carton of milk way past its expiration date.

"And you're writing a book on Ebenezer?"

"On Hemingway," I said. "I came across Ebenezer's name in my research and I tracked down the younger Milch here. Just following a lead."

"You came all the way out here for a lead?" Elmo said, eyeing me through the flickering flames. "That's a pretty in-depth book."

"I try to . . ." I started, but Elmo cut me off.

"I mean traveling through this terrain," Elmo said, and leaned in close to the fire until it was difficult to tell where the flames ended and his face began. "Risking your life all for a name you came across in your research. I would think this lead would have to be pretty goddamn special. Pretty fucking goddamn special. In fact, if I were a betting man, I'd say it was more than just a lead you were after."

"Shit," Grady said, and tossed his empty plate into the dirt.

Elmo smirked and crossed his legs.

"Yeah, shit," he said. "I'd say a couple of things you boys are short of is a good story and good manners. Here you boys are in my camp as a favor to Sully, and the first thing you do after I give you a home-cooked meal is lie to me?"

"If it makes you feel any better, it was Sully's idea to lie," Grady said.

"And it isn't a lie," I said. "I am a writer and I am writing a book."

"It's the truth," Dutch said. He stepped between us and hopped over the fire. He pulled something rectangular from his jacket pocket. Elmo took it and turned it over in his hand. When Dutch stepped away, the firelight caught it and I could see my Scottish vampire detective with one of his various love interests in his arms. It was the same one Digby had been reading. So that answered the mystery of what he had given to Dutch. There were a few pages that Digby had dog-eared, and Elmo flipped to them. He turned the book to face the fire and I could see black handwriting in the margins.

"This you?" Elmo said, holding up the book. "You Toulouse?"

"Sometimes," I said. Elmo leaned forward and stared me down over the flickering flames. He stayed that way as the wind came up off the desert and the dust swirled around the small circle we sat in. He drew whatever conclusion he was looking for and tugged his hat down on his head.

"You writing one of these books?" he said, holding up *MacMerkin's Folly*.

"No."

"Nonfiction then?"

"Yes."

"About the Hemingway thief?" The moment he said it out loud, I realized that it was exactly how I thought of Ebenezer Milch, the First. I saw the name in my mind, written in Courier New, capitalized and complete with the definite article: The Hemingway Thief.

"Yes," I said.

"Well, if you've come here looking for the Hemingway thief," Elmo said, folding his hands in his lap. "Then you must be looking for his goddamned suitcase, too."

Chapter Twenty-Five

"We're sorry about the subterfuge," Grady said. The word sounded awkward coming out of his mouth. One of those cop words like "ascertain" or "perpetrator." Words they used often, but didn't understand outside their narrow purview. "But Digby felt it was best to keep this operation on the old need-to-know, you know?"

"Who the hell is Digby?" Elmo said, shooting a hard look at Dutch. "You told me Sully sent them?"

"He did," Dutch said. "He goes by Digby now."

"That boy," Elmo said, and laughed. He leaned back and laced his fingers behind his head again. "He's got more names than a phonebook. Got so many names, he gives them to other people. Like his girl, Pieta, goes around calling her *La Dónde*. Way I was brought up, you called your lady *darling* or *sweetheart*. You don't call her something sounds like some Mexican time-share."

"We're not trying to screw anybody is what I'm saying," Grady said, trying to stay on topic.

"I understand, son," Elmo said. "It pays to be careful. But careful can get you killed, too. Don't go around lying to people offering help. Don't be rude to new friends when you already got enough enemies."

"You mean La Dónde," I said.

"For one," Elmo said.

"Some rich guy up north's gotta hard-on for these boys," Dutch said. "Hired La Dónde to do the job."

Elmo lifted his Stetson and scratched his forehead.

"That so? You boys are pretty much dead then," he said, and sucked his teeth. "Pieta doesn't fuck around. If there's a contract on you, it's a done deal."

"Digby said we'd be safe here," I said. "Are we?" Elmo patted the pockets of his duster, settled on one, and pulled out a marbled meerschaum pipe. He took his time lighting it with a wooden match. When he was done, he blew the match out and flicked it into the fire.

"You are," he said. "Pieta could be standing right next to you, and as long as you're in my camp she won't lift a hand against you."

"How do you know?" Milch said.

"Didn't Sully tell you what this place is?" Elmo said, sweeping his hand around the top of the mesa.

"He told us it was like a halfway house for the Monte's reformed criminals," Grady said. Dutch laughed and slapped his knee. Elmo grinned.

"It's become something like that I guess," Elmo said. "But not for the first hundred or so years this camp existed. Back then they did some pretty heinous things; terrible things I can't take back. So now I offer a place for people who are tired of all the killing and violence. It's that simple."

"So you guys just sit around being all peaceful?" Milch said. "Pardon me if I don't quite buy it." I gave him an elbow.

"We don't just sit on our asses, son," Elmo said. "There are a lot of folks out here in the Monte need help. Decent people don't know how to protect themselves."

"Jesus, we're staying with the Magnificent Seven," I said.

"Sure, it's why they're so heavily armed," Grady said. "But tell me, Elmo. Are you Yul Brenner or Brad Dexter?"

"I don't follow," Elmo said.

"It's just that your operation seems expensive," Grady said. "How do you pay for it, if you don't mind me asking?"

"Why would I mind?" Elmo said, pulling deeply on his pipe. "We farm, Grady. We eat most of it ourselves and sell the rest to pay for supplies."

"I don't know many crops that sell well in these parts," Grady said. "At least not the kind you eat."

"We have a healthy marijuana crop, if that's what you're getting at," Elmo said.

Grady smiled and shook his finger at Elmo. "That's what I'm getting at," he said.

"Is that a problem?" Elmo said.

"I'm not sure," Grady said. "You tell me this place is a safe haven from the Monte. You tell me you guys are a band of do-gooders out to do good. OK, but you grow and sell an illegal crop, a crop responsible for most of the violence you claim to despise."

"You need to widen your perspective," Elmo said. "Just because something is illegal doesn't mean it's wrong. We have good product and don't step on anybody's toes, so the cartels leave us alone. We trade with some of the local narcos, and they take it from there."

"And you think people aren't killing over your product once it leaves your camp?" Grady said.

"I've seen you smoke more weed than the entire cast of *Pineapple Express* put together," I said.

"That's my weed that I grow myself, or I get it from someone I know who grows their own," Grady said. "The cartels don't get any of my money."

"But you'll take some of theirs, is that it?" I said. Grady gave me a dirty look. I knew I had gone too far. I had no idea why I went after him like that. Just as he probably had no idea why he had laid into Elmo. Maybe we just hated hypocrisy. Maybe we were just fucking exhausted and a little cranky. I put my hand on my friend's shoulder and gave it a squeeze. I followed it with a nod and, thankfully, he returned it. I hoped too much damage hadn't been done.

"Look, Grady, it's not a perfect situation, I'll grant you that," Elmo said. His pipe had gone cold and he took the time to relight it. When the bowl glowed, he pointed the stem at Grady. "If you were here forty years ago, you'd be saying different. The history of this camp is a dark one. I've pulled it by the neck against the current of evil waters. Considering where we started, this place is fucking Xanadu."

"Yeah, we heard the story about your grandfather," Grady said.

"Take it easy, Grady," I said. He bit his lip and held up his hands.

"It's alright, Coop. Ignoring the past's the best way to make sure it comes around again," Elmo said. He picked up a long stick and poked at the fire. Sparks popped into the air and swirled around us like fairy dust. "It's my great-great-grandfather you're talking about. My grandfather killed a lot of people too, but no presidents."

"Digby told us the whole story," Grady said, ignoring my stare. "Booth escapes the Union Army brigade sent to find him. White House covers it up with a stand-in body. Sounds like a lot of bullshit to me."

"Sounds like bullshit to me, too," Elmo said. "It's possible the John Wilkes Booth who founded this camp was just a good storyteller, and the story he liked to tell made people think he'd done something important, even if it was killing Lincoln. You have to understand though, a story like that, it carries a lot of water in these parts." He took a pull on his pipe and let the smoke drift lazily past his lips. "There's another fable going around says I'm the reincarnation of Jesus Malverde, patron saint of desperados and bandits. I don't like it, but it's useful, so I use it. Legends have power here. There are grown men, tough men, killers, who won't sleep outside without gathering brush around them to keep El Chupacabra away. People don't respect much around here, Mr. Doyle. They certainly don't respect life—but they respect legends."

"Sounds like a convenient excuse for bullshit," Grady said.

"So you like stories," I said, trying to salvage the situation. "We have that in common. Ebenezer too I bet, huh?"

"Oh yes," Elmo said. "He did indeed. And he loved to talk about his time with Hemingway in Paris."

"Where's the suitcase?" Milch said.

"Jesus, Milch," I said. "How about some tact?"

"I've got no use for tact, Coop. I like a man who says what's on his mind," Elmo said, and turned to Milch. "You think you have a claim on the suitcase?"

"I'm the last Milch. I think that makes it mine."

"Perhaps," Elmo said. I was having a hard time getting a read on him. At one moment he seemed like your typical rural macho man with his guns and cowboy hat. Then he would smirk and it would remind me of the look my dad always had after he said something particularly wry and witty. He was playing with us, but not like a cat with a mouse. It was different. He had the information we wanted, he knew it, and he wanted us to work for it. It was like a teacher forcing a student to use the encyclopedia rather than just handing out the answer. It was irritating.

"Did he have the suitcase when he came here?" Grady asked.

"Yes."

"Where is it?" Milch said, and it sounded more like a demand than a request.

"I'm not going to tell you," Elmo said. He leaned back and his eyes drifted to the stars.

"Why the fuck not?" Milch said, and pounded his fist on the arm of his chair.

Elmo sighed, but before he could answer, the walkie-talkie on Dutch's belt squawked and a few staticky words came through in Spanish. Dutch replied and tapped Elmo on the shoulder.

"Juan thinks you should see this," he said. Elmo nodded and eased himself out of his chair. He wrapped his gun belts around his waist.

"You fellas should come along," he said. "This concerns you too."

⚡

If the top of the first mesa looked like a Texas Fourth of July, then the second one looked like a beachhead on D-Day. Wires were strewn across stump-like telephone poles. A small radio station was set up on a couple of overturned apple crates. A jerry-rigged shelter made up of sandbags, canvas, and tent poles housed a couple of men sitting over a boiling pot of coffee. They were dressed in fatigues, the sleeves crudely hacked off at the shoulders, and the legs at the knees. The coffee smelled of chicory.

Elmo nodded to the men and strode to the western edge of the mesa, his duster rolling and flapping in the wind coming in over the desert. A large black man in the same cutoff fatigues as the coffee drinkers was leaning against a platform constructed from plumbing pipes and plywood. The platform was covered with a dull, brown webbing, which I assumed was supposed to be camouflage. The man stood up when Elmo approached, and pulled back a flap of canvas so that we could see onto the platform. There was a pile of rags dumped over the length of it, and extending from the far end was what looked like a thin piece of pale-grey pipe. Elmo hunkered down into a squat and poked the rags with his binoculars.

"Juan," he said. The rags moved almost imperceptibly, and I would have chalked it up to the wind if a voice had not followed it.

"Spotted the rooster tail from the truck about ten minutes ago, Elmo," the pile of rags said in a squeaky voice that denoted neither gender nor age. "Just got to the rock. Black Ford Explorer."

"How many?"

"Three outside the truck. Can't see inside. You got the bitch, you know, out in front. Some big fucker in shades. Old man standing next to the truck dressed like Jungle Jim."

"That's Thandy," Grady said.

I looked out into the inky black night and imagined the decrepit bastard and La Dónde out there. In my mind they were demons with black smoke for bodies and the heads of something so evil I couldn't put a name to it. I shivered.

"How close to the rock?" Elmo asked.

"Close, but she knows where it is. You can tell she's avoiding it. She's checking the tire tracks now. Pointing out where Sully went. Talking it over with the old man."

"She knows the rules, Juan," Elmo said. "She crosses the rock, put her down. Her first, then shades, then the old man. If the Explorer rolls out, let it go."

"What are you talking about?" Grady said. "Just shoot her now." Elmo stood up and stretched his back.

"Why would I do that?"

"Because she's here to kill us?" I offered. Elmo rubbed the tuft of hair under his bottom lip. The only light up there was the small fire at the other end of the mesa top, and I could barely see him. His face was not much more than a purple-black mass of inscrutable features.

"That's her job, though, isn't it?" he said. "Can't fault her for doing her job."

"But . . ." I started, but I felt the old cowboy's hand on my shoulder. It was heavy, like a bear's paw.

"You're safe here. That's what I offered you. She steps over the line, she breaks the rules. She knows that, and then I can put her down. She stays on her side, there's nothing I can do."

"You want money, is that it?" Milch said, pushing past me.

"She's right up to the rock, El," Juan said from under his rags. "She's looking right at me. Fuck me. She's looking right fucking at me." The pile of rags shook.

"Hey, Juan," Milch called to him. "How much to take the shot."

"You're out of line," Elmo said, and placed his hand on Milch's chest.

Milch looked up at Elmo and offered him that soothing grin of his. "Didn't mean to box you out, Elmo," he said. "You get your cut. How much?"

"You're out of line," Elmo said, and his hand curled into a fist that gathered in a chunk of Milch's shirt.

"They're arguing now," Juan said. "The old man is pointing at us. The bitch is just letting him talk. OK, now the old man is talking to Shades. Who the hell wears sunglasses at night? Shades is talking to the bitch. Shades is getting back in the truck now. He's the driver."

"Take the shot," Grady said. His voice broke over the last word and it sounded like pure panic.

"How 'bout just the old man," Milch said. "A bullet through that silver hair of his would solve a lot of problems, know what I mean?"

When I heard the smack, I thought it was a gunshot, but then Milch was on the ground and Elmo's hand was flying up toward the sky with his follow-through. It was only a backhand. Nothing like a punch, but I felt for Milch. A punch would not have been nearly as humiliating. I couldn't blame him for what he did. I wanted Juan to take the shot as much as he did. I just didn't have the balls to ask for it. Milch stayed down, which I was grateful for.

"Old man is back in the car."

"Where is she?" Elmo said, looking down at the chastised Milch.

"Behind the open door. I got her head."

"Take the shot, please," Grady said, but it was only a whisper. Maybe it was a prayer.

"Inside now," Juan said. "Truck's leaving."

"Following Sully?" Elmo asked.

Juan answered in the affirmative.

"Good."

Grady sat down in the dirt and hung his head until his chin touched his chest. Milch's tongue flicked out of his mouth and tasted the blood at the corner of his lips. I felt a deep and intense ache begin to throb behind my eyes.

Elmo looked at the three of us, and when he spoke in his deep, gruff tenor, it sounded like the voice of God. "I'm sorry," he said. "I can't help you here. There are rules."

Chapter Twenty-Six

I was awake when Elmo Booth pushed open the door to my room without knocking. The room was a twelve-by-eight hole with an army cot and an electric lantern hanging from the ceiling. I had been lying there with my feet hanging off the end of the cot, smoking a cigarette and staring at the rock ceiling. When I saw the old man's shadow fall against the wall, I shoved the leather satchel under the cot. I hadn't thought much about the manuscript at all really. It had been so important and then it wasn't. I don't know why I even bothered to shelter it under my bunk. It was just paper with a little bit of ink.

"Saw your light was on," Elmo said. I was as tired as I had ever been in my life, and I hadn't even bothered turning out the light. Sleep was not going to come.

"I thought I'd catch up on my reading," I said. Elmo pushed my feet to the side and sat on the end of the cot. He pulled two books from the pockets of his duster. He held up the first. It was the *MacMerkin* novel Digby had given him.

"Quite a read," he said. He tossed the book to me. It landed on my stomach and I let out a little "oof" sound.

"You don't seem like the romance type," I said.

Elmo sat up straight, slapped his chest with both hands, and laughed.

"Fella dresses this way's either a romantic or an asshole," he said. He took off his hat and propped it on his knee. "So what was the plan?"

"For what?"

"You got Pieta and this other gringo after you, right?" he said. "So

189

you come here. Sully tells Dutch you're supposed to hide out, and look, I'm happy to have you."

"Good," I said.

"But then you go on about the Hemingway thief. You want me to tell you where the suitcase might be. Why, I says to myself. Why would they risk it?"

"We were going to trade it for our lives," I said.

"To Thandy?"

"Yes."

"Think that's a good plan?" Elmo said.

I could tell from the look on his face that he did not. Digby was inclined to agree with him, but I had convinced Grady with little effort. Milch had also been oddly receptive to the idea. My hope was that Thandy's ego would be sated with a show of tribute and that he would call off La Dónde. It may not have been a good plan, it was actually a pretty awful plan, but it was the only one we had. Now that Elmo refused to help us, we didn't even have that. We would be dead as soon as we left Elmo's protection. I was beginning to resign myself to the fact that we may have to start new lives there in his camp. I wondered what sort of pot farmer I would make.

My cigarette had burned down to the filter, and I stubbed it out on the floor. I patted my pockets and realized it was my last one. Elmo reached inside his jacket and came up with a thick, hand-rolled joint.

"I got a story to tell and I want your opinion," he said.

"I'm not in a very critical mood," I said.

"Maybe this will help," he said, handing me the joint. I took it, licked the end, and slid it between my lips. Elmo held his lighter under the tip, and I took a big toke. I was tired and the smoke hit me hard.

"Go ahead," I said, as the unpleasant, fragrant smoke poured out of me. Elmo leaned back across the cot and my legs so that the back of his head rested against the smooth rock wall. His voice rolled and bounced off the walls, sounding like it was coming from everywhere. If characters in a book could hear their omniscient narrator, this is what the voice would sound like.

"The story begins with a talented thief in the first half of the last century. War breaks out. He joins the army to see this world everyone's been talking about. He gets there, sees a little action, and then the war's over. He spends some time in Paris. Then a little more time. Before he knows it, that's where he lives. He has some friends. Makes a good living as a dipper at the racetrack. Life is good, not great, but good."

He paused here to make sure I was with him. The pot was good, maybe the best I'd ever had, but I was picking up what he was laying down.

"So our thief meets a writer. Handsome guy with a little bit of talent. He shows our thief his work, and they talk about things—art, music, literature—that no one ever bothered to discuss with our thief before. Our thief falls in love with the writer. It's more than affection. He wants this man, the writer. Our thief has had these feelings before. Acted on it once during the war when they all thought they were going to die. Our thief knows what he is, and while he is not ashamed, he knows he needs to keep it secret. He often wonders if the writer knows how he feels. He steals things for him, but never gives them to the writer. He wonders each evening as he walks along the Seine whether the writer might feel the same. And if he didn't? What then? But for now our thief is in love, and for a while, that is enough.

"The writer becomes frustrated. He is making a poor living as a correspondent for a Canadian newspaper, but it is fiction that is his real passion. He's written quite a few short stories and is working on a novel, but no one will publish him. This becomes the focus of most of their conversations until it becomes as consuming for our thief as it is for the writer. He thinks about it constantly. How can he make this man whom he loves happy? And then one day, as they are discussing the matter over a couple of cups of café au lait, an idea emerges. It begins as a hypothetical, but it slowly, surely, painfully becomes a plan.

"Our thief will steal a suitcase filled with everything the writer has ever written, save one piece of work. This will be his best story. The writer will tell everyone who will listen about his terrible loss, especially any editors or publishers he may know. The writer will have to really sell the story, and the thief would teach him how. After all, our thief made a very good living as a confidence man back in the States. Then, when he has the hook in an editor, one who seems sympathetic and willing to help, that is when the writer will produce his one remaining story. If he plays it right, some editor somewhere would take pity on him and he would get published.

"It might just work, this plan of our thief's, and if it didn't? No problem. His precious work would be safe in the trusted hands of the writer's friend, the thief.

"'You are the only one I truly trust,' the writer tells the thief. The thief almost swoons, but he is able to finish his coffee all the same.

"The day comes and goes. Not a hitch. There was a moment, at the train station, when our thief is surprised to find that the carrier of the suitcase is the writer's wife. Our thief had met the wife before, and the writer's mistress too. He was fearful, if only for a moment, that she would recognize him, but our thief's unparalleled skill comes to the fore and he manages the purloining without incident.

"Our thief spends two agonizing months in an attic with the suitcase. That was the agreed-upon time, two months. He couldn't see his writer. He could only read his words. In that time he came to love the words as much as the writer. He read them through, one after the other, and when he finished them he started over again. Meanwhile, the writer gets a sympathetic editor to publish his one remaining story, a little thing about a rape, along with a couple of other stories he produced, and some poetry. The plan has worked.

"Then comes the exchange. The money for the goods. It does not go well. Our thief does not give back the suitcase. Instead he flees. He goes home for a while. But the grief follows him and he flees again. This time for the Madres. Then he dies, alone in the desert."

Elmo took the joint from me and took a toke of his own. He held it in his lungs for an incredible amount of time, then let it flow out of his mouth as gracefully as water over garden falls.

"What do you think?" he asked.

"Needs an ending," I said. "And you yadda-yadda'd the best part."

The bud was working well, otherwise I'm sure my response would not have been so measured.

"The thief is Ebenezer," Elmo said.

"Yes, I got that."

"The writer is Hemingway."

"I picked up on that, too."

"I'm just saying because you look confused."

I'm sure I did. I was already dealing with less than a few hours' sleep over the last three days. I had witnessed a few killings. The deadliest woman in the world was trying to kill me. I was lying on an army cot in a cave-room dug into a mesa that used to be an Apache stronghold and was now the home of a group of pot farmers lead by the last descendant of John Wilkes Booth. To top all this off, I had just taken a couple of major tokes off a joint filled with the purest strain of weed I'd ever had.

"If I look confused, it may be because you told us you weren't going to help us find the suitcase," I said. I propped myself up on my elbows and swiped the joint away from Elmo. "And then you demonstrated how much you weren't going to help us by, you know, completely and totally not fucking helping us."

"There are—"

"Rules. Yes, I know," I said. I blew out my smoke, meaning to blow it in his face, but it caught in my throat and I was thrown into a fit of hacking coughs. When I was done, I looked up at Elmo with teary eyes. "What I don't know is why you're bothering to tell me any of this."

"I want you to understand," Elmo said. He was still lying across my legs as if we were two sorority sisters gabbing about our boyfriends. "You see, I was sitting up there in my room, reading your book, and it occurred to me that you're not the only ones after the suitcase."

"It just occurred to you? I mean, it didn't occur to you when you had a sniper aimed at his fucking head?"

"Ebenezer and I became good friends while he was here," Elmo said, ignoring me. "I was just a kid then. My father was still running things. Ebenezer taught me a lot about life, the outside world, things like that. I think maybe if I hadn't met Ebenezer, I would have probably run things the way my Pop did." He looked around the room and nodded at the ceiling. "All of this, what we are now, in a way it's because of Ebbie."

"Were you two, um . . ." I said, and trailed off in what was my version of tact.

"He was a good friend," Elmo said. "You said I skipped over the best part? You mean what happened at the exchange?"

"From a dramatic point of view, that would have been the good part, yes."

"I left it out because Ebenezer never told me what happened. Not completely," Elmo said, and let out a long, hard sigh. He took up the second book from his lap. It was Milch's copy of *A Moveable Feast*. He thumbed through it until he found the page he wanted. He read the words to himself with a gentle, unintelligible mumble. I heard "primitive," "tramps," and "prepared to kill a man" clearly enough, however. When he was done, Elmo nodded and looked me in the eye. "I think if you know anything about Hemingway, you could make a pretty good guess as to what happened. Basically, what he says in here is that when you're out and about in places there might be gays, then you gotta carry a knife."

"Jesus," I said.

"Gotta be able to defend yourself against all those fag rapists who are crawling out of the sewers, you get me? That was his kind of thinking."

"Jesus."

"Yeah, and his buddy Miss Stein had a few things to say on the subject herself," Elmo said, turning the page. "Let's see. Yep. 'The act is ugly and repugnant.' Male homosexuality she means here. Not, you know, lesbians, Miss Stein being one herself. Says these poor bastards are all junkies and drunks because they can't deal with how goddamn disgusting they are."

"Jesus," I said again.

"I think when they met for the exchange, Ebbie and Hemingway that is, maybe Ebenezer told him how he felt, or maybe made a move." Elmo waved Hemingway's book. "You can guess how well that went over."

"Chavez told me Ebenezer kept the suitcase out of love. You're

saying it was spite?" I said. My professor in college had been in love
with the idea that Hemingway was a latent homosexual. He theorized
that this was the reason why Hemingway took on so many uber-manly
pursuits. It was why he drank, why he couldn't stay married, and why
women played such terrible roles in his writing. Perhaps Ebenezer
had picked up on that same vibe and made the mistake of pursuing
it. Maybe Hemingway had put it out there on purpose, trying to lead
Ebenezer on so that he could get a favor out of him. Maybe it was all
bullshit. Maybe I didn't care because I was still thinking about the meg-
alomaniacal book dealer who wanted me dead.

"Maybe at first," Elmo said. "Thin line between love and hate and
all. But when Ebenezer talked about his writer it was always with affection. And he loved the stories. I know that. Even more than Hemingway
he loved the stories."

"You ever see them?"

"No. That's the whole damn point, son," Elmo said, and slapped
the paperback against his knee. "No one can see them. Not ever."

"I don't follow."

"Neither do I, to be honest. Ebenezer was an odd duck, you know,
and I'm not talking about his sexual proclivities. I'm not the type who
gives a shit what a guy does in his bunk, you know?" He waited until I
nodded that I did understand. "Ebenezer followed Hemingway's whole
life. Every adventure, every heartache, every success, every failure. You
know what he told me?"

"No."

"He told me it was the longest con job he'd ever seen. From start
to finish, every part of Hemingway's life was bullshit. An image built
on as much flimsy pretense as a dime-store hood running the Spanish
Prisoner."

"Because he thought Papa was gay?" I asked.

"No," Elmo said, and gave me a disparaging look. "Because it was
all calculated. It was all meant to inform his literature and to make him
a star. It was all craven bullshit, you understand?"

"No."

"The only thing that had ever been real was the theft. At least according to Ebenezer."

"But it was a con too," I said.

"Not if he never got the stories back," Elmo said with a wistful smile. "As long as Hemingway never got those stories back, then it was a real theft. It was really taken from him. And then all the grief and misery Hemingway felt from that loss would be real because the loss was real."

"But Hemingway is dead. What's the difference if anybody sees them now?"

"I told you, Ebenezer was an odd duck. He was insistent that no one besides him should ever see the stories. He tried to burn them, you know. Lots of times. He would tell me about it. Said he had the match lit, hanging right over the pages, but he could never do it. And now they are buried out in the desert, out in that hovel he lived in for the last few years of his life. I think they should stay there."

"Because that's what Ebenezer wanted?"

"Yes."

"And his opinion is the only one that matters?"

"It is to me," Elmo snapped. "I owe him."

"For what?" I asked. Elmo shoved the Hemingway book back in his pocket.

"Friendship doesn't mean much to most people in these parts, but it does to me. Ebbie was a friend, but I don't know how he died. I didn't even know he *was* dead for a year after it happened. He never visited regular, so I didn't think much when he stopped coming around. I was just driving by on my way to somewhere else when I thought I'd stop by. One of the locals had found him. He'd been out in the sun for a few days and the animals had gotten to him. That's all I know. My friend died alone in the desert, Coop. I couldn't do anything for him then, but I can do this thing for him now. I can protect the suitcase."

"But like you said, we're not the only ones looking for it," I said. I pulled my legs up and swung them over the side of the bed. I held my book in my hands as I hunched over next to the old cowboy.

"Yes," he said. "That is why I need you to get it. I need you to get it and bring it to me. I'll keep it safe."

"Why come to me?" I asked. "Milch is Ebenezer's kin. Grady is better at this stuff than I am."

"I trust you."

"Why?"

He stuck his index finger into the inside cover of my book and flipped it open. He stabbed the cover page with his digit, directing me toward one sentence written with a fat-tipped pencil in compact handwriting.

Henry Cooper is OK
                    —Sully

PART 4

The End of Something

Chapter Twenty-Seven

At dawn we were on the move again. Nobody asked any questions about Elmo's change of heart, and I didn't offer up any more information than necessary. I told them we were headed to Ebenezer's old camp and that it would be dangerous. I gave a perfunctory explanation that Elmo had taken pity on us. That seemed to be enough. I kept my deal with Elmo and my plans for the suitcase to myself.

Dutch drove. He was on loan to us, along with a gunny sack full of weaponry from Elmo. The pickup truck we were in was Dutch's and was part of the package. We drew straws for our seats. I was lucky enough to be crammed in the cab with Dutch, the leather satchel tucked between us and out of sight. Grady and Milch rode in the bed, flailing and cursing as we bounced along, with nothing but a thin layer of hay to protect their hindquarters. It was only a fifteen-mile drive, but Dutch thought it would take about an hour. The road was a smattering of dust and rubble spread over a series of rocky shelves that looked like they'd been under mortar attack for the last twenty years. Dutch manhandled the gearshift with gusto, turning the wheel like he was steering a teacup at Disney World. My tailbone steadily made its way toward my brainstem, and I knew I would be at least half a foot shorter by the time we got to the camp.

Sleep would have been impossible even without the cacophony of the truck's diesel and the hammer-and-anvil cracking going on beneath the chassis. Dutch proved to be a dedicated storyteller, and he refused to let the ambient decibel level, or even obvious lack of interest from his audience, dissuade him from spinning tales about his life in the Madres. But he'd given me a pack of cigarettes when I'd only tried to bum one, so I decided to like him.

"I wish I could hire Pieta to kill the mochomos," Dutch said, gunning the engine and swerving around a coyote carcass. Mochomos were the red, swarming, ravenous leafcutter ants that made their home in the Madres. In the epic tale of Dutch's life, the mochomos, like Tolkien's orcs, were a constant threat and convenient shorthand for all the little problems in his world. The mochomos' favorite meal was the marijuana leaf; the same leaf Dutch had dedicated his life to perfecting.

Dutch had been born Moonshadow Kesey Dubois to an obscure beat poet going by the name Denim and working out of the Haight in San Francisco. Denim disappeared a year later during the Rolling Stones concert at Altamont. All accounts confirmed that she had dropped a blotter of acid at the beginning of "Sympathy for the Devil," but by the time Mick Jagger laid tracks for troubadours she had vanished. Young Dutch had been left in the studio apartment of the man most likely to be his father, known to his child and the rest of the world as Monkey Vest. Monkey Vest continued to care for the child while using his horticulture degree to pursue ever more potent strains of *Cannabis sativa*. Dutch credits Monkey Vest as developing the early prototypes of aeroponics, along with a rare strain known as Millennium Vulcan.

"'Course Dad never had to deal with the mochomos," Dutch said. Dutch had been his father's lab assistant and later his salesman. He had been in his thirties when his father sent him on a trip to Mexico to research and sample some of the amazing strains that had been emerging from the region. He was in Acapulco when he received the news that Monkey Vest had been killed. A former Grateful Dead roadie cum ad exec had succumbed to a horrific acid flashback and leapt from the forty-sixth floor of the Transamerica Pyramid. Monkey Vest had been stopped in front of the building, finishing a hot dog, at that very moment.

"Lost both my parents because of LSD," Dutch said with a woeful sniff. "I don't remember nobody ever jumping off a building 'cause they were on mota, ya know?" After the news of his father's death, Dutch wandered around Mexico, hiring out his green thumb to whoever needed it. He had worked for all of the major cartels at one time or another. By the end of the nineties, he had created a niche market for himself teaching wealthy Americans how to set up small, easy-to-care-for, hydroponic labs in the garages of their luxurious vacation homes.

"That's where Elmo found me," he said. "I was setting up a lab for the son of some big shot LA politician. We had been partying nonstop for like a week. Woke up in the pool of one a them luxury resorts in La Paz. The people I was with had bolted and the hotel owner was calling the cops. Elmo was there. Don't ask me why. He was wearing one a them terry-cloth robes and eating a big ole hamburger. He tells the owner I'm with him and buys me lunch. By the time we finished coffee, I was joined up with him. Been battling the fucking mochomos ever since."

Dutch was not excited about taking us to Ebenezer's camp, and I could understand his apprehension. Dutch was a grower, not a fighter. Before we hit the road again, I was hoping that anyone out of Elmo's outfit would be equally adept with a gun as Digby—a leading-man type. Dutch was more of a narrator. It made me nervous. *I* was the Nick Caraway in this troupe, and we didn't need another one. What we needed was a killer.

"And you're a writer?" Dutch said. It took me a moment to realize it was a question. It was the first time Dutch had deigned to include me in the conversation. The pause must have been longer than Dutch cared for because he pushed on without an answer. "You don't want to talk about it, that's fine. Ebbie told me all about it while we were packing the truck."

"What did he tell you?" I asked. Dutch pursed his lips and looked at a crack in the dashboard plastic, mulling over what he wanted to tell me. "Come on, Dutch. What did he say?"

"He said you wrote a bunch of chick books," Dutch said. Then he saw the look on my face and added, "His words, not mine."

"It's alright," I said, and leaned my head back against the headrest's worn fabric. "He's not wrong. They're pretty shitty."

"You think you're a shitty writer," Dutch said.

"Yeah. Every writer thinks they're shitty," I said.

"Do people buy your books?" Dutch asked.

"In droves."

"Then they're not so shitty."

"Dutch, just because something sells doesn't mean it's any good," I said, aware of the condescension in my voice. "That *Transformers* sequel is one of the twenty-five highest grossing movies of all time."

"I never saw that one," Dutch said.

"You're a better man for it," I said. Dutch smiled and downshifted as the suspension contended with another series of boulder-size rocks in the road.

"But this Hemingway guy," Dutch said. "He's big-time, right? Even I've heard of him."

"Yeah, he's a pretty big deal," I said with a chuckle. A hole in the road caught a tire, and Dutch swung the wheel wildly to regain control. "He's maybe the greatest American novelist, although there are a few other contenders."

"So, you've read all his books?"

"I've read a couple," I said. "*The Old Man and the Sea* in high school, and couple of others in a class I took in college. *Death in the Afternoon* was interesting."

"But you own all of his books, right?" Dutch said. "You're going to read them."

"Probably not," I said with a shrug.

"And he's the greatest American novelist," Dutch said.

"That's what they tell me," I said.

"Why?"

"It would take too long to explain."

"You like beer?" Dutch said. I was glad he'd changed the subject.

"Sure."

"What do you drink?"

"Whatever's available," I said. Dutch sucked his teeth and shook his head.

"That's a shame," he said. "'Cause there is some really good beer out there; craft beers with all sorts of flavor. There are some real artists brewing today. I brew my own. Spent the last couple of years learning how to homebrew, refining my palate, learning about what makes a beer good or bad."

"So what makes it good?" I asked.

"It would take too long to explain," Dutch said, in a dead-on mimic of my patronizing voice. "It takes a lot of work to be a connoisseur of beer. Had to study the different strains of hops and their various smells. Had to teach my tongue to get the subtle complexities and fruity undertones of each brew. It's taken a long time is my point."

"I see," I said.

"Still," Dutch said, and clicked his tongue. "Nothing's better than an ice-cold Pabst on a hot afternoon."

"That's comforting," I said.

"Is it?"

Elmo had a reason for sending Dutch as our guide rather than a hard-nosed gun tough. The Monte was a closed society. Your passport was whom you knew, the names and acquaintances you could rattle off when questioned by a stranger. It was uncommon to be allowed into a place you hadn't been before, and it was impossible to do so without at least a reference. Dutch, out of all the men and women in Elmo's camp, was the most well-known and universally liked in the Madres. His wanderings as a traveling weed cultivator had put him in the good graces of everyone from the narcos to the legitimate farmers. He may not have been the best with a gun, but his connections would make it less likely we would need one.

Ebenezer's camp was located on the outskirts of a small village named Pobo. It had been formed in the midsixties when the families that made up the local *ejido* had huddled their homes together for the illusion of security. The *ejido* eventually failed, and the village was taken over by a small-time *narcotraficante* who shared his name with the Mexican colloquialism for the AK-47, El Cuerno de Chivo—the goat's horn. Pobo was the perfect site for El Cuerno's operation, as it abutted the mouth of a small canyon with high, inaccessible walls. The other end of the canyon, where Ebenezer had built his camp, emptied onto a plateau high above a wide river. If anyone unfriendly ever came a-callin', El Cuerno could order his men into the canyon, where they could live off of a cache of supplies kept under the canyon's natural protection. Of course, Dutch had once worked for El Cuerno and was still held in high regard for his rehabilitation of the *ejido* land into a vibrant marijuana plantation.

The town—more of a compound than a village, really—consisted of a series of low-slung wood–and-stucco buildings that all looked like they were about to collapse. A barbed-wire fence extended around the length of the village with a high gate made up of rebar and scavenged highway barriers in the center. When he spotted the gate as it emerged over the horizon, Dutch reached back and knocked on the rear window. Grady opened it and slid his head inside.

"Please tell me we're there," Grady said. We hit a bump and his head collided with the roof. "Fuck."

"Yes, we're almost there," Dutch said. "You should know the last time someone these men didn't know tried to pass through here, they tied him to a chair and hammered a six-inch galvanized nail through his scrotum."

"OK," Grady said, and started to pull his head back through the window. Dutch grabbed Grady's collar, but not roughly.

"Just saying, you might want to try being polite. No cop stuff," he said. "They don't like strangers. Tell Ebbie, too. Just sit in the back. Don't smile. Don't speak. Don't look them in the eye."

"Got it," Grady said. We hit another bump and his head cracked against mine. "Fuck," we said together.

"One more thing," Dutch said. "They tug down on the brim of their hats, you get down flat and hold on."

"Why," Grady said.

"It means they intend to kill us," Dutch said. "It's like a warning. Like a tradition. Don't ask me why. I don't get it either."

Chapter Twenty-Eight

Three Mexicans stood by the gate. Dutch insisted there were more out of sight—at least one sniper. They were dressed alike, in black silk shirts festooned with embroidered skulls and roses, unbuttoned down to the navel. They were bulging and out of shape, but no less menacing for the AKs they held, the stocks propped against their hips and the barrels pointed at the cloudless sky. Dutch slowed to a crawl and stopped fifteen yards from the gate, allowing the men to come to him.

"*Mira, está Dutch*," the one approaching the driver's side said to the others through a mouth missing several teeth.

"*Y otros*," the one on my side said. He poked his head inside, along with the gun barrel, and I could smell several terrible and unidentifiable odors. The third stood in front of the truck and put his snakeskin boot on the bumper.

"*Hola, Jorge*," Dutch said he put his elbow on the open window and poked his head out. "*Cómo está El Cuerno.*"

"He skinned a thief this morning," Jorge said in English. The language shift was clearly for my benefit.

"Not wise to steal from El Cuerno," Dutch said. I hazarded a glance behind me. Milch and Grady were sitting with their legs crossed, heads down, and their hands clearly visible on their knees.

"No, not wise at all, Dutch," Jorge agreed.

"How are the crops?"

"Goddamn mochomos," Jorge said. "You have gringos in your car."

"The old place through the canyon. The gringo in the back is the grandson, uh, *nieto*, to the guy used to live there." Dutch said.

Jorge nodded and stuck out his lower lip, considering this information. "So?" he said.

"Wants to see his grandfather's place," Dutch said. "Might want to take some family items."

"Take?"

"Nothing valuable," Dutch said with a noncommittal shrug. "A suitcase with some old letters. You think El Cuerno would mind?"

"And the others?"

"Ex-pats from the *Estados*. Might want to join up with Elmo. Showing them around," Dutch said.

The unnamed Mexican at my window leaned in closer and sniffed at me.

"Ex-pat? They make you leave?" he said.

"More or less," I said. We were supposed to be wanted criminals lamming it in the Madres. It was a common story, and one El Cuerno's people were likely to believe. The trick was trying to act tough enough to make it believable without pissing them off.

"Why they throw you out, *muchacho*?"

"Bad manners," I said, and looked him in the eye.

"You still got bad manners?"

"You know what they say about bad habits, *muchacho*," I said. I kept my face hard as granite, but it was becoming increasingly difficult not to piss my pants.

"Enough, Paco," Jorge said. "They are with Elmo, no? Show me what you take before you go, Dutch. No tricks. OK?"

"OK," Dutch said. Jorge patted Dutch's arm and stood back from the car. My Mexican pulled his head out of the window. The third removed his foot from the bumper and walked slowly out of our way. Dutch put the truck in gear with a deep, wrenching pull and crawled past the guards. He lifted two fingers to the brim of his 49ers cap and Jorge returned the gesture and added a nod.

"Don't you think you should've mentioned La Dónde might be on her way?" I whispered even though we were past the gate and nearly to the canyon.

"Naw," Dutch said. "Jorge would never let us in if he thought she'd be coming too. Plus, she might not be coming. All the guys who knew Ebenezer Milch are dead or far away by now. Only Elmo knows the secret."

"She may have followed us," I said. "If she does come, will they stop her? Will they be *able* to stop her?"

"Probably not," Dutch said with a queasy grimace. "They guard a gate for a low-rent drug king. It's not like they're Green Berets."

"But she might not come at all, right? She went after Digby."

"We shouldn't stick around longer than we have to," Dutch said, as the canyon walls rose on either side of the truck, enveloping us in a velvety shadow. The rear window opened and Grady poked his head through again.

"How much farther?" he asked. Dutch pointed forward where beams of morning sun poked through the other end of the canyon.

"We climb up and out and we're there," Dutch said. He drove over the small stream running through the center of the canyon and steered the truck up onto a ridge jutting out of the wall. It was just wide enough to accommodate the truck, and it angled upward, becoming steeper, until it seemed we were going to leave the earth and drive right into the sun. I shaded my eyes with my hand, my sunglasses proving to be worthless against the intense light. Dutch did the same.

"It's like driving blind," he said. I felt the front tire on my side begin to sink, and Dutch corrected the wheel. He let out a low whistle and I wondered what would kill us first, La Dónde's bullets or Dutch's driving.

The road leveled out again and we emerged onto a dusty pan extending out for about a quarter of an acre. The canyon was on our right and the mountainside to our left. Dutch drove the truck away from the canyon edge and closer to the cliff at the far end of the shelf. The cliff dropped down about two hundred feet and ended in a broad, torrential river that fed the canyon's stream. On the other side of the river was a green, leafy crop of marijuana the size of a Nebraska cornfield.

"El Cuerno's?" I asked, and Dutch nodded. "Where's the camp?" Dutch pointed out his window at a squat domicile made of red adobe jutting out of the mountainside like a cyst. This was where Ebenezer Milch, the Hemingway thief, had made his final home. The windows were decorated with shabby burlap drapes blowing lazily in the breeze. The door had been cobbled together from several packing crates, and the centerboard declared it to be the property of Pensacola Air Force Base. Ebenezer had built a low wall of cinderblock and mud extending around his home and to the cliff. Along the top of the wall he'd fixed a series of upside-down broken beer bottles as makeshift spikes. The gate in the middle was less foreboding, made from the same crates as the house door and carved into pickets.

We piled out of the cab. Milch and Grady rolled out of the truck bed hunched over and stiff like old, broken men. Grady reached back inside and groaned as he pulled out a long canvas sack. It contained two .22 rifles and a Remington .12-gauge shotgun Elmo had lent us. A cold drop of rain splashed on my neck and snaked down my spine. Dark, angry thunderheads were devouring the bright morning sky.

"Storms come up quick around here," Dutch said. "They go just as quickly, too. Let's get inside." The rain started to fall in fat gobs as we dashed through the gate and burst into Ebenezer's home.

Chapter Twenty-Nine

The air was dead and smelled like a frat-house laundry bag. There was a spindly chair on its side next to a large wire spool Ebenezer had probably used as a dinner table. A potbelly stove sat in the corner, its kinked and dented pipe rising out through a hole in the roof. A hummock of ash and charred wood bits surrounded it. Outlaws, runaways, and fugitives had all called this place home for a night or two in the days before El Cuerno had claimed it, and the red dirt floor was littered with evidence of their stays; a few tins of Dinty Moore here, a pile of cigarette butts there. But there was no evidence of a suitcase or anyplace it might be hidden.

"It's not here," Grady said. Milch's shoulders slumped, and he fell against the wall. His knees buckled and he slid down until his ass rested on his ankles.

"Hold on now. We haven't searched the place," I said.

Grady put his hand above his eyes like he was shading the sun, craned his neck forward, and pantomimed a swiveling examination of the room.

"There," he said. "I searched it."

I started to say something, but he held up his finger.

"Hold on. It pays to be thorough." He repeated his mocking search and when he was done he threw up his hands. "Damn, still nothing."

"I don't think that's necessary," I said. "I'm only trying to help."

"It's not here," Grady said, and adjusted the gun sack strung across his back.

"Let's think about this for a second," I said. Milch was running his tongue slowly over his bottom lip while staring at a Mexican candy wrapper splayed open on the ground. "You okay, Ebbie?" He nodded unconvincingly. I patted him on the shoulder and turned to Dutch. "What happened to Ebenezer after he died?"

"Before my time, Coop," he said. "Elmo was the only one who knew him."

"He never talked about him?"

"Not to us," Dutch said. "How often do you talk about someone who died thirty years ago to a room full of people wouldn't care if he died yesterday? I doubt most people in camp've even heard of Hemingway, let alone his suitcase. Why would they give a shit about the man who stole it?"

He had a point. In our quest to find Hemingway's lost suitcase, I had forgotten that most people had never heard of it. I had been imagining Elmo sitting around the fire, retelling Ebenezer's Parisian adventure over and over again with his band of reformed smugglers, thieves, and murderers sitting in rapt attention. Dutch disabused me of this fantasy and replaced it with the image of a group of barely literate, formerly overviolent men telling dirty jokes and bloody vignettes. Ebenezer had found the perfect place to hide the suitcase: in the middle of a region filled with men who could not begin to express how little they cared about its existence.

"When Elmo tells stories, they're usually about J. W. Booth and how he died fighting the Apaches," Dutch said. "Elmo's a man who knows his audience."

"Fuck this place," Milch said, standing up and sticking a cigarette between his lips. "Let's go. We need to go."

"We just got here," I said, blocking Milch's way to the door. "And not without a little bit of trouble either."

"It ain't here," Milch said. His eyes were red and the corners of his mouth were set in terse, wrinkled triangles. "If the suitcase ever existed, it's at the bottom of the Paris River."

"You mean the Seine," I said.

"Whatever the fuck," Milch said, and pushed past me. He was opening the door when I shoved him. The door closed again as he fell against it. He caught himself before he fell, and wheeled around with a wild fist. If I had been an experienced fighter, I could have easily dodged it. I was not an experienced fighter. The blow caught my ear, and I heard a small pop followed by a dull sound like a distant airplane.

"I owed you one from Tequilero," Milch said.

"Tequilero?" Grady said.

"Forget it," Milch said, and made for the door again. This time it was Grady who stopped him. His punch was faster and more compact than Milch's, out and back like a striking rattlesnake. Milch took a step back and fell on his ass. A small rivulet of blood trickled from one nostril.

"It's forgotten," Grady said. "Now let's think about what we do next."

"We fucking leave," Milch said. He touched the blood under his nose with his fingertip and examined it. "It ain't fucking here. You were just saying it to Coop. That Dónde bitch could be here any second."

"We've got time," I said.

"No, we don't," Milch said in a whine. "It ain't here, Grady, you said so yourself."

"Yeah, but I'm a pessimist," Grady said, massaging the hand he used to hit Milch. "You've been the one who was so gung ho we'd find the case. What changed your mind?"

"A room with nothing but food wrappers and used butts," Milch said. "And an old fucking stove." He kicked his leg out at the potbelly, striking one of the legs with his sneaker. It was heavier than Milch expected and he let out a howl and grabbed his foot. He snarled at the stove, lifted his foot up, and brought his heel down on the center. This time the stove lurched to the side and almost upended. The pipe's connection gave a low, rusty groan, and when the body came back down on all four feet, the stack broke away entirely. An ashy nebula of black soot spilled out and dusted Milch.

"Calm down, kid, or I'm gonna hit you again," Grady said. "The case is probably hidden in one of the hills around here. We just have to look for it."

"Don't you get it? Elmo never even saw the fucking suitcase," Milch said. He wiped the blood from his nose with his T-shirt. "You heard him yourself. He has no proof anything Ebenezer told him was anything more than just another con."

I backed away from Milch, giving him space to have his tantrum. I wanted to throw a fit too, but one was enough. I stuck my finger in my ear and wiggled it. The ringing was starting to dissipate, but my head was swimming like a barrel of eels. I leaned forward, took a deep breath, and noticed a thin rut in the layer of ash next to the stove. It was too linear to be accidental. The ringing stopped.

"He never saw it because it never fucking existed," Milch continued. "It was just a fucking story my uncle told my grandfather. Ebenezer was a loser who died alone out in the desert, and nobody noticed for a whole goddamned year." His shoulders hunched over and he covered his eyes with his hands. His next words came out in a barely-audible croak. We inched closer to hear him, but I kept my eye on the rut in the ash. "Pop never saw the suitcase either," he continued. "I asked Dad why and he said Ebenezer didn't want anybody to see the stories without Hemingway's permission. I asked him why he never went after the suitcase, even after Ebenezer died."

"What did he say?" Grady asked.

"He said the knights never find the Grail. They come close, but they never get their hands on it. They weren't meant to."

"What the fuck does that mean," Grady said.

"It means he knew my uncle was full of shit," Milch said.

"I don't think so," I said. "I think your grandfather understood Ebenezer's story better than any of us."

"Hey, if Milch wants to go, maybe we should go," Grady said, and offered his hand to Milch. Milch moved his arm, saw Grady's hand, and took it. Grady pulled him to his feet. "The suitcase was our only bargaining chip, and we don't have it. Our only chance now is to run like hell for the border."

"No," I said. "The suitcase is here."

"I hit you too hard in that ear, Coop," Milch said. "You're not listening. I'm *telling* you it's bullshit. I'm *telling* you we got to get out of here."

"Hemingway wrote Ebenezer's name down in that manuscript. We saw it with our own eyes," I said. "That wasn't bullshit. He wouldn't remember a guy forty years later unless he meant something. Chavez met Hemingway. Hemingway came all the way down here for a suitcase. The manuscript is real. Ebenezer's stories were real. That means the suitcase is real." I lifted the leather satchel containing the manuscript that still hung off my shoulder. "You came here because of this, because it confirmed your uncle's story. You came because you wanted to have a bit of the legend for yourself, something your grandfather never had the balls to do. You wanted to be a part of it, so you came down here."

"And I was wrong," Milch said. "Nobody has seen the fucking thing."

"Of course not," I said. I wiped my mouth with the back of my hand. My lips were dry and cracked. I ran my tongue over them and it was like sandpaper scraping over sandpaper. "Your uncle was a professional thief. A professional knows how to hold onto his score. Didn't you see *Goodfellas*? What happened to the guy who bought his wife the Cadillac? DeNiro fucking whacked him. That's what."

"Are you losing it, Coop?" Grady asked.

"Why would he show it to Elmo? Fucking guy lives in a mountain fortress full of thieves and cut-throats," I said. "He's supposed to walk in there and say, 'Lemme tell you where I keep my priceless piece of fucking history?' No, he's gonna keep it hidden. And you don't keep something like that hidden in the goddamn hills where the elements can get at it either, Grady. You keep it close. You keep it warm and you keep it dry. The suitcase is here. It is in this house."

"Plenty of people have come through here since then. How do you know one of them didn't take it?" Grady asked.

"Ever see *The Great Escape*?" I said. I was tired of answering hypotheticals, tired of trying to understand the mind of a dead man I'd never met, tired of using logic as an unsuitable substitute for hope. I was tired of arguing.

"Never seen it," they all said in one form or another. I wasn't surprised.

"Surrounded by goddamn philistines," I said. "Great flick. Steve McQueen, James Garner, James Fucking Coburn. Great movie. There's a scene where they're explaining where they hid the tunnels."

"Does this have a point?" Grady asked.

"Charles Bronson was the Tunnel King. This was back before *Death Wish*, when Bronson was an actor, not a joke. He's talking to Dick Attenborough in one of the dorms and he shows him a stove." I edged around the potbelly, dragging my boot through the ash. The thin rut got longer as my boot moved over it. It met another rut and made a corner, then another rut and another corner, until it made a square surrounding the stove. I mimed lifting something heavy and did my best Bronson impression. "No one moves a hot stove, yes?"

"I'm leaving," Grady said. I lifted my foot and kicked at the stove with my boot heel just as Milch had, but I was standing and I aimed for the top. The stove leaned back on its rear feet, and just as it was about to right itself, I kicked it again. It crashed down in the dirt and spilled more ash from its belly. I dropped to my hands and knees and rooted through the ash at the center of the square. My fingers grazed over something cold, round, and hollow in the center. I seized it and pulled. It was a metal ring attached to a chain that ran down into the ash. I wrapped both hands around it and thrust my weight backward until I felt something give, and I landed on my ass.

When the ash cloud settled, we could see that I had pulled up a square piece of board and there was now a hole in the floor where the stove had been. I heard shuffling feet and felt a hand on my shoulder. It was Grady. Milch was at his side, and at the far end of the room Dutch stood with his hand over his mouth. The rain had let up enough to allow some daylight through the hole in the ceiling where the stovepipe had been. A shaft of light the diameter of a fence post illuminated what I had unearthed: a scratched, plain brown, and incredibly old suitcase.

Chapter Thirty

Back then, they would have called it a *valise*. It was cheap and common, the type of suitcase a correspondent for the *Toronto Star* could afford—black fiberboard with thick paper pasted on it to give the illusion of leather. It was smaller than I'd expected. I figured it couldn't have held more than a few large hardcover books. The clasps were tin painted to look like brass, and the paint was chipping off to reveal the rust underneath. It was in remarkable condition for being in a hole for the last few decades—a touch of mold on the side and the beginnings of rot on one corner, but that was it. There was a small stamp near the handle that read "Shwayder Trunk Co." It looked like something you'd find in your grandmother's basement while cleaning it out after her funeral.

"Go ahead, Ebbie," I said, and nudged him with my elbow. We were crowded around the hidey-hole, hunkered down on our haunches like trackers studying signs. Milch rubbed his hand on his forehead, mixing ash with sweat. The corner of his mouth pulled up toward his squinting eye as he considered the package less than a foot away.

"Should I touch it?" he said. "I saw in a movie where Nicolas Cage put gloves on before he touched the Declaration of Independence. You know, because of the oil on your fingers or something."

"Did you bring any gloves?" Grady asked.

"No."

"At least wipe your hands on your pants first, then," Grady said. Milch drew in a deep breath like a high diver about to jump. He wiped his hands on his jeans several times and reached out slowly, tenderly. His hands started for the handle, hovered over the rolled fiberboard, his fingers dancing over it as he thought. He shook his head and reached in with both hands, picking the case up with the gentle ardor and uncertainty of a father picking up his child for the first time.

He carried it to the wire-spool table and set it down. The rusted clasps resisted and he pushed against them with his thumb, his tongue sticking out of the corner of his mouth, until they gave way with a plaintive squeak. Milch wiped his hands again, this time on his T-shirt, set them on either side of the top, and opened the case.

The person who had last packed the suitcase had done so with loving attention. The paper inside was stacked neatly in three columns, one on the left, one on the right, and a third placed on top of the other two so that it sagged in the middle. The middle column was made of onionskins, the translucent paper used to make carbon copies during the typewriter age. The ink was blurry and faded, like a notebook left in the rain. I could only make out one word in the title: *Auteuil*. Milch closed the lid and left his hands there, claiming it.

"You think it's real?" he asked. It was hoarse and whispered, like a parishioner in the middle of communion.

"I don't know," I said, but that was a lie. I knew. I knew the moment the case opened and the words were splayed out in front of me, naked and seductive. It felt like we had peeked into a window and found something private, something not meant for our eyes. Elmo had been right. We were looking at the intimate workings of a man long since dead, a troubled man who led a troubled life. I felt a creeping sensation up the back of my neck, and I knew I would never be able to explain to Milch and Grady what this suitcase really meant.

"But you know people who would know, right?"

"Sure," I said. "But with things like this it's never a hundred percent. There'll always be someone who calls it a hoax."

"And there will be people who will pay for it." Grady said.

"It doesn't matter," I whispered. "No one will see it, but us."

"What?" Milch said.

"Coop, you're being a defeatist again," Grady said.

"We kept asking why Hemingway would have given up the suitcase, you know, the reason for the theft," I said. The room, which had already carried the flavor of death, took on the quality of a funeral parlor; the suitcase, that of a corpse; and my heart, that of a mourning child. "But what never made sense to me was why he brought Hadley into it."

"The fuck are you talking about?" Milch said.

"Why blame her?" I continued. "At first I thought he was just being cruel, but that wasn't it."

"Coop," Grady said. "We should get moving."

"I chalked it up to Hemingway being a woman-hating asshole, which he was, but misogyny doesn't explain why the suitcase was real. Why put real stories in there? For that matter, why even have an actual theft? Couldn't he have just *told* the publisher it was stolen? Wouldn't it make sense to keep the stories in a drawer somewhere so he could pull them out later?"

"Who gives a shit?" Milch said. "Let's go. It doesn't matter."

"It does matter," I said. I traced my finger over the edge of the suitcase, feeling each little tear on the paper lining. "It's the whole fucking point. There's a reason why your grandfather never went looking for it. There's a reason your uncle never showed it to anybody, and it has nothing to do with the value of the stories. It was loyalty—your grandfather's loyalty to your uncle and your uncle's loyalty to Hemingway. Call it love if you want. There was love there between them, and that's something like trust. Then the trust was broken, you see? It was broken, but Ebenezer kept the suitcase safe. He kept it safe and made the theft real. He wanted it to be real."

"I think you're losing it, Coop," Milch said. He wrapped his fingers around the suitcase handle and drew it closer to him. "Why would he care if people read these stories?"

"I started and stopped three novels before I finished my first one," I said. "And the one I finished was pure shit. Everyone writes shit when they start. That's how it works. You write shit and then one day you get a little better, and then a little better than that, until you get good. If you're *lucky*, you get good. That's how it works."

"OK, I vote we get going," Grady said.

"Don't you get it? The theft wasn't just a stunt to get published. It was a purge," I said. "That's why he had Hadley pack everything up and bring it to the train station. He knew he wasn't strong enough to do it himself. He couldn't murder his darlings."

"Coop," Grady said. He walked over and put a hand on my shoulder. "Fuck Hemingway."

"It should be burned," I said, looking up at him.

"You should see someone, man," Milch said. "You've got issues."

"No shit," I said, and shook my head trying to clear it. "It's still raining. We shouldn't carry the suitcase out there without protection."

"Didn't you say you wanted to burn it?" Milch asked.

"It was just a thought," I said. It was more than that, though. It was the truth. I finally understood what Elmo wanted with the case. I had already agreed to bring it to him, but now I knew why.

"I got a plastic tarp under the front seat," Dutch said.

"I'll get it," Grady said, and he was out the door before we could answer. I picked at a splinter on the wire-spool table. Milch drummed his fingertips against the suitcase. Dutch became interested in a stain on his denim jacket.

"You made a deal with Elmo, didn't you?" Milch said, after the silence had become too acute to abide.

"What?" I said, snapping my head up to look him in the eye. He had a sad, weary smile on his face. I looked to Dutch for help, but he was still consumed by the contents of his jacket.

"Don't bullshit a bullshitter," Milch said. "Last night Elmo didn't want to do shit for us. Then this morning he loads us up with transportation, guns, and a guide. Come on. Tell me. What'd you two work out?"

"He wants the suitcase," I said with a dry mouth. I kept at the splinter, worrying it with my fingernail.

"Why?"

"I believe he means to burn it," I said.

"Why?"

"I don't think you'd get it."

"No," Milch said, scratching his chin. "I don't think I would. What do we get?"

"He'll get us out of Mexico."

"You think a border is going to stop someone like La Dónde?"

"I think we have a better shot up there, yes," I said.

"What else?"

"Twenty-five grand each."

"That's not much."

"Sounded like a lot to me."

"I meant comparatively," Milch said.

"Compared to what?"

"If it makes you feel any better, I do feel guilty," he said. I felt the air in the room cool a few degrees, and I shuddered from the chill. He stood and held the suitcase at his side like a man waiting for a train.

"Guilty? About what? Ebbie, what are you talking about?" I got a good hold on the splinter, pulled, and it came up in a long strip.

"Take your jacket off," Milch said.

"Huh?" I said. Milch reached behind his back, under his jacket, and pulled out a gun. It was my derringer, the one Digby had given me.

"Where did you get that?" I asked. I was calm, more than I should have been. Perhaps I was getting used to being on the wrong end of a gun.

"I'm a thief, remember?" he said. "Picking pockets kind of goes with the territory. Now take off your jacket. I need something to wrap the case in."

"You might want to think about this, brother," Dutch said.

"Fuck off, hippie," Milch said. I took off my corduroy jacket and tossed it to him. He wrapped the suitcase in it and clutched it to his chest.

"What about Grady?" I asked. Milch gestured with the gun.

"Let me worry about Grady," he said. "Don't look at me that way. Seriously, Coop, you didn't see this coming?"

"I have to admit, I didn't," I said, feeling foolish. "I mean, what's your play here? You still got La Dónde after you."

"You're not the only one who can make deals," he said. His tongue flicked over his lips like a reptile, and he laughed a hoarse, choppy snicker that was without joy.

"Chavez's place," I said, closing my eyes and cursing myself.

"Yup," Milch said. "Thandy was there, up in the private box Samantha took me to. He was up there sitting like a king, you know. See, he'd gotten there first, already heard Chavez's story, and he knew Elmo was the only one who knew where to find Ebenezer. So he waited to see what we would do. Then you go and tell Chavez you know a guy who can get you in."

"You were watching us," I said. Milch smiled and gave me a salute, touching the barrel of his gun to his temple.

"Cameras. Hell of a setup that Chavez has."

"What did he offer you?" I asked.

"One hundred grand."

"He'll never pay you."

Milch shrugged.

"Gave me his word as a southerner," he said. "Also, he wants you and Grady dead a lot more than me."

"You stole the manuscript."

"You tied him up with his own pants and kicked him down a mountain."

"Goddamn it, that was Grady," I said.

"I don't think Thandy is the kind of man who splits hairs on shit like that, you know?" Milch said.

"So the plan was for you to wait until we have the suitcase, and then you double-cross us?"

"You're one smart cookie, Mr. Velour," Milch said. "Yeah, that's about the size of it. Then that bitch Samantha decides she doesn't want to play the waiting game. That was a close one. And the whole time I thought you were going to figure it out anyway."

"Well, yeah, now it seems fairly obvious," I said. "I have to admit I feel pretty stupid."

"Don't feel too bad," Milch said. "I'm a professional."

"Professional dick," Dutch said.

"That's not helping, Dutch," I said. "So how do you expect to get out of here?"

"It pays to think ahead," Milch said, and pulled a small plastic instrument that looked like a cell phone out of his pocket. "GPS."

"You've killed us," I said.

"I prefer to think of it as saving myself."

"You think Thandy's just going to forgive you for stealing the manuscript?"

"Who gives a shit about the manuscript while I have this?" he said, hoisting the jacket-wrapped suitcase under his arm.

"You can't trust him," I said. "We should just go back to Elmo."

"Elmo keeps his word," Dutch said.

"I thought I told you to shut the fuck up, Cheech," Milch said, and slapped Dutch across the face with the derringer. Dutch's hands went to his face, and he stumbled back until he hit the wall. Milch grimaced at his handiwork and made his way to the door. I took a step toward him, and he raised the tiny pistol again.

"You step out there with that case, and you're a dead man, you know," I said.

Milch laughed and opened the door. His hand rested on the knob, and he paused.

"You gonna come after me, Coop?"

"Ebbie, I don't have the experience you have, but I do know you can't trust a man like Thandy, even if he gives his word as a southerner."

"Oh, come on," Milch said. "You think I don't have that old man where I want him? And his killer bitch, too? You think he's scamming me? I'm scamming him, Coop. Don't you get it? Can't you see, I'm a fucking profess—" There was a loud crack, too close for thunder, and Milch's head pitched forward violently. His knees bent and he reached his arms out, still holding onto the case, and hit the floor. There was a second crack, and Dutch screamed as he spun around. His legs hit the overturned stove, and he fell over it and out of sight.

"The door!" Dutch yelled. "Get the door!" I reached out casually and closed the door, still not registering what had just happened. Dutch army-crawled around the stove and kicked the back of my knee. I collapsed to the floor between Dutch and Milch. Milch was lying prostrate, his ass in the air, his face pressed into a mound of ash, and his arms spread out in front of him as if he were worshipping the fallen stove. A chunk of his skull from his eyebrow to his hairline was missing, replaced by a gaping maw from which a steady flow of blood ran down to mix with the ash, forming a paste. No more Milch.

"She's here," Dutch said.

Chapter Thirty-One

I got Dutch sitting up and leaning against the stove. He was shot in the shoulder. There was a small bloodstain on the front of his shirt and a large one the shape of Ohio just above his shoulder blade. The bullet had gone through, which, Dutch assured me, was a good thing.

"Take a peek out the window," Dutch said. "Let's see what we're dealing with." I used my elbows and knees to crawl across the room. There was a small hole at the bottom of the burlap curtain. I screwed up into a crouch and put my eye to it.

"There's a Jeep next to our truck," I said.

"What kind?"

"I don't know cars," I said. "One of those SUV things. It's big and black with tinted windows."

"Gunners?"

"I see two Mexicans in matching black suits and sunglasses. Jesus, one of them is huge."

"Fat?"

"No, you ever see *Enter the Dragon?*"

"No."

"The big Chinese guy who fought John Saxon at the end?"

"I never saw it."

"This guy looks like that guy. Except he's Mexican. It's the Mexican version of that big Chinese guy." I turned around and leaned back against the wall, with my head just underneath the windowsill.

"Do you see her?" Dutch asked. He pulled a handkerchief from his pocket and held it against his wound.

"No," I said. "Maybe she went after Digby."

"If she was out there, you'd never see her," Dutch said.

"Then why'd you ask?" I said. The Mexicans stood on the other side of their Jeep. The smaller one, who was probably my height, rested a long, scoped rifle on the hood. The big one held two astronomically large pistols in each hand. I scanned the edge of the canyon and the cliff that dropped down to the river, looking for a glint of glass in the sun that might betray a sniper. Nothing. Then it occurred to me—where the hell was Grady?

The smaller Mexican set his rifle down and reached below my sightline. He came up with a large, black shotgun with a host of shells secured to its side. He nodded to his partner, and they walked around the car and toward the house. I told Dutch.

"Take a shot at them," Dutch said.

"Grady's got all the guns," I said. "Unless you count the derringer." I tried to figure out how Grady could have escaped. The only way out was through the canyon. I couldn't believe La Dónde's men would have missed him even if he were on foot. He could have scrambled up over the hill behind the house, or maybe he pulled a Butch Cassidy and jumped into the river. Whatever happened, I was beginning to fear Thandy had been right about Grady from the beginning. When it came down to it, I had trusted the wrong man.

"Here," Dutch said, grunting as he reached behind his back and came up with a revolver. It was the size of fat squirrel, with a walnut stock and a long barrel. He slid it along the floor through the blood and ash, and it came to rest between my feet.

"That thing looks like it's from World War I," I said.

"It is." Dutch motioned with his hand for me to pick it up. "It was my grandfather's, a Webley. Don't worry. It works."

"What am I supposed to do with it?"

"Shoot at them."

"I can't shoot worth shit, Dutch," I said, and picked up the Webley. It felt too heavy to hold, let alone aim.

"You don't have to," Dutch groaned. "Just shoot out the window.

Let 'em know we have it. They won't be so quick to come inside if they think we can shoot back."

I held the gun up and examined it in the little light coming through the window. I thumbed back the hammer and shoved the barrel through the windowpane, shielding my eyes with my sleeve as glass tinkled down. The rain was falling harder and louder now. The Mexicans paused at the sound of the window breaking, but only for a moment. The large one tapped his partner with the back of his hand and they started toward the house again. I sat on my haunches, holding onto the windowsill for balance. I didn't bother aiming and fired just as they reached the wall. I felt the shot in my balls, and the goddamned ringing started up in my ears again.

The bullet hit one of the beer-bottle pikes on top of the wall, and it exploded like an auburn grenade. The Mexicans raised their arms as the glass tore into them. They backed away, firing wildly at the house and wiping away the tiny streams of blood running down their faces. Their shots knocked out the remaining windowpanes, blew a good-sized hole in the door, and dug huge chunks out of the adobe.

"How'd it go?" Dutch asked, after the firing stopped.

"Better than expected," I said. The large one took off his Ray-Bans and bent his head back to let the rain wash his face, shaking his head and whipping his long hair like a shaggy dog after a swim. He leaned against the Jeep's fender and pounded two hard knocks on the rear door with his pistol. The tinted rear window dropped down a few inches, revealing a tobacco-colored fedora bobbing sharply as its owner spoke.

"Thandy's here," I said.

"Can you shoot him?"

"I can shoot *at* him," I said. "The rest would be up to God." The large Mexican holstered one of his pistols and opened Thandy's door. The old bookseller was obscured by the door and the Mexican's body. The Mexican pointed back at the house with the revolver, and I could hear him speaking over the rain. His voice was loud and angry. Thandy may not have been completely in charge.

After a moment, the Mexican stomped his foot and swung the door wide. Thandy stepped out, holding his hand out in a calming gesture. He reached back into the Jeep and pulled out a green golf umbrella. He opened it and I could see the outline of a map of the United States, with a flag pin springing out of what would have been Georgia—the official logo for the Masters. He conversed with the large Mexican, who continued to gesture at the house with his pistol. Thandy patted the man on the shoulder and took a few steps toward the house.

"Mr. Cooper," he shouted. The moment he spoke, there was a quick blast of light and sound from under Dutch's truck, shotgun fire. The smaller Mexican had been standing next to the truck. His feet kicked out from under him, and he landed on his ass. Another blast tore apart his abdomen and ripped his shirt into gory shreds. He didn't fall over but sat with his legs spread out and his head forward in a gruesome parody of the stereotypical Mexican siesta.

The other gunman reacted quickly, aiming his dual pistols and firing shot after shot in the direction of the shotgun blasts. A shadow under the truck rolled away as the Mexican approached and bent down next to his compatriot. He tucked his pistol under his arm and reached out like a man trying to coax a cat out from under a car. Grady materialized on the other side of the truck, racked his shotgun, and fired, decapitating the Mexican. The headless body fell next to its partner.

Thandy watched the whole thing while holding his umbrella. He didn't move except for his feet, which shuffled up and down like he was trying to warm himself in the cold rain. The rain let up as Grady bounded around the truck. He racked the shotgun again and leveled the barrel at the old man's chest. He took a step forward, and the bookseller smiled. Grady cocked his head and lowered the shotgun an inch. Something at the edge of the canyon had caught his attention.

A small fountain of crimson flared out from the back of Grady's shoulder as he was knocked off his feet. His gun fell from his hand and skittered away under the Jeep. He rolled onto his stomach and pushed up with his good arm. He got his legs under him, and he lurched toward the dead Mexicans and their weapons. He took two steps before his left calf and then his right blew open as unseen and unheard bullets ripped through them. He let out an agonized scream and clutched his bloody legs, trying to stem the flowing claret.

"What happened?" Dutch said.

I told him.

"I told you she was here."

He was right. La Dónde, Pieta to some, emerged from behind a rock at the edge of the canyon, holding a rifle. There was a canister at the end of the barrel, which I assumed was a silencer. She wore a military shirt tucked into black jeans. The body the clothes covered deserved better. Her dark hair was pulled back from a cherubic face, the color of ice melting in bourbon. I took comfort in the idea that she was probably going to be the last thing I would see on this earth before I died. It was not a small comfort.

Thandy took a few careful steps toward Grady. He stood over him, still holding the umbrella like he was reading a putt on Amen Corner. La Dónde set her rifle down on the truck's hood and pulled a pistol from the holster at her hip. She reached down, grabbed Grady's collar, and pulled him up into a sitting position. At least he wasn't dead. I related this to Dutch.

"Mr. Cooper," Thandy called in a sing-song voice. "Can you see us, Mr. Cooper?"

"I see you, asshole," I called back. Dutch was looking drowsy.

"Do I have to explain the situation?" Thandy asked.

"Maybe," I said.

"Give me the suitcase."

"You think we have it?"

"You'd better, for your friend's sake," he said. "I'm willing to trade him for the suitcase. I'm aware he isn't in mint condition, so I'm going to throw in your life as well."

"Don't trust him," Dutch said.

"No shit," I replied. I crawled over to Milch's body and reached for the suitcase. The corpse was not willing to part with it, and I had to pull the case with my hands and push with my feet against his shoulders to wrest it away. I kept the jacket wrapped around it for protection. I also hoped La Dónde wouldn't shoot me until they were certain I actually had the suitcase.

I pulled the door open a crack and then pushed it wide with my toe. I considered taking the Webley but decided against it. Bringing it would mean using it, and I didn't want to pick a fight. I tucked the suitcase under my arm like a football.

"Be careful," Dutch said.

"I'm not sure that's an option," I said, "but at least it stopped raining." A car horn started blaring, and I could hear the rumble of radial tires over loose rock. Dutch tilted his head back and laughed.

"We're not so fucked," he said. I returned to the window. A black GMC van with a red stripe on the side launched out of the canyon road and landed, going about forty toward the cliff. The driver hit the brake and swerved left, dragging the back wheels through the mud until the truck had completed a 180. The rear wheels dug through the wet sand until they found purchase, and the van lurched forward until the driver hit the brakes again, stopping thirty feet from La Dónde and her hostage.

"It's the A-Team," I said. Thandy backed up against the Jeep and spread his arms against it for balance. La Dónde circled behind Grady, putting my friend between her and the newcomer.

"Sully," Dutch said.

"You gotta be fucking kidding me," I said. The van's door opened and closed. Digby emerged with his jacket off, his sleeves rolled up, and his gun tucked into a holster hanging at his hip. He came around the front of the van and tipped his hat back on his head. He looked around, assessing the situation, his thumbs hooked into his gun belt.

La Dónde let go of Grady's collar, and he tumbled onto his side like a scarecrow. She slid her pistol back into its holster and let her hand hang loosely next to it. Digby took a step closer, and she did the same. Their lips parted to take a breath, their eyes blinked, and their forefingers ticked against saddle leather in perfect unison, a mirrored connection between anima and animus. The post-rain ozone was thick in the air, and it added a syrupy mise-en-scène to the two former lovers standing less than a bullet's flight apart.

"Pieta," Digby said.

"Michael."

The guns roared, and they were on the ground. Dead.

"What happened?" Dutch asked. I could answer it only with my best guess. I surmised they had both drawn because I could see their respective pistols in their lifeless hands. Figuring out who had pulled first would have been impossible. I assumed they had responded to some mutual signal deep in their loins. The bullets had passed each other briefly, the closest their hearts had been in some time, and then lodged into their waiting bodies.

"They pulled and shot each other," I said. "No preamble or nothing. They just fucking shot each other."

"I suppose they said everything they had to the last time," Dutch said, scratching his nose. His eyes were closed now and his breathing was labored.

"Yeah, but Jesus," I said. "All this buildup and then nothing? It was a little, I don't know, anticlimactic."

"That's how people die."

"I guess."

"You're telling me you're disappointed?" Dutch asked.

"A little."

Thandy scrambled over to La Dónde's body and gave it a tentative kick. There was no response. He took a step toward Digby but stopped and covered his mouth with his hand. He crouched down to pry La Dónde's pistol from her fingers. Properly armed, he leaned forward and up on his toes to get a better look at Digby's lifeless body. When satisfied he was dead, or at least as satisfied as he could be without a tactile inspection, he folded his umbrella and tossed it through the open window of the Jeep. He dropped to his knees, took hold of Grady's collar, and pulled him back to a sitting position, using Grady's torso as a merlon.

"The situation has not changed, Cooper," Thandy yelled.

"It's changed a little," I said. Thandy pressed the gun barrel to Grady's jaw. Grady let out a groan and a few expletives. Again, I was relieved he wasn't dead.

"Bring out that fucking suitcase." Thandy's genteel accent had devolved into caricature. Each word scraped out of his mouth like it was coming from a defective bullhorn. "Bring it out or I'm gonna spread his brains all over the mud."

"He says he's gonna kill Grady," I said to Dutch.

"I hear him," he said. "You think he'll do it?"

"Yeah." I picked up the Webley and tucked it between the suitcase and my chest, leaving my hand on the grip.

"You think you can do it?" Dutch asked. "You think you can shoot him?"

"No, but he doesn't know that." I took a deep breath, recited what I could remember of the Our Father, and stepped out into the yard. The sun shone down through the clouds in shafts, bouncing off the puddles and illuminating the dead in a shimmering glow. I moved slowly. The mud sucked at my boots like hands begging me not to take another step, but I moved on.

Thandy had his bony hand wrapped around Grady's throat. The gun hand was shaking, but it was probably from the cold rain that had passed over us. His face was set and hard, no nerves there. When I was close enough, I lifted the leather-clad suitcase and showed the Webley underneath. It was aimed, I hoped, at the spot between Thandy's rueful eyes.

"It looks like we have what the pulps call a Mexican standoff," Thandy said. His tongue slithered over his cracked lips.

"Maybe," I said. I dropped the suitcase in the mud; the nearly century-old lock broke with the impact, and it opened. Thandy gasped as he looked on at the cardboard sinking into the mire. The pages, covered in scribbles and faded type, blew listlessly in the wind. Any moment, a good gust could take the whole thing away.

"You pick that up, you son-of-a-bitch," he said with a jeering snarl.

"You know," I said, and pulled Dutch's pack of cigarettes from my pocket. I drew the last one out with my teeth and tossed the empty pack into the suitcase. I kept the gun leveled on Thandy as I fished out my Zippo and lit up. I took a nice, long draw and smiled at Thandy. "Those old onionskins, I hear they make pretty good tinder in a bind."

I tossed the lighter onto the frail, old parchment, and it caught in an instant. The top pages curled and blackened, and then the suitcase itself caught. The smoke wafted up, and it was spiced like cloves and cherry tobacco. The paper turned the same color as the ink, dissolving the words, sentences, thoughts, and dreams back into the ether from which they came. Thin slices of the soul of the man that was Hemingway in Paris immolated in the mud like a funeral pyre.

Thandy screamed, and it came out a guttural squeal; he dropped the gun and launched himself at the conflagration. Grady fell over in a hump. I took a moment to enjoy the old man pounding at the flames, bits of paper and ember floating up into the air like fairies dancing in the moonlight. A few glowing pieces dropped to the puddles with a soft, satisfying hiss. The doddering fool sobbed over the flames as if his tears could put them out. When I'd had my fill, I walked up to him and placed the barrel of the Webley against his gray temple.

"You destroyed it," Thandy said with snarl. "How could you? How could you just destroy it?"

"I made it real," I said, and kicked the case over. The paper that had not burned took off in the breeze. The cardboard case crackled and spit, and the fire died into a picayune hillock of ash and pulp. No more Hemingway suitcase.

"And now you'll kill me, is that it, Cooper?" Thandy said. It was a pathetic little croak. He was on his knees, his suit ruined. I shrugged and motioned with the revolver for him to stand.

"I remember someone telling me about a tradition down here," I said, aping his aristocratic speech. "It seems, Thandy, that when a body's got a body in a position like this, you can give the prisoner three choices."

"Fuck you," Thandy wept.

"Oh, so you know about the *Bota*, the *Lena*, and the *Plomo*," I said. "Problem is, I don't have a prison to put you in, and I don't see any two-by-fours around."

"Please," Thandy said, and held his hands up in a prayerful pose.

"Makes your options a little limited. Tell you what. I'll give you to the count of ten to get in your Jeep and get the fuck out of here before I blast your sorry ass all over the canyon. One."

"Please, no."

"Two."

He got to his feet and staggered back.

"Three."

Thandy gasped and scrambled around the front of the Jeep. He got the door open and dived inside.

"Four. Oh fuck it," I said, and fired a bullet into the rear window. Thandy shrieked like a woman and threw the truck into drive. I could still hear his screams echoing in the canyon long after the truck was out of sight.

I scratched the back of my head and looked down at Grady.

"I hope you know what to do about your legs, because I don't know fuck all about first aid," I said. Dutch stood in the doorway, holding onto the jamb for support. I waved him on to join us.

"It's not as bad as it looks," Grady said.

"Good, cause from here you look like shit," I said. Dutch fished a first aid kit from the back of truck and knelt down next to Grady.

"If we can stop the bleeding, he should be OK," he said. "We got a doctor back at the camp. You're gonna have a hell of a limp, though."

"He's been looking for an excuse to do less walking," I said.

"Fuck," Grady said, grunting as Dutch tied a bandana above his left calf. He waved his hand at the mound of ash that had been the Hemingway suitcase. "It was all for nothing, huh?"

"I still got my story."

"I'll tell you this much, Coop," Grady said.

I walked back to Dutch's truck and flipped the top off of the cooler in the bed. The beer was still cold.

"What?"

"John Fucking Grisham never had a day like this."

Chapter Thirty-Two

We took the van. I drove and Dutch stretched out in the back. He had showed me how to dress his wound and stop the bleeding. Grady insisted on riding up front with me and the open window. He had lost a lot of blood, and I had to give him an elbow every once in a while to keep him awake. The rain had come back and it blew through the window, soaking Grady's shirt and beard.

The guards were waiting for us at the gate. I slowed to a stop, rolled down the window, and whizzed through my smile Rolodex, coming up with the one I use for turning in late manuscripts. Jorge bent down and stuck his head inside the truck. I could see Thandy's black Jeep just over his shoulder, parked up against one of the bungalows.

"All set," I said. "Thanks for the time."

"El Cuerno wants to talk to you," Jorge said, and reached past me to turn off the engine. "Looks like you still got bad manners." He pulled the key and leaned back, placing the barrel of his AK-47 on the windowsill. There was a house, newer than the others and in much better shape, up on the hill, with brick stairs leading down to the gate. A portly middle-aged Mexican dressed in white emerged at the top of the stairs. He had a servant on each side of him. One held a green Masters umbrella over the head of the man in white, and the other had an AK slung over his shoulder. Obviously the man in white was El Cuerno. He took the stairs slowly, limping and relying heavily on a wooden cane.

"Hello," El Cuerno said with only the slightest accent. "Busy afternoon up at the old place, huh? Jorge tells me first you three come through with a fourth man. Then Pieta, her men, and an old man they did not know. Then Sullivan, who I thought was dead, comes through in this van. All these people come into my camp. We are open like Disneyland, I suppose." Jorge's head hung low and he wiped his face with a red handkerchief.

"Tourist season, I guess," I said with a weak laugh.

"Then the old man comes back down. No men. No Pieta."

"I see his Jeep over there," I said.

"No, no, you see my Jeep. I just got it today. What do you think?"

"It's a lovely vehicle. I'm sure you could get that window fixed real easy," I said. "Did you get it at a good price?"

"For me, yes. Not for the old man," he said. "I see you have Dutch. Hello, Dutch."

"How is your crop this year, El Cuerno?" Dutch said from the back. He reached up to shake the narco's hand but could only manage a few inches with his shoulder injury. El Cuerno reached the rest of the way and took Dutch's hand, shaking it gently.

"Damn mochomos are driving us mad," he said. "Is your friend dead?"

"Getting there," Dutch said.

There was a commotion toward the back of the van. Jorge and a second guard opened the side door and pulled at the edge of the tarp back there. El Cuerno held up his finger and limped over to see what they had found. I kept my hands on the wheel, flexing them for something to do. El Cuerno appeared in the open frame of the side door.

"There are two dead bodies back here, *amigo*," he said.

"Yes," Dutch said.

"I know Sullivan. Who is the other one?"

"The nephew of the man who used to live up at the old place," I said.

"Pieta killed them?"

"More or less," I said.

"And where is the lovely Pieta?"

"Dead. They killed each other, Sully and her," Dutch said.

"That is the way it would have to be with them, huh. And where is she?"

"Back there," I said, moving my head back toward the canyon. "Coyotes gotta eat, right?"

"That is right, *amigo*," El Cuerno said, and burst into laughter. He tapped his servant's shoulder with the back of his hand. The rest of the men joined in the laughter. "And they are mighty hungry around here, eh." I let him finish laughing, holding his belly, and tapping his cane against the ground. I smiled politely and nodded.

"I guess we'll be on our way then?" I asked. El Cuerno picked at his teeth with his thumbnail. When he was finished, he spat on the ground and kicked dirt over it.

"Your friends here, Dutch," El Cuerno said. "They are dear to you?" Dutch squinted and looked up at the brightening sky.

"Dear enough, El Cuerno," he said.

"We need help with the mochomos."

"I can be out next week," Dutch said. El Cuerno tapped his cane against the ground vigorously.

"A new Jeep, no more Pieta, and Dutch to take care of the mochomos," El Cuerno said. "*¿Jorge, está un día bueno?*"

"*Sí, Jefe,*" Jorge said. "*Está muy bueno.*"

"He has to say that," El Cuerno said. "Everything that happened today is his fault. I will see you next week, Dutch." He whacked Jorge on the knee with his cane. Jorge reached into his pocket, pulled out the keys, and tossed them to me. I had them in the ignition and turned before the sound of their jingling stopped. The gate was open and we were free to go. Dutch closed the side door, and I pressed down on the accelerator.

"Don't know what all the fuss is about," Grady said. He reached his cupped hand out the window and splashed some rainwater on his face. "These cartel guys ain't so bad."

≋

"You thought I'd abandoned you, didn't you?" Grady asked. We were sitting in deck chairs at the top of Elmo's mesa. Grady's wounds, while painful, weren't nearly as fatal as we thought. Elmo's doctor had pulled a small-caliber bullet from each leg, but the shoulder slug had passed clean through, as it had with Dutch. Elmo had given us half of his original offer of twenty-five thousand each, which was only fair, as we hadn't given him any proof the suitcase was destroyed. I had given him the manuscript, though. When I handed him the satchel, he had tossed it next to his gun belt on the ground, not even bothering to look inside. He had asked us to stay until Grady recovered, but Grady begged off, citing the upcoming Baja 500 and getting back to his hotel. We ignored the doctor's advice to lay off the rum.

"The thought had crossed my mind," I said.

"Crossed mine, too." He raised his glass of rum.

I touched mine against his and took a swig.

"I like this ending," I said. "For the book I mean."

"It's a little depressing," Grady said. "Losing Digby and the suitcase. The thing with Milch."

"That's what I like," I said. "Not the part about Digby, but the suitcase."

"It's no good. All that death and nothing to show for it. We got some cash, but how long do you think that'll last? Even Hemingway let the old man have his damned fish."

"You should finish that book when you get the chance," I said, and took a sip of rum.

"How long will it take you to write it?"

"Don't know," I said. "I promised Ox another *MacMerkin* first."

"So you're not going to kill Toulouse?"

"No, he's not such a bad guy. There are worse ways to earn a buck, you know?" I said. "And I'm not so cavalier about killing as I was last week."

"Good," Grady said. "I like that vampire. I want to see what happens now that he's moved to Las Vegas."

"What?" I said, turning in my chair.

"I've been reading them for years," he said with a grin. I laughed and looked out at the yellow-orange incandescence across the horizon. The stars were poking out and the rum felt good in my belly.

"I like this ending," I said.

"You should change it," Grady said. "People like a happy ending."

"I'll think about it."

Acknowledgments

Here is a list of people who helped. They know why, and they know, I hope, that I can never truly thank them enough. This is in no particular order except that my wife is first because she is. Teddy and Ginny are not on here because they did not help and the first draft was written before they were born. But I love you guys all the same.

(1) Anne Harris
(2) James Harris
(3) Jayne Harris
(4) Brent Taylor
(5) Jessica Negrón
(6) Uwe Stender
(7) Professor Walton Collins
(8) Dan Mayer
(9) Grant Gholson
(10) Tony Bondi
(11) Dan Stalilonis
(12) Jade Zora Scibilia
(13) Cheryl Quimba
(14) The good people at Bretton's Village Trunk Shop, especially Churchill Barton
(15) Everyone at Seventh Street Books

About the Author

Shaun Harris grew up in New England and has a degree in American studies and film and television from the University of Notre Dame. He now lives in rural Wisconsin with his wife and two kids.